IS NEW YORK
BURNING?

LARRY COLLINS
AND
DOMINIQUE LAPIERRE

ISBN: 1-597770-520-7

Library of Congress Cataloging-In-Publication Data Available

Book Design by: Sonia Fiore

Printed in the United States of America

Phoenix Press
9465 Wilshire Boulevard, Suite 315
Beverly Hills, CA 90212

10 9 8 7 6 5 4 3 2 1

"RIGHT," SNAPPED PAUL ANSCOM, CHIEF OF
THE HOMELAND SECURITY DEPARTMENT'S
EMERGENCY RESPONSE TEAM.
"LET'S GET CRACKING, GENTLEMEN. THE FATE OF
NEW YORK CITY AND A MILLION OF ITS INHABITANTS
IS NOW IN YOUR HANDS. IT'S ALL UP TO
YOU. GO SAVE NEW YORK!"

TABLE OF CONTENTS

AUTHORS' NOTE

CHAPTER 1
NORTHWESTERN IRAQ
Early Spring 2003...*1*

CHAPTER 2
WAZIRISTAN, PAKISTAN
Over One Year Later *11*

CHAPTER 3
PORT ELIZABETH, NEW JERSEY
A Container of Basmati Rice..............................*45*

CHAPTER 4
WASHINGTON, D.C.
The Crisis—Day One.......................................*59*

CHAPTER 5
NEW YORK CITY
The Crisis—Day Two.......................................*95*

CHAPTER 6
**NEW YORK CITY, WASHINGTON, D.C.,
JERUSALEM, KARACHI**
The Crisis—Day Three....................................*151*

CHAPTER 7
WASHINGTON, D.C., NEW YORK CITY, JERUSALEM
The Crisis—Day Four *193*

CHAPTER 8
NEW YORK CITY, WASHINGTON, D.C., JERUSALEM
The Crisis—Day Five......................................*237*

POSTSCRIPT..*275*
ACKNOWLEDGEMENT *277*

AUTHORS' NOTE

If the authors of this book have allowed themselves to mix reality with fiction and have permitted themselves to employ public personalities in the pages of their work, they have employed only the names and certain well-known facts of the public and political lives of the individuals involved. The rest, and most notably, the flow of the action and incidents growing from it are the work of the authors' imagination.

*To the victims of terrorism in whatever its forms,
and to the men and women of good faith
who strive for truth, justice and peace.*

CHAPTER

1

NORTHWESTERN IRAQ

Early Spring 2003

The black Cadillac, its window shades drawn, sped through the moonless night along the hard-packed desert road that since biblical times has been the principal link between Damascus and Baghdad, the cities of the caliphs. The car was one of the personal vehicles of Iraqi dictator Saddam Hussein. With the American invasion of Iraq clearly only days away, it was equipped with electronic devices capable of jamming the radar of any American fighter jets seeking to disturb the 435-mile (700-kilometer) journey of its occupant.

On the outskirts of the Iraqi capital, the car pulled to a halt in front of a palatial residence. That was not, however, to be the destination of the car's passenger. A pair of uniformed guards escorted him to a second Cadillac which set out immediately for another palatial residence where the process was repeated a second and then a third time. Like the first vehicle, the second and third Cadillacs were equipped with tightly drawn window shades. In these tense days, visitors to Saddam Hussein were not going to be able to identify for the benefit of an American CIA agent which of the dictator's many residences and offices was used for their meeting. Furthermore, Saddam made it a point never to receive visitors during daylight hours.

The visitor's lengthy journey finally came to an end at the guard post of yet another imposing palace where half a dozen security officers in black combat gear took him into a small anteroom. There, much to his distaste, he had to put up with a full body search and strip. That completed, he was turned over to six officers of Saddam's personal bodyguard in olive green uniforms. They escorted him down a long corridor, its walls decorated with yellow and blue mosaics of the famed lions of Babylon and of the ancient capital's great monuments.

At the end of the corridor they entered a small private elevator. While its downward journey lasted only seconds, the plunge was so swift and steep that the visitor's ears popped like in an airplane coming in for a landing.

The elevator's door opened onto a communications center full of computers, radios, television screens and telephones. The visitor was now placed in an electric cart similar to those used to shuttle disabled passengers around an airport and, accompanied by another pair of armed guards, trundled down another seemingly interminable corridor lined with still more mosaics of ancient Babylonian vistas.

Finally they stopped before a locked door that gave onto another locked door that led at last to a large office. There, at the head of a long table of highly polished oak, sat the Iraqi dictator. He was wearing the olive green, jacketless uniform in which he had become familiar to television viewers around the world. Unlike many dictators who were forever awarding themselves decorations for wars in which they had not fought, no battle ribbons adorned the dictator's shirt. His only identifying marks were a pair of gold eagles on his shoulder boards and the dark blue tattoo of his Tikriti tribe on the back of his right hand. His forehead was lined with deep furrows and his eyes were sunk deep into their sockets. He looked thoroughly exhausted.

He beckoned to his guest to be seated. "May Allah shower his blessings upon you, brother," he said in a greeting that was for him more ritual than religious. "Thank you for paying me the honor of accepting my invitation to visit me here in Baghdad in these perilous times."

The visitor smiled. "It is a privilege, *ya sayed*—yes, sir. The real honor is in being shown just how well protected you are here."

Saddam smiled in return. "Bush and his American jackals are ready to invade my nation any day. It is their goal to capture or kill me. Believe me, I shall not make their task easy."

"Pray they do not succeed, my brother," the visitor replied.

"It is because they are about to invade that I asked you to undertake this difficult trip," Saddam continued. "You see, I have something very important to give you, my brother, and I know of no one who will know how to use it better than you."

The visitor acknowledged his words with a kind of half bow. He was a forty-three-year-old Lebanese-born Shiite Muslim of Palestinian descent. His name was Imad Mugniyeh and until 9/11 the CIA considered him America's most wanted war criminal. Indeed, the ghastly death toll of 9/11 aside, no one was responsible for as many American or Western deaths as Mugniyeh: 63 Americans killed in the bombing of the U.S. Embassy in Beirut in 1983, 241 U.S. Marines and 58 French foreign legionnaires blown apart in their Lebanese barracks a few months later, 114 victims in the 1992 bombings of the Israeli Embassy and Jewish Community Center in Buenos Aires, 19 American airmen at their Khobar Tower barracks in 1996—all those bloody incidents were the work of this short, slightly built terrorist.

Mugniyeh avoided publicity as a cat avoids water. Not for him interviews on Al Jazeera television or videotapes smuggled to

Lebanese TV channels. Indeed, Western intelligence agencies had only two small photographs of the man, a thick mop of hair pushing over his forehead, a sparse beard circling his chin.

He was born in a village near the Lebanese coastal seaport of Tyre and enrolled at an early age in the training camps of Yasir Arafat's Al Fatah. There he learned his trade alongside kamikazes of Japan's Red Army, Shiite warriors bent on overthrowing the Shah of Iran and fellow Palestinians dedicated to the destruction of Israel. His enthusiasm, his aptitude for violence, caught Arafat's attention. The PLO chief assigned him to his elite bodyguard unit, Force 17.

With Israel's invasion of Lebanon in 1982 and the PLO's expulsion from the country, Mugniyeh signed on with Islamic Jihad and was one of the founders of the Iranian-inspired Hezbollah, a terrorist organization that the CIA's George Tenet held to be even more dangerous than al Qaeda. He was instrumental in developing the organization's use of suicide bombers against southern Lebanon's Israeli occupiers. He was also the architect of the wave of kidnappings in the Beirut of the 1980s that seized people like Terry Waite, the Archbishop of Canterbury's envoy, and the American journalist Terry Anderson, and that led to the torture and murder of CIA agent William Buckley.

The CIA, Britain's MI6, France's SDEC and Israel's Mossad had all pursued him with no success. He was just a myth invented by the Israelis to nourish the paranoia of the CIA, his Lebanese supporters liked to tell journalists trying to meet him. With fluent French, credible English and a smattering of Spanish, supplemented by a mastery of disguises, he moved quite successfully around the globe to strengthen his networks and nurture his contacts. One of them in 1998 in Sudan had been with a fellow hater of the West, Osama bin Laden. While nothing specific came out of their meeting, both knew the day could well come when their work in the holy war against the West would bring them together again.

"Those jackals of the Great Satan in Washington are getting ready to launch a savage attack on this Arabic nation," Saddam prophesied. "They are going to crush our villages and cities under a deluge of their bombs. In spite of the great courage of my soldiers, one must fear they will be trampled under the weight of U.S. arms. As for me, I will eventually become a martyr—unless, of course, the cancer cells my French doctors have recently discovered in my body act faster than the Americans do. Or, God forbid, the American devils take me prisoner."

Mugniyeh listened to Saddam's little speech without any outward sign of emotion until his reference to cancer, which jolted him. "Surely those French doctors are wrong, my brother."

Saddam shrugged in indifference. "No matter. That devil George Bush tries to convince the world that I have weapons of mass destruction here in Iraq. Would that I did, for I would gladly use them now against him and his troops. But, alas, I do not. Once, in 1991 we were so close! My scientists had built a working model of a centrifuge that could have transformed uranium, even the natural uranium we have stocked here, into a working bomb."

Saddam sighed, almost in tears as he pronounced those words. "But after the Kuwait War, the model was destroyed by the UN inspectors and I had to set aside my project.

"However, my brilliant Iraqi and Islamic scientists, who are far smarter than the West wishes to admit, provided me with something almost as good. They pierced the best kept secrets of the Western physicists and designed for me a nuclear weapon that can reduce Tel Aviv, London or New York to dust. Their design, I have been assured, is flawless. I know this because those devils, the inspectors of the United Nations, captured a copy of the design. They acknowledged that it was flawless, that if constructed it could explode with terrifying force."

Saddam gave another short, despairing sigh. "However, to make it I had to have a source of highly enriched uranium and those damned Americans frustrated all my efforts to get it."

Mugniyeh nodded knowingly. He was close enough to many of the extremist mullahs ruling Iran to be aware of the difficulties they were having in getting fissile material for their own nuclear projects.

Saddam meanwhile had gotten up, gone to the wall and taken down an oil painting depicting him riding a white horse and waving a sword. The painting concealed a safe in the wall whose combination lock Saddam now proceeded to open. He drew out a leather case, larger than an attaché case but smaller than a full-size suitcase. He placed it on the table between them and sat down again.

"Brother," he said in a tone so solemn he could have been reciting a couple's marriage vows, "while I do not share the fundamentalist Islamic views you and many of your brothers cherish, I yield to no one in my hatred of America for the evil they are preparing to wreak on my people and for the evil they and their Israeli allies have already visited on our brothers in Palestine."

Saddam pushed the case across the table to Mugniyeh. "And so I am giving you today this case, my brother. In it you will find an exact copy of my scientists' plan with all details for each step necessary to construct an atomic bomb of awesome power. All you will need to convert these plans into a real bomb is twenty-three kilograms of highly enriched uranium. Of course for our national program we needed not twenty-three kilograms but well over a hundred kilos. For you, to find just twenty-three kilos should be easy. Perhaps your Iranian friends can help you, provided of course that you do not tell them I gave you this plan. Not that they would need it. I am sure they have one of their own already. And surely with money and friends you can find what you need in Russia. Take this plan now as my last will and testament. Build the bomb with your brothers and use the bomb against the Americans in one of their cities to avenge my soul, *inshallah*."

Awed and moved Mugniyeh stood and bowed to his host. "*Ya sayed*, for sure you shall be avenged."

Saddam gestured to him to return to his chair. "I am told it should not be difficult to smuggle such a thing into America. Surely your brothers in Hamas and the Hezbollah will know how to do it. Then use the ultimate power these plans can give you to achieve a great victory for our peoples, something that will get true justice for your brothers in Palestine and for my suffering people here, something they and the world will accept and recognize as being right and just. And for me—Revenge! Revenge! Revenge!"

Mugniyeh rose and once again bowed respectfully. "Fear not," he swore, "you shall be avenged. We will make this bomb and win justice for all our peoples in your name."

CHAPTER

2

WAZIRISTAN, PAKISTAN

Over One Year Later

It was the usual handful of passengers disembarking from Tehran at Karachi's Quaid-e-Azam International Airport aboard PIA Flight 63—a smattering of Shiite mullahs, two of them wearing the black turbans that indicated they claimed descent from the Prophet, businessmen in lightweight suits for the heat in Pakistan's cities, a few homecoming couples with children, and a solitary woman in an all-enveloping black *chador*.

The presence of police agents in and out of uniform reflected the fact that Pakistan was a nation infested with spies and Islamic extremists, both Sunnis and Shiites. Indeed, even the nation's president, General Pervez Musharraf, had recently declined to disembark at the airport on the advice of his bodyguards. However, airport security was in this case both rigorous and swift. The lone woman went to the baggage conveyor belt, declined the offer of a porter and when the bags came up, lifted her suitcase from the belt by herself and left through the airport's main exit, where she paused for a moment.

Among the Pakistanis waiting to greet the arriving passengers was a young man in an embroidered, pillbox-style hat. Seeing the woman in her chador, he sauntered over to her. "The believers are fighting," he murmured.

"On the paths of Allah," came the reply. There was nothing feminine about the voice that uttered it, however. It belonged to

Imad Mugniyeh, the Hezbollah terrorist to whom Saddam Hussein had delivered his plan for an atomic bomb.

His arrival in Pakistan represented for Mugniyeh a defeat of considerable magnitude. He had proven totally unworthy of the sacred mission Saddam had given him. The Iraqi dictator was now a helpless prisoner of the Americans, his nation occupied by U.S. troops. The design for an atomic bomb which Saddam had given Mugniyeh as an instrument of revenge remained unused in his suitcase. In months of wandering Russia and the other states of the old Soviet Union, he had failed to find so much as a single gram of highly enriched uranium—and that despite the aid of Chechen rebels and the fact he was ready to dish out vast sums of cash for the precious metal. For Mugniyeh, this flying visit to Osama bin Laden, the fellow Islamic extremist he had met briefly in Khartoum in 1998, represented a last hope of realizing the sacred mission Saddam had confided to him.

With proper feminine deference, he allowed the young man to take his suitcase and followed him to his parked car. Their destination was a residential quarter in the heart of Karachi called the Defense Colony. Most of its inhabitants were retired Pakistani army officers. Al Qaeda had used its contacts in the military to establish in that neighborhood a network of safe houses as well as its operational headquarters for southern Pakistan. Mugniyeh was of course expected at one of the safe houses.

Forty-eight hours after his arrival, he was off again in a Toyota 4x4 escorted by three *mujahideen*, their AK-47s carefully concealed under their seats. He had discarded his female disguise and was now dressed in the flowing robes of a northern Pakistani tribesman and a cream-colored turban. Their destination was the legendary city of Peshawar at the foot of the Khyber Pass, once the northern gateway to Britain's Indian Empire.

In the years since the Soviet invasion of Afghanistan, the city had become a focal point for Islamic extremists, drug dealers, ex-Talibs evicted from their homeland and old *mujahideen* warriors whose AK-47s were now available to the highest bidder. It took two days of hard driving to get from Karachi to the city, whose teeming bazaars had welcomed giants of history such as Alexander the Great, Marco Polo and the Mogul emperors Babar and Akhbar.

Mugniyeh was installed in one of the al Qaeda safe house. While his escorts made the arrangements for his onward journey, he wandered the city's alleys and famous bazaars. They were crowded with Pashtun warriors in green turbans and loose-fitting *salwars*, Baluchi peasants pulling camels loaded with multicolored carpets for sale, horsemen from the high plateaus of the Pamir in search of tea and spices. In the 1960s those bazaars had swarmed with hippies looking to score a hit of hash. Spot a pale face there now, it was joked, and it probably belonged to a CIA officer operating undercover.

Prowling those bazaars, Mugniyeh's practiced eye spotted a staggering array of arms, from U.S.-made Stingers to locally produced AK-47s. There was a full range of U.S. military equipment, from first aid kits to infrared night vision goggles scavenged from the battlefields of Afghanistan and Iraq. He was intrigued by the dozens of posters pasted on the city walls that bore the likeness of the man he had come to see. They promised a $25 million reward for his capture, dead or alive. He noted with an approving smile that the passing Pakistanis were apparently indifferent to the posters.

In the nineteenth century, Peshawar had been made the capital of British India's North-West Frontier Province and the city had retained that distinction at the birth of an independent

Pakistan. It was a singularly hollow honor, however. The city's control of the province it was supposed to administer had always been more symbolic than real. The British had never made any serious efforts to bring the fiercely independent tribesmen of the province under their rule. Now, in 2004, the national government in Islamabad was simply irrelevant in the province. Both the North-West Frontier Province and the neighboring Baluchistan Province were governed by a three-party coalition, the MMA, Muttahida Majlis-e-Amal (the supporters of the popular assembly), that was much closer in ideology to extremist Islam than to the government of President Musharraf. The province's so-called Pakistan Frontier Corps, ostensibly responsible for policing the province and the nation's borders, was in fact a disorganized, underpaid, ragtag militia barely capable of policing the streets of Peshawar itself.

The final stage of Mugniyeh's journey began at nightfall after a three-day wait in Peshawar, in another 4x4 driven by a Pashtun warrior armed with a locally made AK-47. They had barely left the city when the driver stopped, whipped out a pair of U.S. Army infrared night vision glasses bought in the bazaar and began to scan the sky.

"Americans! Americans!" he muttered over and over again as he peered into the night sky. Finally convinced they were safe, he resumed their journey, explaining to his passenger how the Americans had recently swept in under the cover of a thick fog forcing Osama to flee to a new hideout. In any event, he said, the leader never stayed in the same place for more than a few nights. He and his followers also developed a new technique to frustrate their American enemies. They never used telephones of any sort so that the NSA's spying ears in the sky could not intercept their conversations. In the mountains and valleys of the Hindu Kush, the marvels of modern electronic communications were replaced for Osama bin Laden by messengers on mule back.

Forty-eight hours after their departure from Peshawar, Mugniyeh realized he was approaching his journey's end. Their vehicle was stopped by a half dozen warriors who had slipped across the Afghan border at night. One delivered a package for the al Qaeda chief to the driver. In it were several flasks of insulin, a packet of syringes and a bottle of medicine for Osama's ailing kidneys. The group's leader ordered the pair to dismount, move into a shack beside the road and remove their clothing.

"Hey," Mugniyeh whispered to his driver, "they're speaking Russian. How come?"

"They're Uzbek. They belong to the Islamic Movement of Uzbekistan that's responsible for the chief's security."

Once in the shack, they were each placed under a shower of scalding hot water and roughly scrubbed down with brushes.

Contemplating his red and bleeding chest, Mugniyeh barked angrily, "What the hell was that for?"

"In case someone has placed chemicals on your body that the Americans could pick up with their satellites and then follow you to the leader's location," the guard replied in halting Arabic.

At that moment Mugniyeh glanced down and saw an Uzbek reaching for his testicles. "Hey," he shouted, "and what do you think you're doing?"

"Security," was the answer. "In case you're carrying something in your scrotum. You wouldn't be the first to try that."

"Security! If I knew we had to go through all this just to see Osama, I would have stayed in Tehran where only a woman can touch my balls."

The journey reached its climax that night when they arrived at a tiny mountain village called Mirim Shah on the flanks of the Hindu Kush. Mugniyeh, his driver and their Uzbek escort left their 4x4 and set off on foot for a three-kilometer climb up a steep incline to the mountain retreat of Osama bin Laden. No grinding motor noise, no engine vibrations, no excessive emanation of body heat was going to reveal the passage of the men to any hidden American sensors in the area.

The meeting between the two most important global leaders of Islamic terrorism took place shortly before dawn and the *muezzin*'s call to morning prayer. Mugniyeh was shocked by Bin Laden's physical appearance. He looked drawn and he supported himself on a pair of canes. His left arm seemed to be bothering him. Clearly the turbulent decade since their Khartoum meeting had taken its toll. There Osama had seemed lithe and muscular, always ready to go for a ten- or twenty-minute gallop across the Sudanese countryside. He's not doing that anymore, Mugniyeh thought.

"May Allah bless your arrival," bin Laden proclaimed in a voice whose vigor belied his fragile appearance. He led Mugniyeh into the interior of his provisional headquarters, a natural cave sliced deep into the mountain's core. The floor and the lower part of the walls were covered with carpets, one of which was white, bearing the words *Allah Akhbar* in large green Arabic letters. Books, papers, pistols, chargers, AK-47s and a computer littered the carpets. Mugniyeh wondered how Osama could exercise the worldwide leadership of his organization, of his struggle to reinvigorate the Islamic world, in such chaos. Mugniyeh began to have doubts. Had he perhaps made a mistake? Had he come to the wrong place, to the wrong leader in his desperate efforts to carry out the sacred charge Saddam Hussein had given him?

Then he reassured himself. The man before him may have aged since their last meeting, might be suffering from the frailties of the body, but he was still the most dynamic, the most charismatic leader Islam had produced for generations.

After all, this was a man against whom, for the first time in history, an American president, Bill Clinton, had actually signed a death warrant. This was the man who had led George W. Bush to issue a top secret memorandum of notification calling for him to be captured or killed on sight. This was the man whose secret training camp in Afghanistan was blasted by sixty-five American satellite-guided missiles at the cost of almost fifty million dollars. And what had they achieved with all those millions? Killed a few rabbits—because a high-ranking admirer of Bin Laden in Pakistan's ISI, Inter-Services Intelligence agency, had warned him the attack was coming. Bin Laden and his followers were able to vacate their camp well before the missiles struck.

Here he was, calm and still in firm command of his international *jihad* to restore Islam to the glory it had once known. The air of chaos about this cave was understandable after all. He and his lieutenants had to be ready to pack up and rush to a new hiding place in minutes, didn't they? From such an unlikely hideout, protected by devoted tribal leaders in the Pakistani mountains and by his inner circle of Uzbek bodyguards, he had commanded bombs in Bali, Kuwait, Riyadh and Morocco. And the Americans with all their millions in reward money? Where were they? Nowhere to be seen. No, Mugniyeh thought, he had indeed come to the right leader for help.

The two men sat down cross-legged on one of the few empty carpets. A servant brought them tea, hard wheat biscuits and a pot of *labneh* cheese. Mugniyeh listened attentively to Osama's welcoming discourse. Then he ceremoniously placed Saddam's briefcase on the carpet between them and began the speech he had prepared for their meeting.

"Just before the Americans launched their treacherous attack on Iraq, our brother Saddam Hussein invited me to Baghdad. He presented this case to me as his last will and testament. It contains the most precious gift he could bequest to the *jihad*, to your brave struggles in the righteous cause of Islam. It is a complete, detailed plan drawn up by his nuclear scientists for the most powerful of weapons, the atomic bomb."

Osama solemnly nodded his head to acknowledge the importance of his visitor's words.

"Making the bomb from this design requires highly enriched uranium, which," Mugniyeh continued, "our brother did not have. He might have succeeded in obtaining it had those disciples of Satan not invaded his lands. It was his most fervent hope that I might succeed where he had failed and that I might then use this bomb on the Americans to avenge him. It was his final gift to the struggle, the inheritance he would leave to the Iraqis before his nation was crushed by the Americans and he was killed or captured."

Mugniyeh sighed, encapsulating in that sound all the frustrations he was about to reveal. "I spent almost a year in Russia, working with our Chechen brothers, seeking to purchase this uranium. Alas, I must confess to you that I failed."

"That is not surprising, my brother," Osama said comfortingly. "I too tried to get the material we needed for a nuclear bomb this way. Our brave brother Jamal al-Fadl, who you may have met in Khartoum, was ready to pay a million and a half dollars on my behalf a decade ago for uranium but the supposed sellers were imposters. Another of my agents was caught in a trap set by the police in Germany in 1998. I have told the Chechens I will give them thirty million dollars for this material. What have they delivered me? Nothing."

Osama stirred from his half-reclining position to sit up erect, legs crossed in front of him on their carpet. "I am now convinced that is not the path we must follow to obtain the great arms we seek. That path leads only to criminals, to imposters, to those who seek to rob and betray us as we follow the divine path of the *jihad*. Ours must be another path, an Islamic path."

He glanced at the suitcase that Mugniyeh had opened as he was talking, but Mugniyeh was surprised by his host's lack of curiosity.

"The Musaylama—false prophet—of the present time, George Bush, says that Iraq is the foreground for war against terrorism. Well, if killing those who kill our sons is terrorism, then let history be witness that we are terrorists. If we kill their innocents, I say it is permissible in Islamic law and logic. I salute our steadfast brothers in Iraq, the heroes of the land of the two rivers and I say to them, you are eminent among the Arabs and the defenders of Islam. It's almost two years since the invasion and yet the invaders have not been able to implement their plans. This is thanks to your *jihad*. May Allah reward you in the best manner."

Osama again bowed briefly at his invocation of the Divine's name, then continued. "But we too must aid and reward our Iraqi brothers. You are no doubt aware of the *fatwa* I have published. It is the sacred duty of the Muslim peoples to obtain these arms the infidels call 'weapons of mass destruction.' The American people can expect nothing from us except *jihad*, resistance and revenge. The Lord of the worlds gives us permission to take such revenge. After all, the Americans were the first to make and use these weapons. Why should they be immune from their horrors?"

Osama paused again and glanced skyward as if to invoke a divine blessing on his next words. "On that blessed Tuesday, September 11, 2001, with our splendid and courageous operation, the likes of which mankind had never witnessed before, we rubbed America's nose in the dirt and dragged its pride through the mud."

"The next attack must be this size," he vowed, extending his arms wide from his chest, "and it must be done with the very weapons the Americans themselves unleashed on the world—these arms they call 'weapons of mass destruction.' What was accomplished in Madrid and London was praiseworthy, but those attacks on trains, subways and buses didn't reach the scale we need. They did change the government in Spain. But the London bombings were not spectacular enough to do likewise in Britain. The problem, my brother, is that conventional explosives cannot produce the level of panic that reroutes the course of history. To bring victory to our cause in Palestine and Iraq we need more—we need the explosive power of the atomic bomb.

"I swear by Allah Almighty, who lifted the sky without effort, that America will never enjoy safety until safety is assured to our brothers throughout the Muslim world.

"If our next attack kills four million Americans, it is our right to do so in response to the evil they have inflicted on Muslims." The voice with which he uttered his bloodcurdling threat was, Mugniyeh thought, calm and matter of fact. There was no effort to be dramatic, no emotional emphasis, and none was needed. Osama was indeed the leader he had admired for so long, his force, his readiness for action undiminished by time.

"The blood pouring out of Palestine," Bin Laden continued, "must be met with revenge of equal power."

Mugniyeh nodded, just the faintest suggestion of a smile on his otherwise dour features. He had been physically engaged in the struggle with Israel for twenty-two years. He was well aware of the fact that the plight of his fellow Palestinians had not been at the forefront of Bin Laden's concerns until his fourth call to arms on October 7, 2001, when the Americans began their bombing campaign against the Taliban in Afghanistan.

The appearance of one of Osama's men interrupted the leader's discourse. The man made a respectful bow, then leaned down to whisper something in Osama's ear.

"Ah!" Osama declared. "The infidel soldiers have crossed into our lands from occupied Afghanistan and are moving through Mirim Shah where you left your vehicles to come up here. Do they suspect we are here? I doubt it, but come, we must take precautions." Moving with surprising speed on his canes, Osama led the way to yet another cave cut into the wall of an adjacent mountainside. Behind him his followers rushed to pack up his headquarters' litter in case an emergency evacuation became necessary.

The second cave was illuminated by the light of a single candle, and a large stone was rolled across its entrance to seal it off from the outside world. The aide who had alerted them to the Americans in the valley below remained with them. Once they had settled in the darkness on another pair of carpets, he drew a syringe from the folds of his cloak and proceeded to inject a dose of insulin into Osama's forearm.

"Ah," the leader said, shaking his arm, "you see the conditions in which these Americans force me to live?" Then he smiled and blew out their single candle. "I care not. Pain on the path of the *jihad* is the purest of pleasures. Today *jihad* is obligatory for the Islamic nation, which is in a state of sin because we rush madly after the comforts of life and have discarded the Book. We let Jews and Christians tempt us with their cheap pleasures and their sordid and materialistic values."

He waved a spindly white hand in the cave's darkness.

"To return, my brother, to the great dream which brought you here. We worked toward such a goal in Afghanistan before the American invasion. We had laboratories in Kabul, Jalalabad and Kandahar, and Russian scientists working with us. It is only when we have those weapons that we will be able to meet the enemy on equal terms."

Osama paused, allowing an eerie silence to envelop their blackened cave. Then, his voice dropping to something like a sepulchral whisper, he resumed. "Islam is in retreat because the people are not walking in the path of the Prophet. Love of death in the cause of Allah has deserted our hearts. It is not in the path of thieves and infidels that we will find the arms we need. Ours must be the path of Islam. We must find brave fellow Muslims who are ready to walk with us in the vanguard of the *jihad* and secure these weapons, Islamic weapons. Those weapons now exist. They are in Islamic hands, and I have found three believers among those who control them. With them we will have the means to achieve our goal. They will be here in forty-eight hours, and you will stay here as my honored guest to meet with them. Together, we shall gain the arm that will give us the vengeance we seek."

*　　　*　　　*

It was, indeed, exactly forty-eight hours later that Mugniyeh was summoned back to Osama's presence in the same cave where their first meeting had taken place. Looking at Osama, he understood instantly just how important this meeting was going to be. The Islamic leader was wearing a brand-new turban, its white folds so pristine they almost glowed. His beard had been freshly trimmed, and the streaks of gray which usually marked it had been carefully dyed. Even the most devout among us, Mugniyeh thought with a smile, is not immune to the stirrings of a little masculine vanity.

The two men awaited their guests just far enough inside the entrance to Osama's secret cave that no prowling American Predator spy vehicle could catch a glimpse of them. Exactly on schedule, Osama's two guests arrived on mule back escorted by two Pashtun warriors, members of a tribe to whose chief Osama paid a regular and generous protection fee. The first man to dismount was short and slim but carried himself with the erect posture of a military man. The second visitor had a rather melancholy expression and a neatly trimmed mustache. He wore his still-plentiful hair combed back from his forehead. Mugniyeh recognized him instantly. It was Abdul Qadeer Khan, the architect of Pakistan's atomic bomb, a man revered by Pakistan's citizenry with a fervor equal to that bestowed on the nation's founder, Mohammed Ali Jinnah. Osama rushed to greet him. From the warmth of their embrace, Mugniyeh understood immediately that the gossip of the bazaars was true. The two men were close and dear friends. The hugs they were exchanging were not ritual gestures but the manifestations of a deep and genuine affection. For sure the rumors were correct. Khan and Osama had worked together on the development of the Pakistani bomb in Kabul before the Americans had invaded.

Osama led the pair to Mugniyeh to introduce him. The shorter man was Major General Hamid Gul, former commander of the Pakistan Army's elite ISI, Inter-Services Intelligence. This secretive organization's responsibilities now included safeguarding the warehouses in which the warheads of Pakistan's nuclear force were hidden. His name, if not his face, was familiar indeed to the Lebanese terrorist.

What Mugniyeh could not know, of course, was that Gul was considered by the CIA to be the most dangerous man in Pakistan. And yet for ten years Gul had fought with courage and determination alongside the CIA's operatives in their war against the Russians in Afghanistan. They had baptized him "the BLG"—Brave Little General—both for his size and his valor in battle.

But for Gul, his American colleagues had become the ultimate traitors when, after the Red Army's defeat, the U.S. governments of Ronald Reagan and George H.W. Bush imposed sanctions on Pakistan for its nuclear program—a program to which the United States firmly closed its eyes during the decade when it needed Pakistan's cooperation in fighting the Russians in Afghanistan. One of his American colleagues said that Gul had become like "a woman scorned." As "hell hath no fury like a woman scorned," so Gul's fury at his former allies had no limits. His son had been enrolled, with CIA help, at Texas A&M and Gul promptly pulled him out. No son of his was going to be schooled in a university of the Great Satan. He quit the Pakistan Army and the ISI and joined an Islamic extremist movement, the UTN, the Umma Tameer-e-Nun, the Reconstruction of the Muslim Umma (community).

Working closely with UTN leaders he had organized a series of secret cells inside the officer corps of the Pakistan Army. Many were high-ranking officers of the ISI, including some of those responsible for safeguarding the nation's nuclear arms.

Osama led them into the cave where a meager but well-intentioned welcoming banquet awaited them. Mugniyeh could not suppress a smile at how tidy, how well ordered the cave now was compared to the chaos he had noted on his arrival. The notebooks, cartridge clips and computer disks had all been packed away, and kerosene lamps, not candles, illuminated the place. Osama, ever the good host, waited to formally open their discussions until his guests had eaten and mint tea and coffee had been served.

"My brothers," he said, "I asked you to join me here today because I firmly believe the time has come for our *jihad* to rise above the guerrilla tactics we have employed in the past. It's no longer enough to swear, as we once did, that with an AK-47 and the Koran, Islam can triumph. Brave martyrs driving trucks filled with high explosives into the barracks and embassies of the infidel, into the markets of the Jews, placing bombs in the discotheques of their decadent youths, even flying jets into the skyscrapers of the Great Satan, were acts of courage and nobility. But now we must escalate our struggle to a new dimension.

"Today," he continued, "the *jihad* must employ those very weapons the infidel's scientists developed to impose their rule on our universe. The Americans are embarked on a war of extermination against the peoples of the *umma*, our Islamic community. Look at what they did to Iraq. Look at how they help the Jews enslave our brothers in Palestine. And what have our leaders done? Nothing!"

He sighed as if to underscore the enormity of that failure. "The Koran orders us to give Muslims the strongest means of defense. Our leaders' failure to do so is an act of treason, a rebellion against the very injunction of Allah. I say 'let this Bush suffer the horrible punishment of God for what he has done.' We must take revenge upon him. We must strip him of his sense of security and stability."

Osama paused, took a sip of his coffee—a calculated, dramatic hiatus—as he drew toward the climax of his little oration. "Thanks to the inspired work of our great brother Abdul Qadeer Khan and his respected colleagues, the Sword of God now waits to be seized by our avenging hands. You, Dr. Khan, believe as I do that the atomic bombs hidden in the arsenals of this great nation are not Pakistani bombs. They are Islamic bombs. They belong to the community of the faithful. The time has now come to use these weapons against the powerful tyrants who oppress us. Is that not so, dear friend?"

Khan coughed to clear his throat. "My brothers," he declared, "I agree with Osama when he says ours is an Islamic bomb, not a Pakistani bomb. When Prime Minister Bhutto first asked me to work on it in a secret meeting in his office in December 1974, I immediately saw it as an Islamic bomb, not as he did as a means of defending Pakistan against Indian aggression. I thought: 'The Americans have the bomb. The Jews have the bomb. The Chinese have the bomb. Why is it we, the Muslims, are the only people forbidden to have it?' Today, thanks in large part to my work, we have fifty-two bombs in our nuclear arsenal. They are, as Osama says, Islamic bombs. They do not belong to one nation but to the *umma*. They provide us Pakistanis, as Prime Minister Bhutto wanted, with a means of deterring Indian aggression on our subcontinent, be it against Kashmir or any place else. But what else might they achieve for us?"

"Surely our arms could destroy the Zionist oppressors of our brothers in Palestine, could they not?" Osama asked.

"Certainly," Khan answered. "We could fire a dozen of them on Israel and feel sure at least three would reach their targets. Israel is geographically a very small nation and three well-placed atom bombs would destroy it. And we would still have all the arms we need to defend ourselves against India."

Smiles came to Osama bin Laden's ascetic features about as often as snow does to the tropics, but those words brought a glow to his face. "There, my brothers," he said, "is our answer."

"No," Khan replied, "unfortunately it is not. Israel's

nuclear force is larger than ours, larger than India's, larger even than England's. They have over two hundred nuclear arms. Most of their bombs are fitted onto their Jericho missiles in hardened underground silos in the Judean Hills. They will survive our attack. Our bombs may kill three million Israelis but some will have lived to fire those missiles at us. They will eradicate our nation and kill forty million of us. We will have turned our Pakistan into a massive state suicide bomber. I built my Islamic nuclear bomb to defend our nation not to hasten its destruction."

A respectful silence greeted his words. No one in Pakistan had a greater right than Khan to debate how the nation's bombs should be employed. Born in Jullundur, in the Punjab, he had been driven with his parents from India into the new nation of Pakistan in the bloody fighting that had accompanied the Partition. He was embittered at his experience and devoted his life to Islam and to a scientific career. He vowed that he would help bring his new nation the best of modern weaponry so that its people would never undergo another experience like his.

In 1972 he went to England to study metallurgy and then moved to Düsseldorf to work for Urenco, a Dutch, German and British firm that focused on developing high-speed centrifuges to enrich uranium.

Stung by Pakistan's humiliating defeat in 1971 when East Pakistan, aided by India, had become the independent nation of Bangladesh, Prime Minister Zulfikar Ali Bhutto sought to equip his nation with atomic arms to counterbalance India's superiority in conventional weapons. He asked Abdul Qadeer Khan to join that effort in the secret 1974 meeting in his office. They agreed and Khan returned to work with Urenco in both Germany and Holland, where for a year he advanced his knowledge of centrifuges, translated classified German documents, then abruptly left for Karachi in March 1976, taking with him an enormous storehouse of knowledge. By July, he was running a Pakistani uranium enrichment program in Kahuta.

While the CIA was well aware of those activities, the Reagan Administration chose to ignore them in return for General Zia Al Huq's cooperation in fighting the Soviets in Afghanistan.

By 1981 Pakistan's first centrifuges, thanks in large part to Khan's work, were beginning to produce enriched uranium. By 1984, one thousand centrifuges were working and Pakistan's scientists ran "cold" computer tests for the design of an implosion bomb.

After the Russians left Afghanistan in 1990, President George H.W. Bush invoked the Glenn-Symington Amendment placing sanctions on Pakistan because it was producing nuclear weapons. But by then it was too late. The horse was out of the barn. Pakistan had close to a dozen nuclear weapons comparable to the one dropped on Hiroshima.

"Then what can this great weapon, this scientific triumph, achieve for us?" asked a dejected Osama.

"Let me as a military man answer that," declared General Gul. "Dr. Khan is right. It is true that our Ghauri-III missiles can reach Tel Aviv. We were able to develop them thanks to the aid our North Korean friends gave us in return for the help Dr. Khan's laboratory gave to them in developing their atomic weapons. But first we must recognize that the Israelis have an excellent missile defense system, the Arrow, which they developed with the Americans. They just tested it against an intercontinental ballistic missile—and shot the missile out of the sky with it. We might be able to score several hits with the Ghauri if we fire them on a very precisely timed schedule so they would fly into Israeli airspace out of the sun so as to very briefly create a blind spot in the Israelis radar systems. But as Dr. Khan indicated, the Israelis would know from their radar where the missiles came from and their retribution would be certain and overwhelming."

"No one in this cave loathes the Americans more than I do," Gul declared, "but as a soldier I understand and accept Dr. Khan's position. That is not the way to use the great weapon he and his fellow scientists have put at our disposal."

"Then what is?" asked a disheartened Osama bin Laden.

Gul leaned back on his carpet and sipped at his strong black coffee. "I assume that most of you followed as I did the recent American presidential elections."

The members of his little audience nodded.

"Bush and Kerry could agree on only one thing—the greatest danger America faces is a weapon of mass destruction falling into the hands of so-called terrorists, people like us, ready to employ it to threaten an American city. Cheney, Bush's vice president, called it 'America's nightmare.'"

Once again the cave dwellers nodded their agreement.

"Well, my friends, I propose we make that little nightmare come alive for those damned Americans. Shatter their dreams of enslaving our Islamic *umma*."

Another sudden smile burst over Osama's face. "*Aywah, aywah*—yes, yes!" he murmured.

"When the Americans set out to destroy the Taliban," Gul continued, "that traitor Musharraf sold our country to them for their war. At the same time he took our nuclear devices from their warehouse in Kahuta and dispersed them to six secret new locations. One of them is at Tikrim Mir, not far from here. As you are aware, I have created a clandestine organization inside the officer ranks of the ISI. These fighters for Islam are men who share our ideals and the conviction that we need *jihad* in these terrible times. The ISI officer in charge of the installation at Tikrim Mir is one of my fighters for Islam."

Gul reflected for a moment and added, "I believe I can convince him to let us spirit a bomb out of his facility in the middle of the night."

"Now as most of you do not realize, our bombs and the detonator sets which explode them are kept in separate locations. The detonators are in Chasma. I suggest Dr. Khan and I go to Chasma and fit out our stolen bomb with an appropriate detonation system."

"Certainly we could do that," Khan agreed. "No one would be surprised to see me in Chasma or ask questions about what I was doing there. I think we should marry the detonation device to a mobile telephone that we can purchase in Karachi. I could set the detonator to respond to the number we have programmed into it. The bomb will only explode if the secret number is called. Osama and no one else will have the number."

Osama bin Laden had been studying the scientist's face as he spoke. There had been no indication of emotional conflict. Although Khan, as Bin Laden knew, was a man who loved poetry and flowers, his hatred of Americans was such that killing a million or so of them with one of his bombs would not disturb him.

He looked next across the carpet to Mugniyeh. "I am sure that among your followers are brave young men who crave death so that eternal life will be given unto them as martyrs. Men who with the help of my organization and our knowledge of international customs and travel regulations would be prepared to smuggle this weapon to the land of the Great Satan."

At his words, Mugniyeh's thoughts went to the horrors of the Ein el-Hilweh Palestinian refugee camp in southern Lebanon. It was by far the most horrible of those horrible camps, a sinkhole festering with hatred and despair, where hope was an illusion not a promise.

"Yes, my brother, I do, and they will be people who can speak fluent English and glide among the Americans as one of them, believers who have spent their lives studying and preparing for the opportunity God had not yet given them."

Once again, Gul took over the discussion. "What is critical," he said, "is that the Americans do not know where the bomb came from, that this is in fact a Pakistani bomb." He looked at Mugniyeh. "Our brother Osama has told me that you have with you a design for a bomb which Saddam Hussein gave you. It is clearly a copy of the Iraqi plan the United Nations inspectors seized in 1995. The Americans know that plan. We must send them a copy of it saying this is the bomb we are using. They will know immediately that it is a valid design—an Iraqi design."

"Yes," Mugniyeh agreed, "but how are they to know we were able to make it? They could say this is just a hoax, that no such bomb has been smuggled into their country."

"Very good point," Gul agreed. "I suggest we send them some enriched uranium along with the bomb design and say this is what we made it with." The beauty of this scheme is that the Americans for all their atomic might and power will not be able to retaliate, because they will not know who to retaliate against. They will be blinded by the circumstances.

"After we have smuggled it out of the arsenal and fitted it with its detonator," he concluded, "the entire device will weigh a little more than fifty kilograms. I will pack it into a large wooden crate like the kind that would contain, for example, a dishwashing machine. You will be able to transport it without difficulty on a camel's back."

Osama and Mugniyeh listened fascinated, indicating their approval with enthusiastic nods of their heads. The irony of moving an atomic bomb on a camel's back was not lost to them. "Shipping the bomb directly to Karachi to put it on a U.S.-bound freighter would present us with a double risk," Gul warned. "The first is that between Chasma and Karachi it might somehow be intercepted by CIA agents or Pakistani police in their pay. From that, the second risk—the Americans would then be able to determine that the bomb came from our arsenal and that would be a catastrophe. We must make sure that until the bomb is on a ship bound for the U.S. it stays as much as possible on Indian soil."

"Of course," Osama agreed. "Since the border crossings between India and Pakistan are all officially closed, we must pass the bomb in one of the camel caravans that slip across the Rajasthan desert. Those smugglers pay off the police on both sides of the border and nobody ever bothers them. My men smuggle drugs that way all the time. With the growth of opium poppy cultivation in Afghanistan we are once again financing our struggle by using drugs purchased by the rotten youth of the West. While the Americans have spy satellites studying caravan traffic crossing the desert, there is no way they could detect an atom bomb hidden under a pile of carpets on the back of a camel. A team of my al Qaeda men will meet the caravan in Jaisalmer, and they will arrange to smuggle the crate into the United States. This is something in which we have much experience, using loyal Muslim shipping companies operating out of India. There they are much less under surveillance than companies in Karachi, for example."

"Where do you propose we hide it once we've gotten it into the United States?" Khan asked Osama.

"I would like to see it placed in New York. New York is the symbol of everything we all loathe in America: their power, their greedy, grasping hands strangling us financially, their corrupt, decadent television and entertainment industry. And after all there are more Jews in New York than there are in Tel Aviv. You told me in Kabul that the most awesome aspect of a nuclear explosion is the heat it generates, killing people for miles around the blast and setting thousands of fires. So be it. Let us burn New York. Reduce that evil citadel to ashes with the scourge of fire."

Mugniyeh found himself assigned a far greater role than he had imagined possible when he had voyaged to Osama's secret hideaway. "*Sayed*—sir—may I make a suggestion?"

"Of course."

"What will hiding and then detonating the bomb in a great American city achieve for our cause?"

"It will tell the Americans one thing—what you have suffered until now was only the initial skirmish," Osama answered with vehemence. "Now the real battle has started."

"But, my brother, it will lead the Americans to seek blind and brutal vengeance against Muslims. The hate 9/11 inspired will seem mild in comparison. I have learned one thing in the operations I conducted, beginning with the bombing of the U.S. Marine barracks in Lebanon. To be effective, an operation must have a precise objective. In Beirut my goal was to drive the Americans from Lebanon. It succeeded. When Reagan saw how many of his beloved marines had died, he fled."

"So what would you propose?"

"Suppose we tell the Americans, 'The bomb will explode in New York or Washington or Chicago in a week if you do not force the Israelis to promise publicly before the entire world that they will leave all the illegal settlements on the land seized from our Palestinian brothers after 1967.'"

Mugniyeh sat back to sample the reaction to his words. "That is something we could realistically hope to achieve. All the world, even the American people themselves, and many Israelis, see the terrible injustice those settlements represent. Everyone except the fanatics in Israel will agree and support our just demand. If Sharon refuses and if a million Americans die, it will be the Israelis' fault, not ours."

Bin Laden turned to General Gul. "What do you think as a military man? And as someone who knows so well how our nuclear arms are stored. Could we smuggle one out? Is such a plan really possible?"

Gul stretched his legs out on the carpet and closed his eyes in thoughtful concentration. "Yes," he said on opening them, "I think it is possible. It will take some time because it obviously must be done in total secrecy but I know which of my fighters for Islam I can count on to help us."

"Brilliant," Osama said. "Our Islamic nuclear bomb will bring justice to our brothers in Palestine at last, in a way the whole world can accept and understand. How can the Americans do anything but agree?"

*　　　*　　　*

Just over six weeks later, a Toyota sedan bearing the signs of the ISI turned off the Islamabad-Karachi highway some fifty miles past the Pakistani village of Naya Chor. It drove onto a hard-packed dirt track paralleling the Indian Pakistani border along the parched Rajasthan desert. Its destination was the tiny border-crossing village of Qadr, little more than a collection of ramshackle dirt and wood huts.

The driver was a lieutenant colonel in the ISI uniform that was certain to command respect along the frontier. Beside him, in civilian clothes, was retired general Gul. In the back seats were Osama bin Laden and Imad Mugniyeh. All four men were wrapped in a thoughtful silence, thinking of the enormity of the act they were about to accomplish.

Gul's plan had worked exactly as he had hoped. The driver of the car was a member of his clandestine network inside the ISI. He was the officer in charge of the secret Pakistani nuclear storehouse in Kabirwala, a tiny town in the Punjab.

Under the cover of night, and with the aid of a fellow conspirator, he had managed to remove one of the eight atomic bombs assigned to him for safekeeping.

It had been a delicate operation. The ISI had installed a computerized security system in the arsenal so that if any of the eight bombs were tampered with a signal would be sent to the Nuclear Command headquarters in Islamabad. The colonel however had the code that controlled the alarm system and was able to put it on standby long enough to remove one of the bombs. He also had altered its settings so that when he turned the system back on it would show the bomb still in place. Only a physical inspection of the arsenal could reveal that it was missing.

Gul had driven the bomb to Chasma where Dr. Khan had married it to a detonation system wired, as he had promised, to a cell phone. His system was equipped with a sophisticated American-made scanning device programmed to screen out any incoming wrong numbers so that the bomb could not be exploded by error. It would respond only to a call by Osama or Mugniyeh, who would be only ones to have the cell phone's number.

From his seat beside the driver, Gul indicated half a dozen camels gathered around a clump of scraggly, burned out shrubs, the best imitation of a watering hole the Rajasthan desert had to offer.

"There they are," he said.

The driver pulled over, and as he did, three men emerged from under a cloth stretched over four poles just behind the camels. "My men," Gul said. "They know this desert perfectly. They will guide you safely into India."

Gul, Mugniyeh and the driver got out, leaving Osama in the backseat, his familiar face partially screened by the car's shades. Gul opened the trunk. The bomb was inside, packed into a large wooden crate. Two of the camel drivers came over, lifted it from the trunk and carried it to one of their waiting camels where they fitted it into a rope sling suspended from the animal's hump. Of course they had no idea what was in the crate. They tossed over it a red and purple Afghan carpet similar to the carpets the other camels were carrying.

Bin Laden slipped out of the car and went over to Mugniyeh. He gave the Lebanese terrorist a warm embrace, then pressed a small envelope into his hand. "My men will be waiting for you on the other side of the border. They will take you to your destination near Bombay. Everything you will need to know about the rest of your onward journey is here."

He then stepped discreetly up to the bomb under its carpet on the camel's back. He laid his hand on it. "Allah, the inspirer of the Book and the conductor of the clouds, grant the *mujahideen* victory over the infidels wherever they may be. Establish firmly our heroes and help them with a victory of yours, for there is no helper for them and for us except you," he muttered in a voice pitched so low that none of the ISI men manning the camel caravan could understand him.

Meanwhile, an ISI officer had helped Mugniyeh onto the saddle of one of the waiting camels. The leader gave a whip-stroke to the animal's flank, and slowly, with their ancient swaying motion, the ships of the desert set off, carrying the most modern of devices toward its distant destination.

Gul, Bin Laden and the colonel watched silently as the six animals plodded their way toward the horizon. Finally, as the last animal disappeared from sight, twisting around a towering sand dune, Bin Laden murmured a kind of invocation to provide closure to what they had done. "At last, the vengeance of the just shall be ours."

*　　　*　　　*

Bin Laden's al Qaeda operatives transported the bomb from Jaisalmer, in India, down to the suburbs of Bombay exactly as their chieftain had ordered. Once there, Imad Mugniyeh confided it to their capable hands for its onward shipment to the United States. He had no idea—nor was he supposed to have any—of how they intended to do that. It was their business, but he well knew that smuggling illegal goods into the United States was relatively easy.

He climbed back into his favorite disguise, his black chador, and with the woman's passport his Iranian friends had given him, headed for Bombay Airport. Then he flew back to Tehran on Air India. In the Iranian capital, his associates arranged for his onward journey to Beirut. There, a mission of considerable importance awaited him—recruiting the three volunteers he had promised Bin Laden—the three who would travel to the land of the Great Satan to receive the bomb when it arrived, move it into an appropriate hiding place, and make sure it was ready to go off in the apocalyptic explosion for which Abdul Qadeer Khan had programmed it.

His Hezbollah associates had arranged a meeting with three volunteers, all fluent English speakers, in the most sordid of Palestinian refugee camps, Ein el-Hilweh, just south of the

Lebanese seaport of Sidon. Nothing quite so filled Imad Mugniyeh's heart with hatred as walking down the mud- and garbage-filled alleys of Ein el-Hilweh. For the terrorist leader, each visit there stirred two conflicting emotions: his hatred for the Israelis who had driven these wretched people from their homes half a century ago, and his shame for the Lebanese whose policies had done so much to compound the misery of their existence.

The camp claimed the sad record of housing the densest concentration of human beings of any of the Middle East's refugee camps. Forty thousand people were crammed into an area not much larger than half a dozen football fields. It was a site without trees, without flowers, without butterflies, without birds— with the exception of a few flocks of predatory crows.

Children grew up in the camp without knowing a shrub, a green forest, an open field or even the sea whose shores were nonetheless close to its western borders—but polluted by the overflow of the camp's sewage system sluicing its waters into the sea. Tuberculosis, malaria, dysentery were prevalent and helped contribute to the low life-expectancy of the camp's inhabitants. It was feverishly hot in the summer, and then the winter rains turned its alleys into muddy lakes.

Mugniyeh and his guide made their way gingerly through the mud, the stench of urine and the hordes of flies buzzing over the human excrement littering the alley. All was stark testimony to the inadequacies of the camp's sewage system even fifty-five years after the first refugees arrived.

Most refugees had to live on the meager rations distributed by UNRWA, the United Nations Relief and Works Agency created in 1948 to care for the Palestinians who had fled their homeland following its division by the UN to create the State of Israel. The unemployment rate was extraordinarily high, primarily because the Lebanese authorities were determined not to allow the refugees to infiltrate their society. The refugees were prohibited from working in seventy-two occupations ranging from the law and medicine to sales, clerical work and accounting without a government work permit.

The generosity of the Lebanese in issuing those permits can be summed up in one statistic: in fifty-three years they had delivered 2,500 permits to a total refugee population numbering 364,000—hence the camp's staggering unemployment rate.

A terrible sense of despair weighed on the population since the Nakba—the disaster—of 1948 when hundreds of thousands of Palestinians had fled or been driven from their towns and villages in the aftermath of the creation of Israel. Three generations of refugees had been born, lived and died in places like Ein el-Hilweh that were a disgrace to mankind's conscience.

The refugee camps had become the wellspring of the hate and violence that for years had nourished the more violent aspects of the Palestinians' struggle. While the camp was well distant from the Israeli frontier, its residents had always provided Palestinian gangs with a steady stream of volunteers for the armed combat against the Jewish state. Many of the shacks of Ein el-Hilweh were decorated with a portrait of a man in a *kaffiyeh* who had given his life in the struggle. Their places of honor had recently been supplemented by portraits of postadolescent youths bearing a black handkerchief on their foreheads. Regularly, the camp's young men had signed on with Hamas, Hezbollah or the al-Aqsa Martyrs' Brigade, whose leaders were able to indoctrinate many of them into giving up their lives infiltrating Israel, stomachs banded by the suicide bomber's belt. The resulting random carnage, even the death of Israeli children on school buses, didn't seem to deter them.

Thanks to the Palestinians' traditional thirst for education and learning, however, many refugees had over the years managed to get university and post graduate degrees. Yet even with diplomas in hand, there was no way to avoid the stringent Lebanese work rules. Men with a master's in physics wound up digging ditches for a living. Frustrated, embittered, those men and women constituted an ideal recruitment pool for terrorist managers like Mugniyeh.

The meeting arranged for Mugniyeh was set in the shack of an attractive thirty-three-year-old widow, Nahed Jihari. Her beloved husband had died during an Israeli air assault on his Hezbollah position in southern Lebanon in 1997.

On the wall of her bedroom, beside his photo in his *fedayeen*'s uniform, Nahed had hung the official document he had given her as his wedding present, a British Mandate certificate of ownership of three *dunums* of land on the seacoast below Jaffa. There was also her own diploma from the American University of Beirut. Her dark eyes were accentuated by the kohl with which she surrounded them and gave her a deceptive image of fragility. She was overjoyed by the visit of the legendary Hezbollah leader who she had not seen since he had promised her vengeance at her husband's funeral.

Waiting for Mugniyeh as well were two men he had asked to see. Omar Tahiri was forty-two, a lean, well-built man with what seemed an expression of perpetual melancholy on his face. His father had brought him to Ein el-Hilweh as a baby. He had lived his childhood and adolescence to the music of his father's constantly repeated promise that "One day we will return to Jaffa and eat the best oranges in the world."

Of course, he had never returned. The only Jaffa orange he had ever eaten was one he had bought at Marks & Spencer's in

London on his way to Montreal's McGill University. Ambitious and bright, Tahiri had won himself scholarships to the American University of Beirut, then to McGill where he had earned a master's degree in architecture.

Back at Ein el-Hilweh, however, he was trapped by the Lebanese work permit restrictions and he had to employ his architect's degree building latrines.

Angry and embittered, he had volunteered his services to the Hezbollah in its struggle with Israel's occupying forces in southern Lebanon. His courage and poise under fire had caught Mugniyeh's eye. The terrorist chieftain had trained him as an explosives expert, until a premature explosion had blown away his left hand in 1996. No one could have been happier to get the word that Mugniyeh wanted to see him than Tahiri. Maybe, he had thought, this was the summons back to action he had so desperately longed for since losing his hand.

The third person waiting for Mugniyeh was the youngest of the trio, Amr bin Khaled, a starkly handsome twenty-six-year-old who was the darling of the camp's few unmarried women and not a few of their married sisters as well.

As a kid growing up, Khaled had become addicted to watching American TV programs from which the bright young man had gained a mastery of colloquial, American-accented English. At eighteen, he had agreed to sign up as a recruit with Hezbollah's fighters battling the Israelis in the south. Three years of constant combat had given him an extensive knowledge of arms and explosives, but above all, a reputation as a fighter. Despite his young age he had shown remarkable ability to remain cool under pressure and was imaginative and resourceful when faced with the unexpected. His shooting down an Israeli helicopter with a Stinger missile had proven to his leaders that he had the audacity Mugniyeh was looking for.

Nahed had laid out for them the best welcoming meal her meager rations would allow. The four all embraced warmly, then sat down to her food on the four spindly chairs she possessed. When they finished their coffee, Mugniyeh began his recruiting pitch.

"What we are going through today is beyond description," he said. "International infidelity led by the Great Satan has joined against the Muslim nation to eliminate our holy strugglers. The time has now come for us to strike back with the most terrible of arms available to us. We will be called 'enemies of humanity' and 'terrorists,' but we must ignore such things. Prophet Muhammad was called worse names, but did he abandon his struggle?

"To accomplish this great task, we require three brave strugglers. I cannot tell you now what the mission will be. All I can say is that it will be far from here. It will require courage, skill and determination, which I know you all possess. You will receive in time the papers and money you will need for the task, and the training to carry it out. Will it be dangerous you ask? Yes, it will. You may well die in executing it. But if you succeed, your names will be forever enshrined with Islam's greatest heroes."

Tahiri looked at his two companions, his eyes asking a question his tongue did not have to articulate.

"For my beloved husband; for him, for sure," Nahed whispered.

"Count me in," said Khaled.

Tahiri turned back to Mugniyeh. "We all thank God for having chosen us for this great matter, my brother," he said with a slight, formal bow.

CHAPTER

3

PORT ELIZABETH, NEW JERSEY

A Container of Basmati Rice

"SS *Jewel of India* outward bound from Bombay and South Hampton requests clearance to enter port."

Lieutenant Bob Farrelly of the U.S. Coast Guard scrutinized the white splotch on his radar screen. It showed that another ship stood poised at the entrance of the Narrows, the channel leading off the swells of the Atlantic into the Port of New York. A quick glance at the computer screen on his desk confirmed the *Jewel*'s expected arrival on this Thursday morning, and her destination, Port Elizabeth's Marine Terminal 4.

"SS *Jewel of India*," Farrelly announced into the radio before him, "your ID is X49Y72. Heave to and await instructions while we process your clearance."

His order was a function of the new procedures set in place after the terror attack of 9/11 to govern shipping entering New York Harbor. They were part of a national effort to prevent terrorists from smuggling arms, people or weapons of mass destruction into U.S. ports. While ships were on the water, the responsibility for enforcing those procedures lay with the Coast Guard. Once in port, it passed to Customs, the FBI, the CIA and, in the *Jewel*'s case, the port authority police.

A score of uniformed Coast Guard officers and enlisted men and women milled around Farrelly in their headquarters perched on top of Fort Wadsworth. The fort, originally built during the American Revolution to prevent British men-o'-war from assaulting New York, was now the vantage point from which the Coast Guard could survey the flow of traffic along The Narrows. A bank of TV monitors screened for them the images of passing ships shot by a dozen cameras stationed along the waterway.

Farrelly tapped into his computer's data bank for the file on the *Jewel*. She was the seventh ship to enter the harbor this autumn morning, bringing to New York its share of the twenty-one thousand containers unloaded in U.S. ports every day. They represented just a fraction of the eleven million containers circulating on the globe's seaways, the product of a shipping revolution which, curiously enough, had begun right in Port Elizabeth in 1965.

Farrelly brought up on the computer screen what was, in a sense, the *Jewel*'s legal dossier, another of the post-9/11 procedures. That dossier recorded any legal incident in the *Jewel*'s recent past, whether it was a pack of heroin found concealed under her deck planking, a drunken brawl involving a couple of her seamen, or any suspicion that she might have been involved in some form of illicit traffic or a violation of maritime law.

Like so many ships in international commerce, the *Jewel* flew a Panamanian flag of convenience. The Ships Registry listed her owner as a Panamanian corporation, Interocean Commerce. That of course was pure fiction. Dummy companies like that were designed to protect ships' real owners from lawsuits arising from oil spills or other maritime mishaps. The Panamanian government simply was not prepared to reveal who really owned the ships that flew the nation's flags to anyone for any reason.

Since she displaced more than three hundred tons, the *Jewel*'s master had been obliged under the Coast Guard's new ATS—Automated Targeting System—to furnish the U.S. port authorities with a detailed manifest of the cargo she was carrying ninety-six hours before her arrival in New York. It had to include a detailed listing of the destination of each of the containers she carried and a full list of their contents as furnished by their shippers.

To further strengthen its control of incoming commerce, U.S. Customs had recently initiated a program called the Container Security Initiative. Under that program, U.S. Customs officers were stationed in foreign ports to work with the local authorities as the cargo containers were loaded. The idea was to be sure none were employed to smuggle arms, weapons of mass destruction or, as had happened recently on an Egyptian ship, a member of al Qaeda bearing detailed plans of U.S. airports.

Farrelly's inspection of the *Jewel*'s dossier was swift and routine. The 20,000-ton vessel called on the ports of New York and New Orleans four or five times a year and she had scrupulously followed U.S. Customs and maritime regulations. The 175 cargo containers, stuffed into her cargo holds and jamming her deck, carried the creations of India's thriving handicraft industries – piles of silk and embroidered shirts, blouses, pants and shoes ordered by the purchasing agents of Gap, Banana Republic and the other clothing dynasties servicing U.S. malls. Some containers were full of furniture, carpets, dishes and glassware destined for the display shelves of stores like Macy's and Bloomingdale's. Still others were packed with sacks of basmati rice from the Punjab, tea from Darjeeling, coffee from Kerala, jars of chutney from Goa, cans of shrimp and crab from Bengal and the exotic spices of the East for which the nations of Europe had once fought their colonial wars.

Her clearance was straightforward. Farrelly tapped it onto his computer and turned his radio on. "*Jewel of India,*" he announced, "your pilot is coming on board and you are cleared to proceed to Port Elizabeth."

The *Jewel*'s master, a forty-six-year-old Bengali named Hari Das Gupta, waved his pilot aboard, moved his engines up to half speed and sailed for The Narrows. Although the master didn't know it, some of the buoys along his route were now topped with detectors meant to pick up gamma ray emissions from passing ships in case someone was trying to smuggle nuclear cargo into the city.

The master's attention was transfixed by the prodigious spectacle that never ceased to enthrall him, the entrance to the Port of New York. He smiled at the Ferris wheel and parachute drop of Coney Island, homeland now to thousands of Russian immigrants.

Minutes later he was passing under the graceful spans of the Verrazano-Narrows Bridge. Then, almost before he knew it, off to starboard was the sight that had thrilled so many over the decades, the green-sheathed Statue of Liberty, lifting her torch at the door to the Promised Land. Behind her, the towers of Manhattan pierced the morning mist, incandescent trunks of a forest of glass and steel, clawing up to the sky.

As they had for three years now, his eyes focused on the glaring gap in that majestic skyline, the place where the Twin Towers of the World Trade Center had once stood. For some curious reason, that sight had always made him think of the gap-toothed smile of his six-year-old daughter in the weeks after she had lost her two front teeth. What a sad sight Lower Manhattan had become without those two proud towers!

Beside him, the pilot gestured to the entrance of the Kill Van Kull and the master ordered his helmsman to come to port and start his passage up the seaway along the shores of Staten Island into Newark Bay. As he did, he picked up his radio to announce his arrival to the Port Elizabeth harbormaster.

"Roger *Jewel of India*," the port's shipping officer acknowledged, "we are assigning you berth seventeen in Marine Terminal Four."

*   *   *

The twin maritime terminals of Port Newark and Port Elizabeth extended along Newark Bay opposite Manhattan. They stretched from the landing strips of Newark Airport all the way to the city of Newark itself. Together they probably represented the largest, and certainly the most modern, container-cargo facility in the world. Their more efficient modern docking facilities had pretty much consigned to history the docks of Red Hook and the Brooklyn waterfront. Those piers on which mafia hoods had once picked their loyal longshoremen at the daily shape-ups were largely empty now, as were the piers of the Brooklyn Marine Terminal from which two generations of GIs had sailed to fight in European wars.

The facilities of the twin ports were a mirror of what was most vibrant and modern in American maritime transport. But since 9/11, they were something else as well—a fragile frontier through which a terrorist's weapon of massive destruction might one day slip undetected. The problem was tremendous.

The nation's scientific centers like California's Lawrence Livermore National Laboratory were working hard at developing new and better detection technologies. But as is so often the case, the desire to get them was as strong as the flow of dollars out of Congress to pay for them was weak. At the end of 2002, the twin ports had received three of the best new devices, strange-looking trucks with long metallic arms carrying powerful gamma ray detectors. The vehicles were designed to run alongside the walls of a container or a truck and hopefully detect the presence inside of a nuclear device. Called VACIS, Vehicle and Cargo Inspection

Systems, those trucks cost a million dollars apiece. They could also provide a somewhat primitive image on a screen of the container's contents in much the same way as a camera scans a passenger's checked baggage at an airport.

The arrival of the first VACIS trucks was heralded at the twin ports as a first victory in the struggle with terrorists, but it was a victory of limited dimension. In twenty-four hours, the VACIS trucks at Port Elizabeth could only screen a hundred containers, representing 2 percent—and sometimes as little as one half of 1 percent—of the daily container inflow.

Early the next day, the unloading process began for the *Jewel,* following a well-oiled routine. Hari Das Gupta, her master, watched with satisfaction as a pair of the port's enormous cranes drew up alongside his ship to unload the 97 of his 175 containers that were destined for the New York area.

It was a swift and efficient process. The cranes, like a couple of immense metallic birds of prey, lowered their claws into the *Jewel's* cargo holds where her crewmen fastened them to a container. The container was then lifted from the ship's deck, swung over her side and lowered to the pier at which the *Jewel* was berthed. Each container bore the white initials INOS, for Indian Ocean Shipping, the name of the company to which they belonged. It also carried a band of four numbers that indicated their contents as set out on the manifest Das Gupta had provided the U.S. Coast Guard before his arrival.

Das Gupta watched fascinated as a team of customs officers scanned each side of the container with a machine that resembled a portable telephone. To Das Gupta's amusement, their inspection of each container took several minutes. "Maybe they think my Bengal shrimp give off atomic rays," he laughed to no one in particular. Never had he seen a customs inspector open a container and crawl inside to personally inspect its contents. Das Gupta well knew that would be an awesome task. Those containers were filthy, tightly packed and often stank. An inspector would have to slither and slide through them on his hands and knees.

Customs therefore had to rely on the cargo manifest declaration he had provided just as he had had to rely on the information given to him by the shipper in compiling that manifest. Trust, Das Gupta mused, was the essence of the American system.

The unloading of the *Jewel*'s New York–bound containers was completed by late afternoon. Shortly thereafter a pair of officers of the U.S. Citizenship and Immigration Services came aboard. Das Gupta assembled his crew in the seamen's lounge so the CIS officers could go through yet another of the post- 9/11 procedures. Each crewman had to present his passport with a valid U.S. visa and his seaman's papers. Once the officers were sure all were in order, they gave each sailor who wanted one an I-95 form that would allow the sailor to go ashore while the *Jewel* was in port.

"No passengers?" one of the officers asked Das Gupta.

The Indian master laughed. "My rust bucket isn't the *Queen Elizabeth*, officer!"

A couple of hours later, three crewmen who had decided to go ashore passed the immigration controls and boarded the bus for the short journey to the Port Authority Bus Terminal in Midtown Manhattan. The sex shops, the peep shows, the multitude of whores that once had beckoned to arriving visitors—all were gone now.

Surveying the scene, the eldest of the three crewmen, Malvinder Singh, sighed and told his younger companions, "You should have seen this place ten years ago. That crazy mayor," he pronounced the name *jooley yani*, "has made visiting New York about as much fun as going to a prayer meeting."

Undaunted, the trio continued to their destination, a Ruth's Chris Steak House, to savor a meal that the crewmen's mess of the *Jewel* did not offer.

After the waiter took their order for three rare double sirloin steaks, he asked them what they would like to drink.

"A Seagram's and Seven," the older seaman said.

"Make mine a double," echoed the man beside him who then turned to the last member of their trio. "Your usual ginger ale?" he asked.

"Why not?" the sailor answered. "While they're coming, I've got to make a phone call." He got up and went to the public telephone and took out his credit card and the scrap of paper on which he'd written the number of a cell phone.

"Hello," he said to the answering machine which responded, "I'm in New York. Everything went fine. We sail on the morning tide, God willing." No one is ever going to get suspicious about that call, he thought, hanging up the phone.

*   *   *

For many tourists, it was the best deal New York had to offer—nine bucks for the ultra-rapid, eighty-six-story elevator ride to the top of the Empire State Building. The tragic destruction of the Twin Towers of the World Trade Center had ironically restored the building to the position of dominance it had enjoyed for seventy years as the tallest building in New York and, for many of those years, in the world.

The 103-story Empire State Building was built on Fifth Avenue between Thirty-third and Thirty-fourth streets by a pair of financiers regarded by their contemporaries as either nuts or visionaries. It was opened in 1931, right at the depth of the Great Depression, and became a potent symbol of American power and determination.

The building was embedded into the popular imagination by the cinematic image of King Kong clinging to its summit while he plucked planes from the sky or, more recently, as a lovers' trysting spot in *Sleepless in Seattle.* It was as powerful a tourist attraction as New York possessed. Every day, its seventy-four elevators whisked up to forty thousand visitors to the observation platform on its eighty-sixth floor.

Since 9/11, that flow of visitors had been, quite understandably, subjected to rigorous security checks by metal detectors, X-ray scanners and a flock of security guards, most of them recruited from the ranks of retiring New York Police Department officers. From the lower floor shopping areas and the art deco restaurant to the summit, it was one of the most secure buildings in the United States.

By eight forty-five on this particular morning, an excited crowd was already waiting for the Observatory elevators to open at nine o'clock. That was hardly surprising. An electric sign promised this would be a day of "exceptional visibility," a day when, according to the old bromide, visitors would be able to "see forever"—i.e., through a circle forty miles (sixty kilometers) in diameter around the platform.

A guide ushered the first elevator-load of visitors to the southeastern side of the platform, where visits now began with a ritual contemplation of Ground Zero and a poignant moment of silence in memory of the two murdered towers. Then the platform tour began, some visitors following in the wake of the guide describing the spectacle below, others conducting their visits according to their own schedules and inclinations.

Federico Gonzales, the security officer on duty at the observation platform, was fascinated as always by the enthusiasm with which his visitors contemplated the spectacle. The great metropolis was sprawled below their lofty perch, the streets choked with honking yellow cabs and delivery vans, the towers of the lesser buildings huddled around the Empire State like a cluster of fawning vassals. In the distance, ferryboats cut across the water to Brooklyn and Staten Island.

Three of the tourists soon detached themselves from the group that was making its way around the platform and pausing to contemplate in silence the splendid vistas spread out below. Gonzales studied them from his lifeguard-style chair. Judging from the color of their skin, he decided they were probably fellow Latinos. Tourists from Central and South America almost always made it a point to visit the building. One of the three was a woman probably in her early thirties, wearing what looked like designer eyeglasses. A schoolteacher type, the guard thought. The second was a much younger man wearing a black leather jacket and blue jeans. Probably anxious to pass himself off to the girls as a native New Yorker, thought Gonzales. The last member of the trio was perhaps in his midforties, well dressed in a dark suit and tie. He had a neatly trimmed beard and a dour, almost melancholy expression. They hardly talked to each other, too absorbed apparently by the spectacular sight below.

Gonzales shifted his gaze for a moment to a more satisfying sight—a half dozen young French girls in miniskirts and tight-fitting blouses. When his eyes had returned to the trio of tourists he assumed to be Latinos, they had stopped by the guardrail looking out toward New Jersey. Fascinated, he watched as the older man took a small cellophane packet from his pocket. The poor guy, Gonzales observed, had only one hand, his right. His left was a stump at the wrist. With considerable skill he twisted the packet open with the fingers of his one hand and scattered what appeared to be dust or ashes over the guardrail. As the morning breeze swept the dust away, the three joined hands, the woman clutching the stump of the older man's left hand.

Ah! Gonzales thought. That was some sort of religious gesture—or perhaps a commemoration of the lost towers with some of the ashes of that horrible day.

CHAPTER

4

WASHINGTON D.C.

The Crisis—Day One

For White House interns assigned to it, the sprawling communications center in the basement of the Executive Office Building was jokingly referred to as the "Cyberspace Soup Kitchen." At its heart was a battery of printers hooked up to receive all the e-mail sent to the old White House e-mail address, president@whitehouse.gov, as well as to the newer website address, www.whitehouse.gov/webmail. Of course, the President had other classified e-mail addresses for serious government business, but they were known only to his cabinet members and top aides. Their e-mails came into an entirely different reception center, in the White House itself.

The printers in the "soup kitchen" clacked out in normal times an average of fifteen thousand e-mails a day. The variety of those messages to the President defied the imagination. They ran the gamut from a farmer in Iowa announcing he was sending a piglet to the White House as a gift, to a mother in Baton Rouge, Louisiana, stating she had decided to name her newborn son "George" after the President. And naturally there were the hatred- and vitriol-filled communications from the President's enemies, political and otherwise.

The e-mails provided the White House with a constantly evolving image of the nation's political pulse. The interns assigned to the center were trained to break them down and classify them into categories reflecting sentiment on key issues such as the ongoing war in Iraq, and with terrorism worldwide, the President's Social Security plan, tax policy, globalization, the budget deficit, unemployment, health care and so on. Each e-mail was identified by the state from which it had come so the President's advisors could see how his message was playing out in different parts of the country.

For example, the President's stands on abortion and stem cell research were getting positive response in the South and Midwest and a distinctly negative one in urban areas and the Northeast.

Anne McCormick, a twenty-six-year-old Vassar graduate hoping to find a permanent slot in the government hierarchy, was in charge of the Cyberspace Soup Kitchen this Sunday morning. She and her fellow interns had developed a reputation as meticulous workers, an unintended refutation of the record of other White House interns of an earlier age.

She was filing a stack of e-mails on the Social Security plan when one of her fellow interns rushed up to her.

"Hey Anne!" she said thrusting an e-mail at her. "I think you better have a look at what just came in on printer four!"

"Oh, dear Lord!" Anne exclaimed reading it. Crackpot messages were part of the daily routine in the Cyberspace Soup Kitchen but this one looked serious.

"We'd better get the Secret Service duty officer at the West Gate up here right away."

He was there minutes later, a fiftyish man, slightly overweight, gasping for breath after his sprint from the gate.

"This just arrived in the President's e-mail," Anne said, handing him the text. "Who knows? This one may be serious."

TO THE SERVANT OF THE GREAT SATAN, GEORGE W. BUSH, it began . . .

ALLAH, THE LORD OF THE WORLDS, SAYS THAT IF ANYONE TRIES TO DESTROY OUR VILLAGES AND CITIES, THEN WE MAY DESTROY THEIR VILLAGES AND CITIES. YOU HAVE TRAMPLED ON THE CITIES AND VILLAGES OF OUR BROTHERS IN IRAQ. WITH YOUR ISRAELI ALLIES YOU TRAMPLE DAILY ON THE VILLAGES AND CITIES STOLEN FROM OUR BROTHERS IN PALESTINE IN 1967. THEREFORE WE HAVE DECIDED TO PLACE IN YOUR GREAT CITY OF NEW YORK THE MOST TERRIBLE OF WEAPONS, AN ATOMIC BOMB. WE WILL EXPLODE IT IN EXACTLY FIVE DAYS AT NOON NEW YORK TIME IF YOU HAVE NOT BY THEN FORCED YOUR ISRAELI VASSALS TO PLEDGE BEFORE THE WHOLE WORLD THAT THEY WILL ABANDON EVERY SQUARE METER OF THE SETTLEMENTS THEY HAVE BUILT ON THE LAND STOLEN FROM OUR PALESTINIAN BROTHERS AND SISTERS SINCE 1967. THOSE SETTLEMENTS ARE A CRIME THAT MUST BE ERASED AND THOSE LIKE YOU AND YOUR COUNTRYMEN WHO SUPPORTED THAT CRIME WILL PAY DEARLY IF IT IS NOT RECTIFIED. FURTHERMORE, SHOULD YOU ATTEMPT TO SAVE YOUR CITIZENS BY ORDERING THE EVACUATION OF NEW YORK WE WILL DETONATE THE BOMB INSTANTLY. SINCE IN YOUR UTTER CONCEIT YOU WILL NOT BELIEVE US CAPABLE OF THIS, WE HAVE LEFT PROOF OF WHAT THIS LETTER THREATENS IN A BROWN SUITCASE IN THE BAGGAGE CHECKING FACILITY OF PENNSYLVANIA STATION IN NEW YORK UNDER BAGGAGE CHECK 102475/04.

It was signed *Warriors of the Jihad* and the e-mail address from which it had come was tombald@aol.com, except *aol* was noted as "Australia on Line."

Looking up from the text, Bill Malley, the Secret Service officer, could read a hint of panic on the young faces around him.

"Listen," he said, "this is almost certainly another example of the fake extortion messages we're always getting around here. Islamic wackos in Australia?" He shook his head in disbelief. "Still, not a word about this to anyone while I deal with it, OK?"

Since the missed hints and warnings of 9/11, a whole new series of protocols and procedures had been put in place to deal with national emergencies and terrorist threats, and government employees, at whatever level, ignored them at their peril. However much this e-mail might look like a hoax, Malley knew his duty was to convey it immediately to the permanent Counterterrorism Control Center at CIA headquarters in Langley, Virginia.

Rather than use his cell phone, he dashed to the secure phone in his West Wing office.

Malley glanced at the threat board on his office wall. It was blessedly bare. Damn, he thought, picking up his phone, that may be about to change.

The duty officer manning the desk at the Counterterrorism Control Center at Langley this Sunday morning was a thirty-two-year-old with ten years of agency experience including a four-year tour of duty in Jakarta, Indonesia. Bill Bernhart would have preferred to be spending his Sunday morning playing tennis at his club at the Washington Hilton—until he started reading the text Malley was already faxing him. Maybe this was the big one all young officers secretly hope they will be called on to handle. The response drill for a situation such as this had been hammered into him countless times. Even before the full fax had arrived, he had punched *Warriors of the Jihad* into the CIA's terrorists database to see if the agency had anything on them. It did not.

He then called the duty desk at the NSA, the National Security Agency, and relayed the full text of the e-mail with all the technical information it contained, so that they could find out to whom, and where in Australia, the e-mail address was registered. Next he alerted the agency station in Melbourne to be ready to get someone onto the owner of that e-mail address as soon as the NSA had located the person.

Then he turned his thoughts to that package in New York. The FBI was the lead domestic agency in emergencies of this sort, so he contacted the duty officer at FBI headquarters in the Hoover Building on Pennsylvania Avenue to request that a New York FBI team be sent ASAP to Penn Station.

Finally, he alerted the Emergency Response Center at the Department of Energy on Independence Avenue. If it turned out that there really was something nuclear involved in all this, they would be responsible for dealing with it, under the overall direction of the Department of Homeland Security.

Within minutes, an FBI car bearing a pair of agents was racing out of FBI headquarters in Lower Manhattan and heading uptown to Penn Station. The stunned Haitian clerk who manned the station's baggage checking facility was terrified at the sight of the agents with their gold badges and red, white and blue ID cards. Immigration, he thought in horror, thinking of his friends and family members who were illegal immigrants. When he learned the real mission of the agents, he was so relieved he could have kissed them as he led them to the suitcase belonging to tag 102475/04. He started to reach for the suitcase, but one of them stopped him.

"Don't touch it," snapped the agent pulling on a pair of gloves. "We'll want to run a fingerprint check on it."

"No problem, man," the attendant acknowledged, "and don't you worry. No explosives in there. We've got a police dog in here every night sniffing the bags for bombs and stuff."

The second agent was already on the phone to the Department of Energy's Emergency Response Team in Washington to report on what they were finding. On the strength of the baggage attendant's declaration about police dogs, the agents were authorized to take down the suitcase and open it.

The FBI men were baffled by what they found inside.

"Looks like some kind of a plan or a design," the lead agent reported back to Washington. "Some computer disks too. And oh, yeah. There's a chunk of metal in there too—kind of glinty, about the size of boxer's fist. There's a note on it. It says 'This is a sample of the HEU employed in our device.' What the hell's HEU?"

"Highly enriched uranium," the desk officer in Washington replied. "Pick it up and describe it to me."

"Christ!" the FBI man said, "it's a heavy fucker. Kinda dark gray metal, almost black."

The two men at the Department of Energy listening to the call looked at each other. "What do you think? Could it really be HEU?" the first said.

"Well, we sure can't take any chances," his superior said. "Listen, what I want you to do," he told the lead agent, "is get that suitcase and everything that's in it to the Marine Air Terminal at LaGuardia as fast as you can. We're going to order up a jet from McGuire Air Force Base in Jersey to fly it out to our lab in Livermore, California, 'tooty sweety' as the French say."

"Damn!" the first officer observed once they'd hung up. "This could really be the big one that we've all been afraid was going to come crashing down on us one of these days."

"It does," his boss agreed, "but I don't think we push the panic button—at least not yet. Let's wait until Livermore has done a preliminary read on that design and the rock." He glanced at his watch. It was almost nine o'clock. "They'll have that chunk of whatever the hell was in that suitcase under a gamma ray spectrometer by five o'clock our time this afternoon. That will tell us if it's HEU or not. I think we have to assume the worst so we'd better set up a meeting of the Emergency Response Team here for five o'clock. I'll pulse all our sources to see if anyone has any reports of HEU missing anywhere in world. And I'll give Andrew Card, Bush's chief of staff, a heads-up right now."

"How about New York? The Mayor, the Governor?"

"That will have to be the President's call. From what I know about him, he won't want to jump the gun. He'll wait until we have a solid assessment of just how serious this thing really is. Now get cracking. Alert the agency, the bureau and the NSA to what we're doing."

*   *   *

By five minutes to five everything was ready in room B26, headquarters of the Department of Energy's Emergency Response Team. Closed-circuit TV conference links had been established with the national laboratories at Livermore, Los Alamos and Sandia in New Mexico, and Brookhaven out on Long Island, and with the CIA, the FBI and the Chief of Staff at the White House. Two senior nuclear physicists attached to the team had been summoned into headquarters from their Sunday pursuits, as had David Graham, the head of NEST, the Nuclear Emergency Search Team. Paul Anscom, the Homeland Security official in charge of the team, was in the conference leader's chair. He was in his early fifties, and with his PhD in physics from Carnegie Tech he could have been making four times his government salary in the private sector. But he had spent his career in Energy and in Defense, mesmerized by the adrenaline shot that inevitably came from life at the center of power.

"OK, people," he announced to kick off the conference, "while we're waiting for Livermore's preliminary analysis on that rock, I'd like to ask our CIA guy if you folks have got anything on these so-called Warriors of the Jihad."

"Negative," came the answer. "We ran that name through all our data banks and came up empty. But I don't think you should read anything into that. These Islamic extremists have a habit of making up names to cover an operation and keep us off balance. Like the guys who 'did in' the UN office in Baghdad—they called themselves the Armed Vanguards of Mohammed's Second Army. Or the Hezbollah when they took out those Jewish institutions down in Buenos Aires a decade ago using names no one had ever heard of before. Or since."

"Would that point a finger at Hezbollah?" Anscom asked.

"It could. Or it could just mean that someone—maybe al Qaeda—has taken a leaf from their book. There's even the possibility that they could be homegrown terrorists, like the ones who took out the London subway stations."

"Gentlemen!" It was the director of the Livermore National Laboratory. A man in shirtsleeves had just moved in beside the director on the TV monitor. "Dr. Paul Mott's here with his preliminary report." The scientist had a rather full beard, its blond hairs liberally sprinkled with white, and rimless glasses.

"That rock is indeed highly enriched uranium," the newcomer said. "My preliminary spectrographic analysis gave a reading of enrichment to at least ninety percent, but I'm convinced that in the lab that figure will move up to a purity level of ninety-two to ninety-three percent."

"In other words," Anscom said, "weapons-grade material."

"No doubt about that. If those people, whoever the hell

they are, have twenty-three kilograms of the stuff, they can have a bomb alright."

"And those plans that came with it. Have your people had a chance to study them yet?" Anscom asked.

"Yes," Mott said. "It looks to us like a very valid working design. In other words, if a bomb was made from that design, and made properly, it will explode."

"Just a moment," a voice interrupted. It was Andrew Card, the chief of staff, speaking from the White House. "It seems to me this has now become the kind of serious development that the President needs to know about. It's probably time to inform him and knowing him, once he's been made aware of the situation, he will want to be involved in these discussions."

"Where is the President?" Anscom asked.

"He returned from Alabama a half hour ago. He's up in the living quarters watching a baseball game."

"All right," Anscom agreed, "let's suspend our session for half an hour."

"Right," said the Chief of Staff, "and when we resume, I'd like to transfer our meeting over here to the White House Situation Room as in all probability the President will want to join us."

*   *   *

The President, one hand clutching a cell phone linking him to his father in Kennebunkport, Maine, the other holding his TV remote, was staring mesmerized at his TV screen when the door to his study opened.

"Excuse me for the interruption, sir," said his chief of staff, "but this is important."

"Important?" the President laughed. "What could be more

important than the Astros having the bases loaded and a three-and-two pitch coming up?"

"This," said the Chief of Staff, handing him the terrorists' threat note and Livermore's preliminary analysis of the materials found in the Penn Station baggage check.

"Damn it to hell!" the President gasped reading it.

"Dad!" he said into his cell phone, "either our ultimate nightmare may be coming true or we have the mother of all hoaxes on our hands. Listen to this." Laura Bush walked over from her writing desk to hear too.

Slowly, he read the text. There was a moment of silence while the elder Bush digested its contents. "Well," he said trying to comfort his son, "it could be, as you suggest, the ultimate extortion threat. Play it very tight until you have the absolute proof that there really is a nuclear device hidden in New York. I'm here any time you need me."

The President felt comforted because, once more, this fatherly advice came from a man who had not only been president but also head of CIA. His regular conversations with his father provided him wise counsel and political and global insights, something he himself frequently lacked. While very little of the contents of their chats ever leaked to the public, they constituted a critically important support for his presidency.

The President heard again from his chief of staff. "I've convened a Principals Committee meeting in the Situation Room. The same people we had for the Iraq and Afghan wars plus our nuclear experts from Energy and Homeland Security. It's scheduled to start in twenty minutes."

"Good thinking," the President replied, hanging up his phone and switching off his TV set. "That will give me a few moments to wrestle with this."

There was no one in whom the President had more confidence than Andrew Card—whom he knew could be counted on to inevitably do the right thing, do it fast, and do it with a minimum of fuss. In short, the perfect staff chief.

As the door closed behind his departing aide, the President leaned back in his chair and closed his eyes. "Dear Lord," he murmured, "let this chalice pass from my lips. May this, I pray, turn out to be a hoax, like Dragonfire was."

His wife said, "How terrible! And what a burden this puts on you! Please God, let it be a hoax like the one you mentioned, Dragonfire. Please remind me—what was that all about?"

"Dragonfire," President Bush explained, "was the code name of an informant who told his CIA controller that al Qaeda had gotten hold of a Russian ten-kiloton portable atomic bomb left over from the Cold War. George Tenet informed us of that at our daily intelligence briefing on October 11, 2001—I remember the date because it was exactly one month to the day after the World Trade Center was hit. We had to assume that if the director of CIA took it very seriously, I had to." We knew that the Russians had lots of bombs of that size in their arsenal, and that they were poorly secured. They couldn't tell us for sure if any were missing."

Laura Bush interrupted him. "I remember now. That was when you sent Dick Cheney and some other senior people to that secure site out in Virginia to make sure we'd have continuity of government. Are you going to do that now?"

"Maybe later," the President answered, "but first we have to find out more about this threat. We don't want to create a panic in New York. The Dragonfire story turned out to be a phony, and this one may be too. We're going to move every resource we have, to try and find out. And we are going to pray. A lot."

His instinctive turn to prayer reflected a deep and mean-

ingful side of the President. His religious beliefs had become a
regular source of strength and comfort for two decades since the
day when, on the urging of Laura, he had given up the alcohol
that had been his constant companion—and major weakness—
since his undergraduate days at Yale. There, he had been president of Deke—the Delta Kappa Epsilon fraternity—a group not
known for its sobriety.

To his cynical critics, it had been "Good-bye, Jack Daniel's;
hello, Jesus," but the President's conversion appeared genuine. "I
wouldn't be president today," he frequently told close friends, "if
I had not stopped drinking, and I was able to do that only with
God's help."

If the startling message the White House had just received
turned out to be something besides a sick joke, he was going to
need a full ration of spiritual strength and comfort in the days to
come. The first nine months of his presidency had been unevent-
ful and notable mainly for their banality, perhaps because he
knew that to many of his fellow Americans—and especially to the
Democrats in Congress—he had been elected not by the votes of
the American people but by those of Supreme Court justices. His
foreign policy in those months had consisted mainly of a visit to
Mexico, studied indifference to the problems of the Middle East,
and dislike of the Palestinian leader Yasir Arafat. To a stumbling
economy, all he had to offer was a tax cut that was going to favor
the nation's wealthy.

Then, just as Pearl Harbor had defined the final term of
FDR's time in office, so the assaults of 9/11 tested him and placed
an indelible stamp on his first term. He had become, in spite of
himself, an effective wartime president. His own military career
had been anything but noteworthy, but he led the nation into two
wars, the first against the Taliban in Afghanistan, the second

against Saddam Hussein in Iraq. Neither conflict was completely over yet, and the most critical one of all, his self-declared War on Terror, was clearly far from being won.

He stood up and stretched, then paced with deliberate strides toward the door. If this turned out to be a real threat, one thing was certain: the decisive crisis of his presidency was upon him.

*   *   *

Even in the darkest days of the Afghan and Iraq wars, this president always opened Crisis Committee meetings with a smile, a word of encouragement to his subordinates and, on occasion, a quip inspired by the morning's headlines.

Not today. Shoulders slumped, face drawn into a taut mask, he took his seat at the head of the White House's Situation Room conference table without so much as a glance at his associates. Most of the men and women waiting for him in the Situation Room had been at his side in the dark hours of earlier crises.

For a site steeped in so much history, the Situation Room in the West Wing of the White House appeared remarkably banal. To many who had worked there it looked like the boardroom of a midsize midwestern bank. As a matter of fact, instead, the wood paneling surrounding the room concealed the most sophisticated, state-of-the-art communications equipment imaginable.

The room was where previous administrations faced their defining crises. It was here that John F. Kennedy had pondered the perils of a nuclear Armageddon during the Cuban missile crisis; here Lyndon Johnson had issued the orders that had sent thousands of Americans to die in Vietnam; here Jimmy Carter had agonized over the failed U.S. mission to rescue the Ayatollah Khomeini's American hostages; and here the President himself had given the order to attack Iraq on March 19, 2003.

His first gesture as he took his seat was to bow his head in silent prayer, a particularly heartfelt gesture this Sunday. His colleagues around the table, well aware that this was how these meetings invariably began, did likewise.

"So," he announced to open their meeting, "the vision that has haunted me since I took office may be upon us—weapons of mass destruction in the hands of a gang of terrorists. Anscom," he asked, waving a copy of the report his chief of staff had handed him in his study, "any new developments we should know about before we start?"

The director of the Department of Energy's Emergency Response Team had half walked, half run to the White House from the Department of Energy headquarters. Paul Anscom, veteran of so many years of bureaucratic existence, was convinced that physical fitness and trim personal appearance were keys to effectiveness in U.S. government service. But now he had the rumpled look of a man who'd left for an important meeting without first benefiting from an inspection by his wife.

"Yes sir," he said, "our nuclear physicists have just concluded that the design we found at Penn Station is for an implosion bomb employing highly enriched uranium—perhaps a copy of the design that the UN weapons inspectors uncovered in Iraq in 1995."

"How do they know that?" the President asked.

"Two giveaways. Whoever designed this bomb—and we must admit they did a first-class job—knew they probably wouldn't be able to test their design so they employed more core fissile material, twenty-three kilos, instead of the twenty you would normally use. It was a kind of insurance that it would work. Second, the plan contains computer codes detailing how they could produce perfectly symmetrical explosions at each detonation point.

The codes used in this design match very closely those in the Pakistani bomb developed by Abdul Qadeer Khan and his team. We know that those were the designs he and others peddled in the Islamic nuclear market to Iran and Libya, and probably North Korea, in return for missile technology."

"Could these so-called Warriors of the Jihad be Iraqis then?"

"Mr. President." It was Milt Anderson, the Arabic specialist head of the CIA he had appointed to replace George Tenet and Porter Goss. "I wouldn't jump to that conclusion. The Islamic world is crawling with extremists who hate you, hate this nation and its values."

Few people in the room knew the Arab world better than Anderson. Brought up in Lebanon, the son of a professor at the American University of Beirut, he learned Arabic on his nanny's knees. As an agency operations officer, he served in the Sudan, Iraq, Bahrain. His clandestine work had been so admired by Bill Casey that he was made the agency's director of operations in the struggle against the Russians in Afghanistan. "We've got a whole world of potential terrorists out there to choose from."

"Dammit!" barked an angry President. "I swore on the Fourth of July a couple of years ago I would attack any terrorist group that threatens the United States with mass murder. How can I attack these people when I don't even know who the hell they are? How about Osama bin Laden? Could he have been behind this?"

"That has to be a real possibility, Mr. President," Anderson replied, raising the massive shoulders he developed playing middle linebacker for the University of Oklahoma. "The text of the threat note is similar in tone to some of his writings. For him Islamic nukes are the one decisive way to reverse the balance of power between Islam and the West. The Germans arrested his top lieutenant, Mamdouh Mahmoud Salim, in Munich in September 1998 with a suitcase full of dollars on his way to try to buy highly enriched uranium from Ukraine. We also have good evidence that he was ready to give the Chechens thirty million dollars to obtain the ingredients for a couple of dirty bombs."

Anderson glanced down at the top secret notebook he brought to meetings like this. "Most worrying, we know that Abdul Qadeer Khan, who's considered the father of the Pakistani bomb, had at least two secret meetings with Osama in Kandahar before the Afghan War. Unfortunately nothing ever leaked out about what went on in those meetings, but you can be sure they weren't talking about *Sex in the City*."

The President sighed and looked down the table to the youngest man in the room, an officer of the NSA, the National Security Agency, the organization responsible for intercepting and decoding the millions of messages flashing every day through the boundless seas of cyberspace. "Have your people been able to pin down who was behind that e-mail address out in Australia?"

"Yes," the young man replied. "The agency got an officer out to the owner of the computer. He's a thirteen-year-old boy in Adelaide."

"A thirteen-year-old kid!" the President exclaimed, a wide smile suddenly breaking over his face. "So this a hoax after all! Another Dragonfire!"

"I'm afraid that's not the case at all," the young man replied. He was frail, shoulders hunched, thick rimless glasses on his face, the kind of guy his friends at Cal Tech called a nerd. As a sort of postgraduate course, he had become a computer hacker. Eventually his skills brought him to the attention of law enforcement and the government convinced him to put his talents to more legitimate ends.

"The boy was the victim of a cyberspace ploy. The real author of that message used a whole chain of relays to disguise its origin. It's a technique known to computer hackers and to savvy terrorists and criminals who have learned how to manipulate the Internet. They break into that kid's computer, send their message to the White House, then wipe the memory on his hard disc so there's no trace of the message or where it came from."

"Fortunately, Australia on Line was able to find the call that came into his computer just before it crashed. We traced it back to a schoolteacher in Dorset, England, who'd been the victim of the same manipulation as our thirteen-year-old in Adelaide. With the help of AOL, and of Wanadoo in France, we were able to work our way back through computers in France, Poland and Germany and eventually to an Internet café in Sanaa, the capital of Yemen. The trail ended there. One of our people just visited the café. Given the time difference, it's past midnight out there. The owner says he has no idea who was using his computers at the time we estimate the original message was sent, and he has no usage records that could give us a lead."

Listening to all this, the President was aghast. Like most men of his age he was baffled by complexities of the cyberspace age, but he understood what the bottom line was.

"So what you're telling me is we're never going to find out who the hell sent us this message?"

"I'm afraid, sir, that's a very real possibility," the young computer whiz answered.

"One thing seems clear to me," Milt Anderson of the CIA observed, "the fact these guys went to such lengths to disguise the origins of their message indicates that whoever they are, they are highly motivated, and dead serious."

"And that's exactly the attitude I expect from you at the agency and everyone else in this room. This is top priority: we have to know who the people are behind this threat so we can deal with them," the President declared in what was uncharacteristically close to an angry snarl. "You all know how faithfully I start every day by reading the daily briefing paper and Threat Matrix report that you send me. Was there even a hint in there anytime in the past week that something like this was coming? Hell, no!"

"I have to admit you're right, Mr. President," Anderson acknowledged. "If this threat is for real we have got to recognize that the people behind it have up until now played their hand like real pros."

Those words provided scant comfort for the President. Here he was presiding over the most powerful nation in the world, the globe's only remaining superpower, a nation whose empire surpassed in a sense those of Rome and Babylon, Britain, France and Turkey combined. He had at his disposal military resources that made the power of all history's Caesars, Genghis Khans, kings and kaisers shrivel in comparison. Yet what good was it if he had no foe against whom to employ it?

Terrorism, as he had noted so often, is the tool of choice of those who would attack the nation. "It's their way of leveling the playing field. And by hiding behind a cloak of anonymity they turn us into a helpless giant, and all our deterrent power becomes useless."

The President was a man who since his conversion led a remarkably disciplined life: no booze, an hour of solid exercise every day, in bed at ten o'clock with his wife—no precocious interns in his administration. Yet in times of crisis, he was a gut player, a man who relied on his instinctive reactions. Those reactions, some of his aides noted, were in a way his second religion and a key to his success in politics. Something in his innermost self was whispering to him now that maybe, just maybe, this one was for real.

"So, Gentlemen and Madame," he said, bowing toward his secretary of state. "Four questions. One, if this threat is genuine and not some kind of sick joke, what are the chances these terrorists, whoever the hell they are, succeeded in getting their hands on the highly enriched uranium they needed to make the bomb on this plan of theirs?

"Two, if they did, could they have smuggled it undetected into this country?

"Three, while we are trying to determine if this is a real threat or simply an extortion, what do we do about New York? Who do we inform up there—Mayor Bloomberg? Governor Pataki? The police? Senator Schumer? Hillary Clinton, God forbid?

"And four, if such a device really exists and it is in New York, what kind of destruction could it cause?

"You all know I believe in results so let's attack these questions. I want answers, not speeches. Anscom, the first one's yours."

The head of the Department of Energy's Emergency Response Team sat up a little bit straighter as bureaucrats tend to do when they address the president.

"For the past four years, Mr. President, our efforts here in this room have been focused on nuclear proliferation, preventing 'Axis of Evil' nations like Iraq, Iran and North Korea from becoming nuclear powers. To be a nuclear power, you need not one but at least a dozen bombs and most important, your own source of fissile material. However, to be nuclear terrorists, as these people claim to be, all you need is one bomb made from someone else's fissile material."

"So," pressed an impatient President, "where do they get it?"

"The first place to look is Russia and Ukraine. We've pulsed our sources in both countries despite the time difference. Gram quantities of weapons-grade material have gone missing over the years. We're aware of seven cases of people trying to smuggle material out, but always in quantities far below what would be needed for a bomb. As of last night, our contacts have no reports of a significant amount of bomb-grade material missing."

"Can we be sure of that?" the President demanded.

"No we can't," Anscom answered. "The Russian nuclear watchdog agency admits that their security programs are under-funded and weak and that the danger of theft or terrorism is strong. You may remember, sir, that Homeland Security requested thirty-eight billion dollars in 2003 for our cooperative U.S.-Russia threat-reduction program but we only appropriated one billion dollars. We've been pushing Putin to buy into the Nunn-Rudman Nuclear Threat Initiative and there has been some improvement in the situation. Just before the Chechens seized that theater in Moscow in October 2002, for example, they tried to hit an old Soviet nuclear site but the Russians shut them down completely. Frankly, sir, nobody really knows how good our information on the Russian situation is. But our feeling is that this would be a tough nut for a bunch of Islamic extremists to crack."

Anscom paused, knowing how unwelcome his next words were going to be. "There are unfortunately sites in this country too that are still not properly safeguarded and are vulnerable to insider-assisted theft. Tons of HEU are practically unguarded in fifty-year-old storage buildings in Oak Ridge."

"What!" the President exploded. "Why the hell aren't those sites secure?"

"The same old story, sir," Anscom answered. "I'm afraid that this administration and our congressional allies have been long on rhetoric and short on cash to back up our words."

A grim-faced President let Anscom's remark pass. "China?" he asked.

"Our and the CIA's penetration of their nuclear program is very limited but their security is so tight that it in itself would argue against their being the source. And besides, they have an ongoing struggle with their own Islamic separatists."

"North Korea?"

"Their program employs primarily plutonium, not highly enriched uranium."

"India?"

"Fundamentally the same situation."

"Pakistan?"

"That has to be a real concern in spite of the good relations you have enjoyed with General Musharraf since 9/11. You heard what Milt Anderson said about the scientists who are behind their bomb. Their chief of staff, General Mohammed Aziz Khan, is on record as saying that 'America is the number one enemy of the Muslim world.' Some of their military and scientific leadership like to refer to their weapon as an 'Islamic bomb, not just a Pakistani bomb'—implying that it could be employed in conflicts beyond India and Pakistan."

"In other words," a frustrated President said, "we haven't got a clue where this damn bomb—if it really exists—came from."

"Well, not yet, Mr. President, but with a little luck we may get an answer   before too long."

"How's that?"

"Our scientists out at Livermore right now are using a series of nuclear forensic techniques on that chunk of highly enriched uranium that was left at Penn Station. There are very few large-scale uranium enrichment facilities in the world. By studying that metal's radioactive signatures—the characteristic balance of the isotopes it contains—our people ought to be able to come up with a good idea of how and where it was created."

"How long is that going to take?"

"Hopefully, not too long. Hours, maybe."

"OK," the President acknowledged, the grimace that had clouded his face since the meeting began easing ever so slightly. "Now if this bomb really exists could these so-called Warriors of the Jihad have somehow managed to get it into New York?"

The Deputy Commissioner of U.S. Customs took the question. Larry Schorr was thin, frail almost, but a bushy mustache drew attention away from his physique to a round, florid face. Supposedly not a pair of Italian designer sunglasses, a Japanese car, a French camembert cheese or a Bible printed in Bangladesh could enter the nation without passing the formalities, however vague, of his service.

After 9/11 and the creation of the Homeland Security Department, Customs had become an integral part of emergency response planning. "Mr. President," he declared, "as I am sure you know, preventing the smuggling of nuclear weapons or radiological materials into this country is the highest priority of U.S. Customs. We now require a detailed cargo manifest from all ships calling on U.S. ports ninety-six hours in advance of their arrival. In addition, under the program developed by Commissioner Bonner, we now have U.S. Customs officers stationed in thirty foreign seaports to work with local authorities checking the contents of U.S.-destined freighters as they are loaded."

"Oh, horseshit!"

The outburst shocked the room. It came from Andy Mears, the director of the White House Office of Counterterrorism and a thirty-year veteran of service on the National Security Council.

He had been transferred to the White House at the President's request at the beginning of his administration. Theirs, however, had not been a happy marriage. Mears, a registered Democrat, liked to joke that he was the "in-house liberal," but the disillusionment with the administration's policies and rhetoric that had swept over him in his White House years was no laughing matter.

"The amount of container cargo coming into this country unchecked is simply staggering. We inspect every suitcase arriving at JFK and Newark airports but we let thousands of containers into Port Elizabeth without so much as a glance. Just think of that. Thousands of huge containers, unchecked except by reading a piece of paper, the ship's manifest. Customs is going to try to tell you that they physically check over two percent of those containers. The real figure is closer to half a percent."

"Is Mears right?" an angry President asked.

"Mr. President," the embarrassed Deputy Commissioner of U.S. Customs answered, "manufacturers and merchants in this country, from General Motors to Wal-Mart, are completely reliant on goods shipped in from abroad. If we try to pick apart every one of the twenty-one thousand containers hitting our ports every day, we will create economic chaos. GM will have to shut down production lines. Wal-Mart stops—and they are our largest employers, over one million people."

"But how about all this new technology we're supposed to be developing to detect nuclear devices?" the President asked.

"Mr. President." Mears just wasn't going to let go. This was a subject he'd labored on for weeks—and with few positive results. "A well-shielded nuclear device is going to slip right by even the most sophisticated screeners we have in place today. Make no mistake about that."

"I asked about the new stuff we're supposed to be developing."

Mears was well aware he was digging his political grave with his words but he pressed ahead anyway. "Nothing's being done. We spend eight billion dollars a year on a strategic defense system designed to protect us against missiles that may not even exist and less than six hundred million on port security. In this War on Terrorism, our deeds have never come close to matching our words. We've just been feeding the people a bunch of malarkey when we tell them how much we're doing to protect them from the dangers of terrorism."

Anscom saw the President's face reddening in anger. He rarely lost his temper, but when he did his outbursts were legendary and Mr. Mears was going to be looking for another job soon. Better step in and defuse things if it's not already too late, Anscom thought.

"In fairness to our friends at Customs," he said, "we've had tremendous problems coming up with detectors that can localize the emissions we really want to register. The radioactive emissions given off by highly enriched uranium are thin and weak. Homeland Security has been equipping our customs officers with little handheld portable detectors. But what are the chances they could walk alongside a truck or a container and pick up an emission from a bomb inside? Practically zero."

As Anscom was speaking the Marine Corps major administering the room's communications facilities raised his hand for attention, a bit like a student in a classroom anxious to answer a question or ask for permission to go the john.

"Gentlemen," he announced, "Livermore has requested an immediate TV feed." A large TV screen came down from the ceiling. Within seconds the two men who had appeared earlier on the Department of Energy's screen, the lab's director and his bearded aide, Dr. Paul Mott, faced the White House conference.

"Dr. Mott has completed his analysis of that chunk of highly enriched uranium the FBI recovered at Penn Station," the Director announced. "Paul, over to you."

"Our isotopic analysis revealed that the piece of HEU in question was enriched by a technique developed by the Urenco enrichment facility in Anselm, Holland, in the midseventies," Mott revealed.

"Holland!" mumbled an incredulous President.

Mott of course had heard his comment and addressed it directly. "Sir, at least two of the senior scientists who developed the Pakistani bomb worked at Anselm. It is widely believed that they took back to Pakistan a whole series of working blueprints for an enrichment plant when they returned in 1976. In any event, the limited studies we have been able to conduct on Pakistani enriched uranium all indicate that they employed enrichment techniques similar to those used here. It is our conclusion, therefore, that this particular piece of enriched uranium came from the Pakistani stockpile."

Paul Anscom intervened at his words. "Mr. President, let's step back a moment. Sure, all this is enormously troubling, but we mustn't allow it to rush us to premature conclusions. What exactly do we know? That these terrorists have gotten their hands on a scientifically viable design. And that they may—or may not—have had access to a source of enough highly enriched uranium to employ in that design. But to marry the two, to actually build a reliable working bomb would require a level of scientific skill and sophistication I somehow don't see these people possessing."

"Well, I'm a lot less sanguine," Milt Anderson, the CIA chief, interjected. "For me, this report opens up a whole new concern. Suppose these terrorists had accomplices inside the Pakistani military and they helped them smuggle a bomb or two out of their stockpile?"

"Just how likely is that?" the President asked.

"Very damn likely, I'm afraid," Anderson answered. "I know a lot of those guys from my service with them in Afghanistan. Some of them hate our guts and are convinced we are Islam's real enemies. We estimate Pakistan now has between thirty-five and fifty bombs. For security reasons, they keep the fissile cores of their bombs and their detonation devices in different sites, the bombs in Kahuta, south of Rawalpindi, and the detonators in Chasma, near Islamabad. We know very little about those sites and just how secure they really are. The Paks are paranoid about letting foreigners near them. But we have every reason to believe some of the extremists in their military are among those assigned to protect their bombs. Some of them also were very supportive of Abdul Khan when he was peddling nuclear technology to Iran, Libya and God knows who else. What guarantee do we have that they wouldn't be involved in something like this? None at all."

The President glanced at his watch. "I reckon it's almost seven in the morning out in Islamabad. Musharraf's an old soldier, an early riser. I'm going to put in a call to him right now. If anybody can help us in this God awful dilemma, it's him. Let's adjourn for dinner and reconvene here in exactly one hour."

*   *   *

The President took a handful of his top aides up to the living quarters to join him for dinner. The others drifted off to a considerably less elegant meal at the White House mess. Anscom slipped into a seat by himself. As he finished his macaroni and cheese, he quietly drew his wallet out of his hip pocket. He slipped a photograph from it, contemplated it almost reverently then bent to kiss it. It was the photo of his nineteen-year-old daughter, a junior at Hunter College in New York.

As the President had requested, the crisis meeting reconvened at nine o'clock sharp. "President Musharraf was most distressed and promised us his full cooperation," the President announced to open the meeting. "They are doing an immediate physical survey of their nuclear stockpile, bomb by bomb. Now, for the moment, let's turn our attention to New York."

"Mr. President," Anscom said, "we have placed all one thousand members of our NEST, Nuclear Emergency Search Team, on alert and have ordered an advance party to link up with the FBI in New York. In view of what was said in the threat note about not starting an evacuation, we are for the moment saying this is a drill."

"Good work," the Chief Executive said, ready to follow up on that. Just then the Marine Corps major in charge of communications glided up to his elbow.

"Sir," he said, "President Musharraf is on the phone in the Oval Office."

The President excused himself and left to take the call. He was back in three minutes, his face ashen, his voice hoarse with tension.

"President Musharraf has just informed me that an atomic bomb is missing from the Pakistani stockpile."

"Oh my God," exclaimed the Secretary of State. "Then we have to assume this threat is for real!"

There was not a sound in the Situation Room as the truth sank in. For the first time its occupants found themselves forced to face the full horror, the catastrophic dimensions of a nightmare that had suddenly become a reality. Appropriately it was the President who broke the silence, his voice now thin and drawn.

"Clearly this is as grave a crisis as any this nation has ever faced. I suggest we all pause a moment to ask for supreme guidance as we deal with it." He bowed his head then turned to Anscom. "Paul," he asked, "if these so-called Warriors of the Jihad have managed to get this bomb of theirs into New York, what will be the consequences if they detonate it?"

"Almost unimaginable carnage, Mr. President," Anscom answered. "We've been studying that question since the threat came in. Our estimate, based on the bomb's design, is that it would produce an explosive yield of between ten and twelve kilotons, close to Hiroshima and Nagasaki."

With a gesture of his head, he beckoned to a pair of men sitting in chairs, their backs to the Situation Room wall. "Mr. President, I have asked two of our experts to address the matter for you."

One of the two men took a seat beside Anscom, placing a small blue pocket computer on the desk before him. The other set an enormous six-foot-square map of New York on a stand at the head of the conference table. The pair, Jerry MacPherson and Tom Fraser, had spent the better part of their professional lives studying the horrendous effects nuclear and thermonuclear bombs might have on America's cities. For them the horrifying statistics of the unimaginable were as familiar as temperature changes are to a weatherman.

MacPherson turned on his pocket computer. Everything he might need to answer any of the questions soon to be fired at him was stored in it: the pressure per square inch that would break a window, burst a blood vessel, twist an iron bar out of shape; the degree of surface burns a ten kiloton bomb could cause on an exposed human being five miles from ground zero, the kind and intensity of radiation that would be found thirty miles away.

"We have been asked to describe the effect of the detonation of a ten to twelve kiloton device on Manhattan Island. The situation there unfortunately is unique," he began employing the tone of an archaeologist getting ready to describe the vestiges of a lost civilization. "There is absolutely no doubt it would be devastating. We have assumed the bomb has been hidden somewhere in Mid-Manhattan." He gestured to the map on its stand, with his assistant standing beside it with a pointer. "The primary effect of the explosion would be total devastation within the area of a circle approximately two kilometers in diameter."

His aide indicated the innermost of four red circles traced on the map having Times Square as their center. "Inside that circle the blast overpressures would run from one and a half to five pounds per square inch. Virtually everything would come down. The heat from the blast would ignite paper and other combustible material inside the circle and there is the real possibility it would set off a firestorm like those that gutted Hamburg, Dresden and Tokyo in World War Two."

"Staggering," murmured the Secretary of State, who as National Security Advisor had worked on damage estimates before, but had not become hardened to the thought of Armageddon. To think that those sparkling ramparts of glass and steel from Wall Street to Rockefeller Center—and everyone in them—could disappear in a second! And, as she well knew, such an image was not the demented product of some bureaucrat's brain.

"Casualties?" the President asked.

"The average residential population of Manhattan is about fifty thousand people per square kilometer, but in the daytime, with incoming workers and tourists, that figure jumps by a factor of almost ten so we would be looking at close to a million casualties just from the explosion itself."

"A million!" gasped Condoleezza Rice, her voice almost a sob. The uncle and aunt who had brought her up after her parents' death were this very morning attending a congress of United Baptist missionaries in Greenwich Village, well inside the red tracings of the first circle.

"And we estimate probably another two hundred to two hundred fifty thousand casualties outside the blast area from radiation. There won't be an empty hospital bed within a hundred miles of the city. New York, from the Battery to Fifty-ninth Street, the Hudson to the East River, would become a pile of ash and rubble. Our nation's financial center will have ceased to exist. The damage will be in the trillions of dollars. This nation and our way of life will have been changed forever."

The nuclear expert's words struck the men and women in the Situation Room with what might be described as the force of a verbal nuclear explosion. The President's shoulders sagged and he slumped in his chair almost as if he had been hammered with a physical blow. Michael Chertoff, the director of Homeland Security, on whose department the heaviest burden was certain to fall in the hours and days ahead, kept shaking his head in stunned disbelief.

Not surprisingly, it was Andrew Card, the President's chief of staff, who forced the gathering out of its horrified stupor and compelled its participants to face the decisions that now had to be made.

"Mr. President," he said, "I think you've got to do what John F Kennedy did when the Cuban missile crisis broke. He was campaigning in Chicago and feigned a sore throat in order to get back here to take charge of our response. I think we'd better have Dr. Shaugnessy give you some kind of intestinal disorder so we can cancel all your public appearances. You will have an excuse to isolate yourself here in the White House for the next week so that you can manage this crisis twenty-four hours a day."

"Right," the President agreed, "set it up with Shaugnessy. No need to lie," he continued, regaining a trace of his sense of humor, "this damn business is making me sick anyway."

"Next question," Card continued, "what do we do about Governor Pataki, Mayor Bloomberg? And New York itself in view of that threat of detonating the bomb if we start an evacuation?"

"Get Pataki and Bloomberg on the phone right away and tell them I've got see them down here tomorrow. Say it's top secret. National Security. They'll go along with that," the President ordered.

"How about Senator Schumer? Hillary Clinton?"

"Chuck Schumer's a good guy. We can trust him but I don't want Hillary within a mile of this. She'll blabber it all over town."

"And New York?"

"For the time being we've got to sit on this. After all, we have five days. But suppose these damn terrorists, whoever the hell they are, decide to go public with this themselves. How are we going to look in front of those folk up there in New York if they learn we sat on this for days without telling them to get out?"

The President emitted a painful groan. These were the moments when leadership exacted its price.

"Mr. President, how do you propose to handle Ariel Sharon and the Israelis on this?" asked Donald Rumsfeld. "When do we bring them in on what's happened?"

"Well, not now. It's the middle of the night out there," the President replied. "Can we trust them to keep their mouths shut on this? We'll have to make that decision in the morning."

"Mr. President," interjected Condi Rice, "I think you can count on Sharon. But some of those Likudniks he's surrounded himself with? I doubt it. For them, those settlements go right to the heart of their justification for existing. It's going to pose an appalling dilemma for them. And therefore for us."

"Yeah," said the CIA's Milt Anderson, "and can you imagine the firestorm of hate and anger that's going to erupt in this country if a million Americans die for those damn settlements? Settlements that were opposed by every American President since LBJ and most particularly by your father?"

The President shook his head in despair. "And how the hell do we find out who these Warriors of the Jihad are? Open up some channel of communication so we can try to talk some kind of reason to them?"

"The danger is that these guys are going to be impervious to reason and logic," Anderson said, "but I think Musharraf's the key here. That investigation he's running into how their bomb went out the door may give us the clues we need."

"How about the allies?" Rumsfeld asked. "What do we tell them?"

"For now, nothing," the President answered.

"Not even Tony Blair? The Brits?"

The President reflected a moment. "No. For now I want this crisis to stay right here in this room." He looked at Michael Chertoff, secretary of Homeland Security. "How are we going to find that damn thing and disarm it, Michael?"

"As soon as we adjourn here, I'm sending Paul Anscom to New York to open our Emergency Operations Center there. I will order a full deployment of our NEST teams and the FBI's bomb squad experts to the city. Paul will meet with Police Commissioner Kelly and his Chief of Detectives later tonight to decide how we go about searching the city without starting a panic and alerting the press. We will mobilize our customs inspectors to start immediately scrubbing out the manifests of every ship that has entered Port Elizabeth in the last thirty days to see if we pick up any hint of suspicious cargoes."

"All right," the President declared. "We are all of us here going to be facing in the coming days and hours the worse crisis in the history of the Republic. Activate everything we've discussed and we meet here at nine AM tomorrow. Try to get some rest if you can. You're all going to need it."

CHAPTER

5

NEW YORK CITY

The Crisis—Day Two

With his neat little gray beard, his long, ill-combed hair, his all-enveloping brown smock, the man looked more like a Greek Orthodox monk on Mount Athos than a king of the international food trade. Yet Charlie Birbaki, fifty-four, born of Turkish parents who had come to New York for the World's Fair in 1939, was in fact one of the largest distributors of oriental gastronomic products on the eastern seaboard of the United States.

His catalogue was mailed out every month to thirty thousand clients from Maine to northern Florida. Ensconced in the little glass booth of his Brooklyn warehouse that served as his office, he watched a steady parade of customers leaving his premises every day. Their arms, or the baggage carts he provided, were crammed with sacks, boxes and cartons of his delicacies: basmati rice from India and Pakistan, coffee from Yemen, Sumatra and Kenya, frozen shrimp from Bangladesh, frozen Egyptian artichokes, green lemon jellies from Syria, pistachios from Turkey and Jordan, chutney from Ceylon, couscous from Tunisia and Morocco. To those products he had recently added a line of European specialties, such as the famous *cassoulet* from Toulouse in France and *foie gras* from Perigord.

The warehouse in which he kept them stored was a cave of delights, reeking of spices and grilled almonds, divided into alleys named after the products they sheltered in carefully arranged ceiling-to-floor stacks.

For over a decade, Charlie had brought his imported merchandise into the United States via containers off-loaded at Port Elizabeth. They came from ports all over the East—Malaysia, Alexandria, Latakia, Istanbul, Karachi, Bombay, Singapore—all brought in via his shipping agent up in Albany. The system worked to perfection. When the containers got to INOS, the Albany shipping agent, he got a call and the next day a truck delivered his containers straight to his Brooklyn warehouse. On this September morning he was expecting four containers: two filled with bags of basmati rice, one with Turkish pistachios and a third containing a mixed assortment of goods.

It was a rather special delivery. Four months earlier, one of his clients who loved Turkish pistachios had come to him with a "Godfather" offer: let him add a crate into his shipments of rice once a month. He would pick it up at the warehouse and give Charlie a wad of bills—twenty-thousand-dollars worth to be exact.

Now Charlie was no dope. The guy who always showed up in his New York Yankees baseball cap had to be a Turk, right? So what was Turkey's primary export? Heroin, right? So that's what you'd figure was going to be in those crates. Well, 20K was 20K and above all it was 20K the IRS was never going to know about. If there were assholes out there who took that shit, the hell with them. What concern was it of Charlie's?

As always, Albany's containers showed up at his warehouse right on time. He set his men to work unloading them, holding until last the second basmati rice container. To his surprise it was not his Turkish pal with the New York Yankees cap who showed up to make the pickup but an attractive young woman, wearing a white kerchief, accompanied by a rather distinguished-looking guy of about forty. She drove their rented white van.

"We're here for that case you're expecting today," the woman explained. "Don't worry. Everything's in order." She smiled. "And, of course, I have your envelope."

Charlie ordered his men to open the basmati rice container and they found the crate they were looking for packed as usual in the rear behind stacks of burlap bags full of rice. It was a bit bigger than the usual consignment.

Again the woman smiled. "Bigger package, bigger envelope," she said, pressing Charlie's money into his hands. His touch told him it was almost twice the size of his usual 20K packet. Then as she and her partner moved toward the crate, Charlie noticed that the guy's left hand had been amputated at the wrist.

"Hey," he shouted to two of his workmen, "help these people put their crate into the van." They did, its weight requiring the solid efforts of both men.

A few minutes later the woman waved a friendly hand to Charlie and he watched as her Easy Rent van headed out of his warehouse toward Flatbush Avenue.

*   *   *

This has got to be the seediest place in all of New York City, Paul Anscom thought driving across the potholes and exposed cobblestones leading into the parking lot of 11 Water Street, an aging, windowless warehouse built into the base of the Brooklyn Bridge's Brooklyn Tower adjacent to the East River.

And yet, as he well knew, those tacky surroundings enclosed the most sophisticated, hi-tech, post-9/11 counterterrorism headquarters in the United States and almost certainly in the world. Officially, the place was labeled the New York City

OEM—Office of Emergency Management. The first OEM had been built by Mayor Rudi Giuliani on the twenty-third floor of 7 World Trade Center, a decision much criticized at the time for setting such a critical site in so evident a terrorist target. And indeed the first OEM had been destroyed almost at the outset of the 9/11 bombings.

The new OEM was the creation of Police Commissioner Ray Kelly. Kelly was serving an unusual second term as police commissioner. In his first term under Mayor Dave Dinkins, he had been largely responsible for the dramatic fall in crime in New York City, although his successor grabbed most of the credit for it. In his years out of the commissioner's office, Kelly had broadened his knowledge of the world, serving as the U.S. representative to Interpol in Lyons, France, and as an expert in money laundering at the Treasury Department and Customs.

Nine-eleven hit him personally since he and his wife lived in Battery Park City, just south of the World Trade Center, and for weeks they could not return to their home. So when Mayor-elect Mike Bloomberg asked him to return to the commissioner's office he accepted immediately, vowing to make sure the catastrophe of nine-eleven would never be repeated.

Stepping out of his car onto a pavement littered with old candy bar wrappers, cigarette butts and empty beer and Coke cans, Anscom told himself that Kelly had put his OEM in a location no self-respecting terrorist would want to visit. And yet, once past security, the building's doors led into the command center's heart, a huge, open space uncluttered by pillars or dividing partitions, half the size of a U.S. football field, gleaming with futuristic electronic equipment. At its intelligence center, computer screens displayed digitized maps of Moscow, London, Tel Aviv, Jerusalem, Riyadh, Islamabad and Baghdad. The maps were regularly updated by satellite imagery.

In its Global Intelligence Room, TV monitors carried live newscasts from Al Jazeera, Al Arabiya and other critical TV channels. The recorded newscasts were monitored by Arabic, Urdu, Farsi and Pashtu speakers who did their best to provide running translations of the programs. That was Kelly's doing. At the time of 9/11, the police department had only one Arabic speaker—an Israeli from Jerusalem.

On each side of the central aisle dividing the OEM were five work areas separated by ranks of black computer consoles. There was a working desk and a set of four chairs for each console, and it was identified by the owner's initials in white tape—*CG*, for example, for Coast Guard.

The telephones at each desk were equipped with keys that, when activated, automatically encrypted the conversations. Each computer had access to a score of constantly updated databases, and to the latest intelligence reports and to briefing books on the world's known terrorist groups.

The computers were also wired into an electronic photo library, built up since 2002, that provided up-to-date satellite photographs of every square foot of the city. An operator could zoom in on and identify a couple embracing on the corner of, say, Seventy-fifth Street and Amsterdam Avenue. At the center of the cavernous room was a raised square platform, the command center itself, labeled *ASOG*—the Alternative Seat of Government. All around the platform were computer desks similar to those elsewhere in the room: desks for the NYPD, the FBI, Homeland Security, the NYFD, the hospital services and Customs. There was also a TV monitor that could be linked to the White House Situation Room. The desk at the center of the circle was meant for the mayor but in this crisis it would be Anscom's.

Kelly himself was waiting for Anscom inside the headquarters, anxious to show him the resources that would be available for the crisis confronting them. He liked to boast that "New York City was safer than it has ever been" and indeed, no city in the world from Washington, D.C., to London or Paris could offer its citizens the facilities that Kelly had provided New Yorkers. Kelly was a former Marine Corps captain and as usual was impeccably dressed in a freshly pressed blue suit with a white handkerchief in his vest pocket. The few hairs remaining on his bald head were neatly combed and his face was set in an appropriately serious expression. With him were his key aides, Dave Cohen, the deputy police commissioner for intelligence, formerly the head of the CIA's Operations Division; Deputy Police Commissioner for Counterterrorism Mike Sheehan, formerly a State Department counterterrorism expert; and the officer in charge of the OEM itself, Deputy Police Commissioner John Odermatt.

Also invited were Kevin Donovan, the director of the 1,100 FBI agents in the New York bureau, and his deputy, Joe Billy, the agent in charge of 125 agents assigned to the FBI-NYPD's Joint Terrorism Task Force, the JTTF. Anscom had briefed Kelly by phone from Washington on Sunday night. He now had the full team seated on the Alternative Seat of Government platform and had just provided them with a similarly complete briefing.

"All right, gentlemen," he said in conclusion, "the problem we face is straightforward—how do we save New York from destruction?"

Commissioner Kelly, inspired by his days at Customs, had already been reflecting on the problem. "First thing we do, right now, in the next hour, is assemble a team of fifty customs officers and fifty of my officers and get them over to Port Elizabeth to scrub out the manifests of every ship that has docked there in the last thirty days. I want them to check everything, the manifests, the details of every container they off-loaded, where those containers went, to whom, what they contained, every damn thing imaginable. I want them to scrub out everything suspicious, every anomaly, anything that seems out of line. Forget the fantasy about Customs checking incoming cargoes—it's just a bad joke.

"Second, and most important, I want to alert all my key people, right now. But in light of what was threatened in the note that came into the White House, what am I going to tell them? That there's an atomic bomb hidden somewhere on Manhattan Island?"

"Do that," growled Michael Sheehan, the deputy police commissioner for counterterrorism, "and you run the risk of creating a panic. Your guys are only human. Some of them are going to call their wives and say 'Get the kids out of school and get the hell up to your mother's house in Vermont.' The word will leak out and the evacuation of the city will start all on its own, and probably on a larger scale than on 9/11. Then we run the risk that these terrorists detonate the bomb as they've threatened to do if we evacuate the city."

"Yes," Anscom agreed, "the President is very concerned about that. He's meeting this morning with Governor Pataki and Mayor Bloomberg. In view of the terrorists' threat, he wants to put out a cover story: 'Unidentified terrorists have hidden a barrel of deadly chlorine gas somewhere in Manhattan.' We need the Governor and the Mayor to agree on that."

"That might work as a starter," Commissioner Kelly said, "but what are we going to tell the press when they see some of your technicians going around with Geiger counters? That they're looking for chlorine gas? How long do you figure that's going to hold up?"

"It's a critical problem," Anscom agreed, "but I think

there's a way to handle it. We say that the barrel was probably stolen from a lab in India that exposed metal containers of dangerous chemicals to different radioactive isotopes as a back up to the labeling of barrels, so that if it became illegible for any reason they could identify the contents by analyzing the barrel's radioactive signature. Therefore we can check for that weak radioactivity with Geiger counters. Maybe we can come up with a better cover story, but for now let's go with that. That damn threat note doesn't give us much choice."

"OK," Kelly agreed, "we'll have to see how long it will fly. But remember my guys aren't like Kevin Donovan's FBI agents. They don't come from South Dakota or Oregon or Montana. They come from Brooklyn, the Bronx and Queens. They've got their wives, their kids, their mothers, their girlfriends, their dogs, their cats, their pet canaries right here in the city. They aren't supermen. But if the Mayor agrees, OK, we go with your chlorine gas story."

"Are you well wired into the Islamic community?" Anscom asked.

"Pretty well," Kelly replied. "It's been a high priority for us since 9/11. A lot of things go down at the Grand Mosque on East Ninety-sixth Street that was built with Saudi money in—of all places—the old Ruppert Brewery where the beer was made that financed the Yankees baseball team.

"What we've got in front of us, albeit on a massive scale, is just solid police work, the kind of thing my officers do every day—pulse all the informants we've got, run down whatever leads we can pick up from them, and ditto for any leads from your people in Washington."

"We've got to mobilize immediately the full FBI-NYPD Joint Terrorism Task Force, all 250 of them," the FBI's Kevin Donovan said. "We'll need to back up the Commissioner with whatever additional investigative work is needed."

"As I told the Commissioner last night, we're bringing in right now our NEST—Nuclear Emergency Search Team—to give us the absolute top-of-the-line technological and scientific support in our hunt for this damn weapon," Anscom said. "We are also flying in, as I speak, four brand-new mobile vans from the Lawrence Livermore National Lab out in California. They've built into them the very latest state-of-the-art gamma ray detectors that the lab designed for use in crises just like this one. This will be their first deployment."

"Most threats of this nature that come in don't name a precise place," observed Dave Cohen, the former CIA officer who was now the deputy commissioner for intelligence. "At least this one does, which I guess is something to be thankful for."

"Right," snapped Anscom. "Let's get cracking, gentlemen, the fate of New York City and a million of its people is in your hands."

*   *   *

Not quite fifteen kilometers east of the OEM, in a small auditorium of Our Lady of Sorrows elementary school in Glendale, a sad and solemn little ceremony was about to get under way. Sister Mary Francis Duchelle shepherded half a dozen children onto the room's stage. The spastic uncertainty of their movements or a tongue rolling around in a half-open mouth bore witness to the common affliction cursing their little bodies: they were all mongoloid children.

To help them come to grips with their burden, all children had been assigned a poem to memorize and recite regularly over the summer recess. Now, as a confidence-building gesture, they were to recite their poems to this select audience of parents and friends.

Sister Mary Francis stepped forward to address the gathering. "Katy O'Neill," she said, "is going to open our program reciting the first lines of Walt Whitman's great Civil War epic, 'O Captain! My Captain!'"

She reached into the circle of uplifted faces and took the hand of a ten-year-old girl, her black hair tied into pigtails that fell below her shoulders. Gently she led the child to the center of the little stage, then withdrew a few feet, leaving her alone before the assembly.

The little girl stood there a moment, terrified. Then she opened her mouth, but the only sound that emerged was a shrill "peep". She began to shake her head violently, sending her pigtails swirling about her face. She stamped her feet in fury and frustration. Then, as she had been taught to do, she took a deep breath.

In the first row of spectators, a heavyset man in a gray suit stroked his sweating forehead. Each of the girl's gestures sent a tremor of anguish through him. He was her father, Detective Lieutenant T.F. O'Neill of the New York Police Department. He stared out at her as though somehow the intensity of the love radiating from his face might calm the tempest sweeping her little figure.

It did. She opened her mouth into the perfect O he had practiced with her so often over the summer and the words began to come tumbling out:

> O Captain! my Captain! our fearful trip is done;
> The ship has weathered every rack,
> The prize we sought is won;
> The port is near, the bells I hear,
> The people all exulting.

An enormous sense of pride swept over O'Neill as she

poured out the tragic concluding words, *my Captain lies, fallen cold and dead.*

At almost the same moment, he heard the faint jingle of a bell from inside his suit jacket. He pulled out his cell phone and saw immediately that it was an urgent call. O'Neill was the commanding officer of the Manhattan South Detective Squad. The callback number was from the Chief of Detectives. Something big is going down if he's calling me, he thought, I'd better answer this pronto.

He blew a proud kiss to his daughter and tiptoed out of the room. Although he couldn't know it, five hundred police cell phones were ringing all over the city at about the same time in a grisly tintinnabulation of the bells. "The Chief wants you here at Police Plaza forthwith," an operator told him. *Forthwith* was New York police-speak for "about five minutes ago."

"And," he added, "he wants you to come to the city by the Williamsburg Bridge and check out those sensing devices we put in there a year or so ago."

*   *   *

As he had done every day since taking office, the President had begun his day with a careful reading of the "President's eyes only" daily briefing paper from the CIA. That paper, his father had advised him, would be the most important document that would cross his desk each day. Perhaps, but to his dismay it did not contain on this Monday morning the slightest advance on what he and his advisors had known at the conclusion of their meeting the night before.

At least, he noted, the media had not yet picked up even a hint of the crisis facing the nation. His "intestinal disorder" had attracted a minimum of comment. Probably, he mused, the press corps was delighted to learn something was giving him a bellyache.

"OK," he said, taking his seat at the head of the Situation Room conference table as the grandfather's clock chimed out nine thirty, "what do we have?"

"Three things," his chief of staff, Andrew Card, replied, "Governor Pataki and Mayor Bloomberg are on the way. Paul Anscom is ready to give you a report on the action they're taking up in New York. President Musharraf called from Islamabad fifteen minutes ago with news he wants to convey to you: they've have made progress in their investigation into their missing bomb."

Clearly, the President thought, Musharraf's call takes precedence. "Let's pipe the call to Musharraf onto the squawk box down here so everybody can hear what he has to say."

"Mr. President," Bush began, "I want to thank you for all the help you're giving us in this terrible crisis."

Musharraf acknowledged his thought and plunged into his briefing. "We have arrested the ISI officer who commanded the arsenal from which the device was stolen. He has confessed to doing it because of his membership in a secret Islamic order, the Lashkar-e-Toiba, run by a former commanding general of the ISI, Hamid Gul."

At the mention of Gul's name the eyebrows of the CIA's Anderson arched skyward in a gesture meant to say "I told you so."

"We are searching for Gul but he has disappeared," Musharraf continued. "We have also learned that our weapons designer Dr. Abdul Qadeer Khan was seen in Chasma, where our detonation devices are stored, on the night the bomb disappeared."

"Do you know where he is now?" the American president asked.

"Yes. He's on vacation in Pyongyang, North Korea."

"North Korea!" Bush gasped. "Who the hell goes to North

Korea for a vacation?"

"Well, Kim Jong Il, their so-called Great Leader, keeps a bevy of young ladies in his presidential palace to help him greet visitors. Perhaps that encouraged our good scientist to drop by. In any event, he leaves tonight for Beijing and tomorrow he flies back to Karachi."

The President couldn't resist a joke. "How come Clinton never went to Pyongyang? Now, can you arrange to pick up Dr. Khan at the airport and sequester him someplace where we can talk with him? He may be our only channel into the people who are behind this."

"Of course," Musharraf assured him. "I've already set that in motion using only the most trusted members of my presidential guard."

The two leaders exchanged mutual assurances that they would remain in close and constant contact during the crisis before hanging up.

"Milt," the President asked his CIA head as the squawk box went dead, "do you guys at CIA still prepare these psychological studies, profiles—or whatever the hell you call them—on important people?'

"No," Anderson replied, "we shut that operation down some time ago.

"Well, I want your people at the agency to put together the best dossier on Khan you can for me. I want everything from his sexual preferences to what he has for breakfast. His strong points, his weaknesses, his likes, his dislikes, anything that might help me establish a bond with the man. I want it on my desk tomorrow morning.

"And," he continued, "just what do we know about the kind of guys who would be behind this? All right, they're Islamic extremists. But what do we know about their psychology, their behavioral patterns—what motivates them?"

"Tough question," said Dr. Lisa Holmgren, an attractive woman in her midforties who for almost eight years had been the National Security Council's nuclear terrorism expert. "We specialists in these questions have felt for some time that the idea of using a device for extortion, as is happening here, was outdated. We concluded that nuclear terrorists would have just one idea—get their device into some U.S. location as quickly as possible and then detonate it. In other words, our current thinking on situations like this is that sheer vengeance would be the motivating factor, like suicide bombers blowing themselves up in restaurants in Tel Aviv or on buses in Jerusalem. We may have gotten ahead of ourselves here."

"Yes," echoed Dr. Clint Hartwell of the Homeland Security Department's Emergency Response Team, who had taken Paul Anscom's place at the table, "we must assume we are dealing here with people who are basically fanatics. People who are ready to die. I believe they will babysit their bomb, protecting it with their lives, ready to die in its explosion, ready to detonate it instantly if they're found. That is what makes this search we've embarked on so desperately dangerous."

"The psychology of so-called suicide bombers has evolved over the years since 1982, when we first saw this phenomenon among the Shiites in southern Lebanon," Dr. Holmgren added. "In the beginning the bombers were in the hands of extremist mullahs, who brainwashed them, so to speak, with the promises of paradise and those seventy-two virgins. But in the last five years in Israel that pattern has changed dramatically. The primary motivation became sheer vengeance and intense hatred of the U.S., its support of Israel and dominant position in the world, and ultimately, the values of our culture.

"Then came the London attacks," she continued, her voice growing more somber. "They were part of a new generation of suicide bombers—not new arrivals or clandestine immigrants, but kids who were born in the West, went to its schools and colleges, and lived among other citizens in its cities. If these are our terrorists, and they are willing to babysit their bomb and set it off themselves, we're in a far worse situation. How do we spot them and their bomb?"

"Yes . . . unreasoning hatred," agreed the President, "that's certainly going to complicate the situation. God knows it's desperate enough, but if what you say is true, there'll be little hope of arguing them out of blowing up New York. But tell me—how does that bomb get detonated if the time comes? By radio? A phone call? A cell phone call? A timer?"

"Any of the above, Mr. President," answered the representative of the National Security Agency, NSA. "Unfortunately, the ways of detonating such a device are almost too numerous to list."

"Can we somehow throw a kind of electronic blanket around New York? Shut down the possibility of any radio signal or overseas phone call getting into the city?"

"That might be a possibility, Mr. President. I'd like to run it past some experts for you."

"Sure," said Lisa Holmgren, "but suppose the bomb is in some apartment in Manhattan and one of the terrorists is out in Queens with the phone number. He gives the apartment a call and since it's a landline, the call goes through. If the detonator is tied to the phone, the bomb goes."

"Can New York Verizon shut down the whole system?" the NSA expert asked.

"They do that and then they tie all our search and relief

efforts into knots, and double the panic," Lisa rejoined. With her PhD in nuclear physics from the University of Michigan, these were issues she had pondered for years. "And what if they're suicide bombers, like the ones in London? They wouldn't need fancy technology, just the willingness to die."

A marine officer from the Situation Room's caretakers appeared. "Sir," he informed the President, "Governor Pataki and Mayor Bloomberg are here."

"Good," declared the President. "I think I'll receive them in the Oval Office." He turned to Condi Rice and Don Rumsfeld. "I'd like you two to join me. The rest of you continue to blue sky this damn crisis with Vice President Cheney and see if you can't come up with some good ideas."

*   *   *

The two men stepping into the Oval Office had at least one thing in common with the President who had summoned them to Washington—they were both his fellow Republicans. That was where the similarities ended. Michael "Mike" Bloomberg, fifty-two, had arrived at Reagan National Airport forty-five minutes earlier, not however on one of the Washington–New York shuttles but aboard his private plane, a luxurious King Star jet. And his point of departure for the flight was not the city of which he was the first magistrate but Kingston, Bermuda, where he regularly spent weekends in his palatial estate.

Bloomberg was the incarnation of the quintessential American dream, the self-made man. Born into a modest family outside Boston in Medford, Massachusetts, he had put himself through Johns Hopkins and Harvard Business School on scholarships. He worked his way to a partnership at Salomon Brothers in New York in just six years. Then, following a change in management, he left to form his own financial information firm. The success of Bloomberg, Inc. had made Mike a multibillionaire. Just about every investment professional had a Bloomberg terminal on his desk and Bloomberg's radio and TV shows had become household words in the financial world throughout the globe. He had, quite literally, bought his way into the New York City Mayor's Office, spending forty million dollars of his own money on his campaign. Yet he drew down only a symbolic one dollar of salary, giving the rest to charity. Not for him the regular ethnic marches down Fifth and Madison avenues of his fellow New Yorkers. He loathed the city's noisy political rallies; had never moved into the mayor's official residence, Gracie Mansion, preferring his own luxurious Seventy-third Street residence. After these many years he still remained a closet fan of the Boston Red Sox in their baseball wars with his city's Yankees.

Governor Pataki was a farm boy, brought up on his family's farm in Peekskill, New York. Like Bloomberg, he put himself through college— Yale—and law school—Columbia—on scholarships. After a spell practicing law, he became a professional politician, serving as mayor of his native Peekskill and for ten years in the New York State legislature before running for governor. He took particular pride in the fact that under his leadership New York had enacted the most sweeping antiterrorist laws in the nation.

Neither man, of course, had any idea of why the President had summoned them to Washington. He swiftly disabused them of their innocence, handing each a one-page text reproducing the terrorists' threat note, summarizing everything the federal government had been able to learn since the note arrived, and detailing the steps being taken to address it.

Bloomberg was horrified. "A million or more of my fellow New Yorkers at risk!" he gasped. "My God, what a disaster! I can't imagine anything that would come even close to this! Damn it to hell! I've been trying for months to get two billion dollars out of you to reinforce my city's counterterrorism measures and all I got was a lot of platitudes! You're giving every citizen in Wyoming twenty-two dollars a year for counterterrorism . . .Wyoming, for God's sakes. Are terrorists threatening the cows up there? And what do you give New York? Three dollars a head. I took over a city after 9/11; I was told that everyone wanted to help and what did I get? Nothing except the empty cash drawers Giuliani left me. I even had to close down some of the stations of our heroic fire-fighters to keep the city running."

"Damn right!" echoed Pataki. "You threw away God knows how many billions on the war in Iraq! But on the war on terror? Zilch! It's the same old game—we're always ready to talk up a storm but never come up with the money to pay for it. You let Mike and me deal with the basic function of government, defending New Yorkers, and this is what happens!"

The President was aghast at the fury of their statements. He had expected a "rally around the flag" reaction. Still, he did his best to stifle the tide of anger rising within him. "Listen," he said, "this isn't the time for arguments and recriminations. We have a crisis on our hands. How are we going to deal with it?"

"OK," said Bloomberg. "First thing. Is there really a bomb hidden somewhere in New York? Do we know that for a fact?"

"No, we don't. But we have to assume it, based on that threat note and on Pakistan's missing bomb. We'd be crazy to do otherwise."

"Then what are our chances of finding the bomb before the terrorists' deadline expires?" Pataki asked.

"We've mobilized all the scientific, technological, police skills we possess and set up headquarters in Mike Bloomberg's excellent

Office of Emergency Management. Will they succeed in finding it? God only knows. Pray that they do," the President answered.

"What about the terrorists threat to detonate the bomb if we go public and start an evacuation?" Bloomberg asked.

"That could be only the mother of all extortion threats," Pataki declared.

Bloomberg followed up with "And yet, if all this is for real and it goes off when we start an evacuation, we'll have the deaths of a million New Yorkers on our conscience."

"And if we don't find the bomb in time and it goes off? We'll still have their deaths on our consciences," Pataki added.

"Gentlemen," the President intervened, "the government feels we must play for time here. We have to strive to keep this a secret on a day to day, hour to hour, even minute to minute basis. I think both Secretary Rice and Rumsfeld will agree with me on that."

His two cabinet members nodded their agreement.

"Have you talked to Sharon and the Israelis yet?" Bloomberg asked. "Not yet. I will shortly."

"Look, I've been a Zionist all my life," Bloomberg said. "But I was always against the settlement program and quite frankly I don't think you stand a chance in hell in getting Sharon to back down in the face of this extortion threat."

"A million dead Americans for his settlements?"

"In spite of his evacuation of Gaza, he remains a fanatic just like the guys who planted this bomb are. Maybe he'll agree to dissimulate, to fake some moves to disarm them. But more than that?"

"Look, Mr. President," Pataki interjected, "for better or for worse, dealing with this has to be the responsibility of you and the federal government. Mike and I will support you in anyway we can. We'll try our best to keep this threat a secret for as long as we can by using this chlorine gas cover story you propose in this paper."

"Yes," Bloomberg agreed, "and I'm going to head up to New York to the OEM right now. If a million of my fellow New Yorkers are going to have to die because of these crazies, I'm going to have to be there beside them. What else can I do?"

*   *   *

Normally, passengers on the Lucky Line Falcon 500 jets out of Las Vegas, Nevada, were lucky high rollers, gamblers at the city's casinos flying home in luxury on their winnings. David Graham, the Falcon's sole passenger this autumn morning, had never been in a casino in his life, yet in a sense, he was the ultimate gambler. Graham was the director of NEST, the Nuclear Emergency Search Team, that Paul Anscom had ordered to New York to provide advanced technological support in the search for the terrorists' nuclear bomb. For the next days, Graham would be gambling that the best scientific and technological equipment available to the U.S. government would enable him and his fellow team members to find the bomb before the terrorists could carry out their threat.

Graham glanced out the window as the jet rolled toward its landing pad at New Jersey's McGuire Air Force Base. Somewhere out there in the base's crowded hangars would be half a dozen C141s that had flown in overnight with NEST's top secret, ultrasophisticated equipment packed into vans masquerading as Hertz and Avis trucks.

In their cargo were also half a dozen of NEST's most modern detection vehicles, trucks equipped with gamma-ray imaging spectrometers, which would allow their NEST operators to find and record radioactive emissions over large areas. The truck's designers at the Lawrence Livermore Lab in California believed their new trucks would provide NEST operators with a tenfold increase in sensitivity in detecting nuclear materials or devices.

The spectrometers were the size of a large television set and installed in the rear of the trucks. Manned by a pair of NEST technicians the vehicles would prowl through the streets of New York searching for the telltale emissions that the terrorists' bomb might give off. The spectrometers were designed to first pick up emissions, then allow the operators to pin down the precise location from which the emissions were coming.

The devices were the result of recent advances in microelectronics that had allowed Livermore's scientists to build a gamma ray camera in which a cluster of miniature gamma sensors worked together to create an image. The result was in effect a digital camera for gamma rays that worked much like the compound eye of a fly. The beauty of the system was that it allowed the NEST technicians manning the device in their truck to eliminate immediately a whole range of "false positives." For example, emissions from construction materials containing elements such as cobalt, or rays from phosphorescent substances such as wristwatches with dials that glow in the dark—or even from a patient leaving a hospital after receiving radiation treatment for cancer.

The trucks were just the latest in a series of detection devices developed at Livermore called "Ultra Specs," for ultrahigh resolution gamma-ray spectrometers. Some of the earlier ones were small enough to be carried on the back of a NEST technician like a hiker's backpack. The spectrometers operated at an incredible one degree above absolute zero Fahrenheit (-459 degrees) and could pick up traces of a single gamma ray. They were connected directly to a computer that could determine with five times greater accuracy than previous methods just what kind of a device was giving off the emissions.

Graham's NEST organization was unique in the world. No other nation had anything even close. All one thousand of its members, men and women, were volunteers, most of them scientists or technical people at the nation's great laboratories such as those in Los Alamos and Sandia in New Mexico and at Livermore in California.

Graham had been summoned from a Sunday night dinner in front of his TV set by an urgent call from NEST's headquarters at the Department of Energy in Washington. Every time one of those calls came, the NEST team members knew they could be putting their lives at risk. If the terrible weapon they were being sent to find was really there and detonated, a large number of NEST volunteers would be among its first victims.

The organization went all the way back to 1964 when a B29 bomber about to crash jettisoned its bombs over the open fields and orchards of Palomares, Spain. Los Alamos dispatched a team of scientists armed with the best detection devices then available to find them. They couldn't.

If we can't find a bomb in an open field or forest, reasoned the team leader Bill Chambers, who was a nuclear weapons designer, how the hell could we find a nuclear bomb hidden somewhere in an American city by a terrorist? With this thought, NEST was born.

Almost fifty times in the years since then, NEST teams had been deployed in U.S. cities in response to nuclear threats. Fortunately, none had ever materialized. In the days following 9/11, NEST teams had patrolled night and day around the White House and other key sites in Washington. Twice since then they had been summoned to U.S. cities following intelligence leads indicating terrorists might have smuggled a dirty bomb into the country.

Yet the press never picked up a hint of their deployment. That was because secrecy and speed were the golden rules of NEST's operations. Secrecy to keep terrorists from learning they were being hunted, and perhaps detonating their device in a moment of fright. Also, of course, secrecy so as not to panic the population. Speed because every moment could be crucial in their efforts to save thousands of lives.

An unmarked government car was waiting for Graham as his plane rolled to a stop. A veteran of over a dozen of these missions, the nuclear weapons designer could feel his stomach tightening into the angry, nauseous knot that was always there whenever he had to lead NEST into action. Graham was built like a tight end, six feet four inches tall, solidly muscled and dressed like a ranch hand in cowboy boots, a broad-rimmed hat, a blue and white checkered shirt—and a Navajo good luck charm hung around his neck on a rawhide cord.

As soon as he had settled into the car, with the driver headed up the New Jersey Turnpike toward New York. Graham closed his eyes and sighed. No one knew better than he how desperately difficult the job ahead was, despite all the technology his team possessed. The tightly packed city blocks of New York were a high-rise forest of glass and steel providing an abundance of natural screening to smother the gamma ray emissions his equipment was designed to pick up. And if the terrorists had wrapped their bomb in lead? Then his men and women would have to be right on top of it to identify it. And the skyscrapers! Sure he had half a dozen NEST helicopters to patrol the city rooftops, to do close-in flybys of the skyscrapers. But what a nightmare job!

He sat back and tried unsuccessfully to sleep. An hour later, they were approaching the New Jersey entrance to the Lincoln Tunnel. There before him across the dark waters of the Hudson was the magnificent skyline of the city he was supposed to save. A line of F. Scott Fitzgerald he had read as a schoolboy came back to him. To see Manhattan like that was to sense in it "the first wild promise of all the mystery and beauty in the world."

Well, on this autumn morning that skyline held out no promise of beauty for him. What was waiting for him over there was perhaps a taste of hell, the ultimate challenge to the techniques he and his teammates had so carefully developed. He would follow all their exchanges by radio, praying he would not hear in his earphones that terrible phrase *Gamma ray four.*
That was the code indicating that indeed a nuclear device was spotted, hidden somewhere in that teeming city where additional millions came each day from the suburbs to work.

*   *   *

Nahed Jihari, her white scarf still firmly knotted around her head, drove her Easy Rent van out of the Brooklyn-Battery Tunnel onto the foot of Manhattan Island. As she steered the vehicle across Trinity Place toward lower Broadway, the usual collection of impatient, petulant or just plain rude New Yorkers were leaning on their horns creating a noisy symphony.

Nahed laughed. "Just like driving in Beirut or Jerusalem." Omar Tahiri, sitting beside her, jerked his head toward the rear of their van. "Well what we've got back there will shut them up soon enough."

The two terrorists, along with their colleague Khaled, had arrived in the United States a few days before. Shortly after they had agreed to undertake their mission, Imad Mugniyeh's trio of terrorists had their photographs taken in the Ein el-Hilweh refugee camp. The photos were hand-carried by a French Algerian member of al Qaeda to Montreal, where they were delivered to a Pakistani master forger-counterfeiter, Farid al Mansour. Mansour was not affiliated with al Qaeda. His artistry was for sale and it did not come cheap. Counterfeit Indian passports, U.S. visas, birth certificates and New Jersey driver's licenses, ostensibly issued in November 2002, when Garden State licenses were notoriously easy to copy, had cost Mugniyeh close to one hundred thousand dollars for his three terrorists.

However, the fake documents had worked perfectly. The three had flown without incident from Paris to Montreal. From there, they had gone by train to that quintessential tourist destination, Niagara Falls. On a Saturday evening, they had ostensibly spent hours gambling in the Casino Niagara, then headed off to Buffalo over the Peace Bridge on a shuttle bus full of American gamblers. Their phony New Jersey drivers licenses were all the ID they needed to slip into the United States with their busload of happy gamblers.

An al Qaeda operative from Rochester met them at their hotel the next morning and drove them to a motel in Yonkers, one in a chain of motels frequented principally by illegal immigrants. Nahed did most of the driving to get herself well accustomed to American traffic.

Now, at Twenty-third Street she turned onto Fifth Avenue to head for the hideaway they had selected for their atomic bomb. They had to double-park in front of the building, but in that part of Midtown Manhattan, everybody did. Indeed, one of the most common criminal actions in the neighborhood was for a robber to pop open a van's rear door and walk away with whatever was valuable inside.

Khaled, the third member of their trio, was waiting for them in front of the nondescript building chosen for their base of operations. It was four stories high, over a century old and its front facade was "decorated" by a green metallic fire escape.

On one side of the building was Mimosa's Pizza Parlor, on the other a souvenir shop selling "I Love NY" T-shirts. The neighborhood was redolent with the odor of the hot dogs roasting on the peddler's stand on the corner.

"Everything went fine," Omar assured his colleague, "except this crate is heavy as hell."

"We'll slip the Super fifty dollars to give us a hand with it," Khaled said. It would not be their first act of generosity toward the toothless old man. They had already handed him six thousand dollars in cash for three months' rental of a two-room flat on the fourth floor. Needless to say, the sum went straight into the Super's pocket. The building's absentee landlord, an insurance company in Texas, would never see a trace of that cash nor was there any official document like a lease or rental agreement.

Khaled and the Super wrestled the heavy crate past the Korean hairdresser's shop occupying the ground floor and into the building's creaky elevator. It was a noisy ride up to the fourth floor that they shared with an Afghan carpet dealer. The intervening floors were filled with a multitude of small shops selling electronic goods and out-the-door stocks of pirated DVDs, TV cassettes and even fake Hermès handbags.

It was a simple affair, a living room, a bedroom, a bathroom and a primitive kitchen. Once the Super had disappeared, the three proceeded to open their crate and remove the protective casing in which their bomb had been stored.

Working with care and precision, they set it up as they had been instructed to do by Mugniyeh's experts in Lebanon. Then with the most delicate of movements, they verified the connection of the cell phone to the bomb's detonator, installing along with it the relay that would divert any false numbers that somehow might come into it. When they finished, Tahiri stood back to admire their work, then looked out the window toward the high-rise buildings across the street.

"There won't be much left of them when this thing goes off," he said. Then suddenly a mother carrying her infant child appeared in a window of the building just opposite theirs. That gave a troubling personal image to the tragedy they were preparing. "Or them either," Tahiri mumbled.

Then he turned to Nahed. "You'd better get that van back to the rental agency," he ordered.

*   *   *

Across Manhattan Island, Detective Lieutenant T.F. O'Neill pulled his unmarked New York police car up to the police command post at the Brooklyn end of the Williamsburg Bridge. He flashed his gold shield at the patrolman on duty and said, "I want to get a look at that scanning device we installed here at the end of 2002."

The device was part of a top secret program set up by the New York Police Department that year. Radiation scanning devices similar to those employed by David Graham's NEST teams but much less sophisticated had been secretly placed at all the entry points to Manhattan Island, in tollbooths, on bridges and at the entries to the Lincoln, Holland and Brooklyn-Battery tunnels. The idea was to pick up any terrorist attempting to smuggle nuclear material into the city. As O'Neill was about to find out, it was one of those ideas that looks great on paper and becomes a shambles in execution.

"That Goddamn thing!" the patrolman said. "We turned it off months ago. It picked up every poor son of a bitch going over the bridge after getting radiation therapy at some hospital in Brooklyn. We even got your chief of detectives one day."

"Well, I'd better get him now," O'Neill said and rang up Police Plaza on his cell phone. There he learned from the Chief of Detective's assistant that those devices had been turned off all over the city. Why? Because in their first months of use, they had turned up a staggering seventy thousand false positives and the police had simply stopped using them.

"The Goddamn program was a shambles," the assistant growled. "Forget about technology saving this city. Still the PC wants them all turned back on to full power right now. And don't forget the Chief expects you down here forthwith."

O'Neill passed the message to the disconcerted patrolman and climbed back into his car. So, he thought, something big is going down, which explains why we have this "all hands to the pumps" at Police Plaza's orders. And if the Chief is insisting all those scanning devices get reactivated immediately that could well mean we're facing something nuclear. Jesus!

*   *   *

"This is it?" the President exploded, slamming the single sheet of paper on the Situation Room table with the palm of his hand. "This is all your stations in Islamabad, New Delhi, Kabul—and your nuclear nonproliferation experts—could come up with on this guy?"

"This guy" was Dr. Abdul Qadeer Khan, the nuclear physicist who led the development of Pakistan's atomic bomb.

"What have you got in here we can use as a lever to open up a dialogue with this guy? He used to stay up all night reciting Urdu poetry? He grew roses when he was a kid? How about all the Dutchmen, the Germans, the Brits he worked with in the seventies? They have any clues to his character we could work on?"

"Mr. President," said Milt Anderson of the CIA—whose officers had been working all night assembling that brief document—"you may be a little harsh here. There are a couple of elements in that report that might facilitate our contact with the man."

"Which ones?"

"First there's the fact Khan is a member of an Islamic group, the Lashkar-e-Toiba—Soldiers of the Cause—which we know has ties to al Qaeda and Osama bin Laden. So we're dealing here with an apostle of the *jihad*. Yet there are contradictions in the man's behavior. He doesn't use alcohol, like a good Muslim, but he's clean shaven. No beard of the Prophet for him. And as far as we know, he's lived a strictly monogamous existence, always faithful to his one wife."

"Despite those trips to Pyongyang?"

"Alas, Mr. President, it seems clear they were scientific not sexual in nature. He seems to be a man of civilized behavior, which may help in establishing a dialogue with him."

"Civilized? Civilized?" exploded Donald Rumsfeld, the secretary of defense. "Just how civilized can someone be who doesn't stop proclaiming that the atomic bomb he developed is not just for Pakistan but for all the Muslim world—and therefore for Islamic terrorists?"

"Look, we're getting off course here," the President said forcefully. "Dammit, the problem before us isn't deciding who Khan built his bomb for. It's finding out how we can convince him to help us solve this crisis. He's obviously a deeply religious man.

Shouldn't we find some Islamic authority to help us open up a dialogue with him?"

"Now we're on the same page, Mr. President," Milt Anderson answered. "We have with us Sheikh Omar Habibullah. He's a Pakistani who runs the Institute of Islamic Studies here in Washington. He's ready to either help you in a conversation with Khan or to talk directly to him himself. Do we know yet if Khan will agree to talk to us?"

Bush looked at the clock. "His flight landed in Karachi an hour and a half ago. Let's call Musharraf for an update on the situation."

A few minutes later, the Pakistani president's image appeared in a direct TV link from Karachi to the Situation Room's closed circuit TV. "Dr. Khan is in the next room," he informed the Americans. "He has admitted to me that the bomb missing from our inventory was taken on the orders of Hamid Gul and his group of extremists. He's also admitted that he himself activated its detonation system so wherever that bomb is, we know it's fully functional. I've avoided for the moment any talk of bringing formal charges against him and at my request he has agreed to speak with you but only to explain the reasoning that led Gul and his associates to perform this terrible action."

Well, the President thought, at least he's agreed to talk. That's something to be thankful for. While the room's technicians had been setting up the TV link, a slight man in a beige *djellaba* and white turban had been ushered into the Situation Room. The President stood, smiled and beckoned him to a seat at the head of the table. The Sheikh, the President knew, had been fully briefed on the situation by the CIA.

He turned back to his microphone. "Dr. Khan," he said, "I want to thank you first for agreeing to talk to me in this hour of crisis."

If the President had imagined courtesy was going to get the conversation off on a friendly footing, Khan swiftly disabused him of that illusion. "Mr. President," he said, "I did so because I want you and of all your people to understand why we did this. It is because your so-called War on Terrorism was never a war on terror. It was always a war on Islam."

"Dr. Khan," the President interjected, "you are, I know, a man of deep religious convictions as am I. The Jesus I worship is acknowledged as a prophet by your own holy book, the Koran."

"Mr. Bush," Abdul replied, "you are a pious fraud. You invaded the land of my Iraqi brothers in search of weapons of mass destruction that never existed. Your so-called road map for Middle East peace was a grotesque joke. You never raised a finger to stop that war criminal Ariel Sharon from slaughtering my Palestinian brothers and sisters with your Apache helicopters, your F15s, your rockets. You stood by and did nothing while his tanks demolished their cities and their homes. Well now, Mr. Bush, an Islamic atomic bomb is hidden somewhere in your nation and if you do not force Sharon and his Israeli henchmen to return to our Palestinian people the lands they seized, every square foot of it, then it is your countrymen who will pay for Sharon's intransigence."

The President was aghast. He wasn't going to be able to reason with this man. Probably his best hope lay in the sheikh, to whom he nodded.

"Good day, sir," the Sheikh began, "it is a privilege to address the honored teacher, the much-admired intellectual benefactor of our great nation, Pakistan."

"Who are you?" Abdul asked in a tone that indicated he had long since learned to ignore flattery.

"A fellow Pakistani, like you born in Lahore. I teach Koranic law at the Islamic Institute here in Washington. The President has asked me to speak with you. I know from studies that you are a devoted follower of our great faith. I speak to you therefore in the name of tolerance and understanding, those virtues extolled and practiced by our great Prophet, God rest his soul. Surely you know these terrorist fanatics who have planted one of your bombs somewhere in an American city."

"No, I don't know them personally."

"Well, surely you understand that if this bomb which exists because of the great intelligence which Allah bestowed upon you explodes, killing hundreds of thousands of innocent people, their deaths will blemish forever the history of our great faith."

"Look, Doctor," Abdul replied, "as I told you I do not know personally these people you call terrorists but I can tell you I admire them and bless their combat. The *jihad* is an act of faith. If Allah blessed me with the knowledge to build this device and then placed it in their hands, surely it is to obtain justice for our Palestinian brothers and install upon their stolen land the blessings of divine justice. I wish for their success."

"Placed in their hands by that bastard Hamid Gul," growled CIA's Milt West in a voice too low for his microphone and hence his listeners in Karachi to pick up.

"My dear Dr. Khan," the Sheik replied, "I'm sure you know as I do the *surats* of our holy book which urge us to tolerance, mercy and forgiveness for our enemies."

"Yes," Khan answered, "and I also know by heart those *surats* which urge us to *jihad* against those who spread injustice on this earth and crush the weak: 'Fight in the path of Allah those who fight you' and 'Those who are attacked are authorized to defend themselves.' The Palestinian martyrs recite verses such as those before sacrificing their lives on their Israeli targets. Theirs are acts of desperation because no one—and particularly your American friends—is prepared to offer them hope, a future. If this bomb is menacing the lives of so many Americans, perhaps it can play a crucial role in giving the Palestinians a future. Perhaps it can force the enemies of Islam to make peace at last. A just peace. That is now up to your American friends and Ariel Sharon. I have no more to say, Learned Brother. God keep and preserve you."

The sharp *click* of a telephone being hammered into its cradle reverberated through the Situation Room. Khan had cut the communication.

"Son of a bitch!" said Vice President Dick Cheney. "There's going to be no reasoning with that bastard!"

A chorus of grunts and mumbles gave an approving echo to his words. For several long seconds the room was reduced to silence, its occupants shaken by the finality of the Pakistani scientist's refusal of a dialogue. It was finally broken by the tones of a feminine voice, that of Condoleezza Rice. "Mr. President," she said, "let's let a few minutes go by and then see if I can get Dr. Khan back on the line."

"Condi," said Vice President Cheney, "with all due respect, that's a terrible idea. That guy is obviously a hard-core Islamic extremist. The last person he's going to accept to talk to is a woman."

"I'm not so sure, Dick," Condi Rice replied. "CIA's report describes him as 'civilized,' right? He had that childhood upbringing under the British Raj and those years in Germany and the Netherlands, so *civilized* might also mean 'courteous.' He could well be more responsive to a female voice than you think. And if he is, I might know how to establish a rapport with him."

There was no one in his government in whom the

President had more confidence than his secretary of state. With her fluent Russian and knowledge of the Soviet Union, she had played a key role at his father's side in the critical days when the Communist empire was collapsing. In his own administration, she had often been the first of his close collaborators to speak to him after she'd finished her morning workout, and often the last to talk with him in the evening.

He much admired her ability to calmly synthesize and analyze the arguments surrounding the issues before his government. And the two also shared a passion for watching baseball and football games on TV in the White House.

"Listen," he told the room, "let's let Condi give it a try. What have we got to lose? Get Musharraf back on the line and see if we can't get him to reestablish contact with Khan."

To everyone's surprise, the Pakistani scientist agreed. Condi began in her warm and husky voice. "I want to thank you for agreeing to talk with me. I was anxious to have the opportunity to speak with you because I think I am particularly well placed to understand and sympathize with some of your concerns."

"Sympathize?" Rumsfeld mumbled, with an angry glower on his face on hearing her words.

"I have read much about you, Dr. Rice," Khan replied, "and as a fellow academic I much admire your achievements."

"Thank you, Doctor, and I too can appreciate the enormity of your scientific accomplishments. We share, I would venture to say, certain common elements endowed to us by history. We—and our peoples—know what it is to suffer the burdens of discrimination by the wider society surrounding us—you as Muslims in an Indian Raj dominated by British and Hindu values; we as African Americans, the descendants of slaves, in a society dominated by the values of its white majority. For both of our peoples, religious faith has been a critically important anchor to which we have clung in our hours of trial, Islam for you, the Baptist faith for most of my brethren. For you, as for me, the pursuit of knowledge was critical in freeing us from the prejudices and hardships our societies imposed on us. We share that just as we share the darker color of our skin that sets us apart from much of our surroundings."

"Ah yes, Miss Rice," Khan interjected with what seemed to the leaders gathered in the Situation Room to be the hint of a laugh, "as you Americans say 'Black is beautiful.'"

The President glowed at his words. Condi's done it, he thought. She's made him laugh.

"Our struggle in this country," she continued, "was often marked by hatred and bitterness for our white brothers and sisters."

"And," Khan added, "the murder and lynchings of your people."

"Indeed," Condi replied, "but it was the message of tolerance and wisdom, understanding and fraternity given voice by great men like Martin Luther King that led us, Doctor, to where we are today."

"King, of course. A disciple of India's Gandhi, whom I saw as a youth," Khan noted.

"Dr. Khan, suicide bombers, however just they may feel their cause is, do not represent the true ideals of Islam anymore than Timothy McVeigh, the Oklahoma bomber, represented those of Catholicism. Islam, the great faith that it is, is no more represented by Osama bin Laden than Christianity's values were represented by the excesses of the crusaders of Pope Urban II."

"Indeed," Khan said, "well put."

"I know, Doctor, that you, like I, are a great lover of poetry."

"Quite true, Miss Rice," Khan replied with what was almost

a sigh.

"I have always liked that Persian epic 'The Rubaiyat of Omar Khayyam,'" she said.

"Ah, yes. Dr. Rice, I share your enthusiasm for that great work."

"I often reflect on that line 'I sing of man's brief life, separated from death by the space of a breath.'"

"How true those words," Khan responded.

"Yes," Condi continued, "and surely you would wish that the harvest of your great scientific achievement will be the triumph of justice and understanding. Not hatred and bloodshed, the stifling of life's short breath in hundreds of thousands of people."

She paused to give emphasis to the plea she was now ready to utter. "Come with me, Doctor, in the footsteps of Martin Luther King. They lead to the broad uplands of human understanding and reconciliation, not the hell of hatred and vengeance the explosion of your bomb will wreak. There is still time, Doctor. Please reflect and help us overcome this crisis embracing us all."

An almost eerie silence followed her words. "You are a powerful advocate, Miss Rice," Khan answered finally, his voice suddenly subdued. "I shall reflect on what you have said overnight. God willing, we will talk tomorrow."

Once again a click indicated that he had hung up his receiver. Then something happened which the somber premises of the Situation Room had not witnessed since Khrushchev signaled his willingness to withdraw his missiles from Cuba: the entire room burst into applause.

*   *   *

Holy smoke, Detective Lieutenant T.F. O'Neill thought looking at the mob crowding the auditorium of the New York Police Department at One Police Plaza, everybody's here but the men's room attendants. There were FBI agents by the hundreds, probably every damn detective in the NYPD, Customs guys, Secret Service, Counterfeit Squad guys, New York State Police troopers. The only thing missing from the city's police community were the women from the Society for the Prevention of Cruelty to Animals!

The brass up on the platform was impressive: the police commissioner, Ray Kelly; O'Neill's boss, the Chief of Detectives; Dave Cohen, the deputy PC for intelligence; the Irishman who ran the FBI's New York office, a couple of "suits"—probably spooks from Washington or Albany. All the flags were on the platform behind them: the nation's, the city's, the state's, the NYPD's, the FBI's. You'd think they were getting ready for a parade down Fifth Avenue.

Commissioner Kelly got up, walked to the lectern and banged a gavel to silence the clamor of a thousand men and women talking anxiously to each other.

"All right, people," he said, "let's come to attention and listen up." For a long moment he stood there staring out at the gathering, ever the Marine Corps officer bracing to send his troops into battle. "Ladies and Gentlemen, we have a crisis on our hands, perhaps the worst crisis this city has ever had to face."

"Worse than 9/11?" an incredulous voice from the audience asked.

Kelly ignored the speaker. "We have solid intelligence information that a group of terrorists has smuggled a barrel of chlorine gas into Manhattan Island. I don't think I need to tell you just how deadly chlorine gas is. Should those terrorists release it into our atmosphere, if their demands are not met, the result could be the death of hundreds, thousands of our fellow New Yorkers."

Kelly's words sent alarm bells ringing in O'Neill's head. They wanted those gamma ray detectors on the bridges and tunnels turned back on full blast to pick up chlorine gas?

As if to answer his unspoken question, Kelly added, "And by the way, there's one possibly helpful aspect to all this: we think the barrel may have been stolen from a chemical plant in India that tagged their barrels of dangerous chemicals with identifying radioactive signatures. They did that so that even if a barrel's labeling was obliterated it could be identified by its specific signature. So we'll be able to use Geiger counters to help us search for that damned barrel."

"I'm sure you all remember from your chemical-warfare training sessions. That damn stuff is deadly. The fact that barrel has been hidden here in Manhattan and we're looking for it must, and I repeat must, be kept a total secret. If it got to the public, we'd risk having a panicked flight of the population like the one we saw on 9/11. I can tell you because you are all responsible, intelligent law enforcement officers."

"What are the terrorists after?" someone shouted from the audience.

"It's an Arab-Israeli thing," Kelly answered. "That's the State Department's concern, not ours. Ours is to get to that barrel before the terrorists blow it up. The lives of one hell of a lot of people will depend on our succeeding in that job. Unfortunately we have very little intelligence on the perpetrators at this moment, but I will turn the meeting over to Deputy PC Dave Cohen who'll give you all we've got."

"This has all the earmarks of an al Qaeda operation," Cohen began, "so we will want to activate every source we have on Arab terrorists and activists. And we will want to look at everything we've got on people who are into providing them with false ID, driver's licenses, credit cards, whatever. This will be an 'all hands' operation bringing in every human resource we have available—Treasury, Customs, Narcotics—the lot. We have already mobilized the joint FBI-NYPD anti-terrorism task force. Inspectors accompanied by federal officers are to begin immediately scouring out potential targets: the Empire State Building, Madison Square Garden, Penn and Grand Central stations, major synagogues, Wall Street, federal office buildings. We have selected fifty senior-grade detectives to leave immediately for Port Elizabeth. There they'll be paired with FBI and customs agents to comb through the manifests of every container unloaded there in the last thirty days.

"We have no physical description of the perps as of this moment. We do not know their number or anything of their movements. But we can assume these people realize it's best to blend in as middle-class folk; do as little as possible to draw attention to themselves. They usually live well but not ostentatiously. They may be native born, maybe not even of Arab descent, like Reid, the guy who tried to blow up a plane with explosives in his sneakers. They don't want for money. They do have a tendency to stay with their own kind so we'll want to check out everything we have on the Muslim communities over in Brooklyn for example. What's called for here is good solid, hardheaded detective work. Let's go. There'll be assignments waiting for you at your precincts. And the fifty guys selected for Port Elizabeth will find their names on the bulletin board in the hall."

"Hell," O'Neill said to himself finding his name on that list. "Here I am running Manhattan South which is supposed to be the most terror-prone place in the city and I have to go off on a junket to glamorous Port Elizabeth for the night!"

*　　　*　　　*

The sense of relief that had swept over the U.S. government officials in the White House Situation Room after Condi Rice's conversation with Dr. Khan had been brief. Now the President and his advisors faced yet another challenge, one which promised to be almost as difficult as the conversation with the Pakistani had been.

"We just can't put this off any longer, Mr. President," Condi Rice said. "You've got to get Ariel Sharon on the line. We've prepared a one-page summary of the situation in Hebrew that we can put onto the closed circuit link by facsimile so he'll have everything in front of him."

The President gave a worried stroke to his forehead. His conversations with the Israeli leader were never easy. This one promised to be a nightmare. "Where is he?" he asked.

"At his residence on Balfour Street in Jerusalem, probably just finishing up his dinner," Condi said.

"Kosher cuisine," smiled the President, "just like we had for him here when he came to dinner at the White House. It's not bad." He turned to the head of the CIA. "Milt, you've studied this guy. Is there anything in his history or background that gives you hope he might be accommodating to us in the face of this threat?"

"Absolutely nothing, Mr. President. His reputation for activism goes all the way back to '49 or '50 when he was a young officer and led his company on a punitive raid into a village in Jordan in which *fedayeen* were alleged to be hidden. I think sixty or so village males were gratuitously killed. He became a full fledged hero in the 1973 war when his division smashed across the Suez Canal and encircled a large part of the Egyptian Army. He was a powerful advocate for action against the PLO in Lebanon because of their raids into Israel. When the war started, he promised Begin he'd stop twenty miles inside Lebanon but, of course, he went all the way to the suburbs of Beirut. If he'd had his way, he would certainly have killed Arafat right there and then, but he was under pressure from Reagan to exercise restraint."

"And, of course, there was that business of killing all those Palestinians in a refugee camp," the President recalled.

"Sabra and Chatila."

"Yeah, wherever. Just how guilty was he really of that, my 'man of peace.'"

A faint ripple of laughter followed the President's words.

"At the best, Mr. President, he was guilty of doing nothing to stop it," Anderson replied.

"And tell me, is he really a believing, a religious, man?"

"He follows outwardly the requirements of Jewish life. Like his kosher dinners here at the White House. Does that reflect belief or political expediency? I don't think I'm entitled to say. However, Mr. President, there is one thing on which I think we at the agency all agree—it's that famous visit he made to the Temple Mount or what the Muslims call the Haram al-Sharif in September 2000. That, we are convinced, was sheer expediency. He could have gone up there any time he wanted to for thirty-three years. His aim on that visit was to blow the Oslo peace process out of the water, which he certainly succeeded in doing."

"And his thoughts on the settlements?" the President asked.

"Oh, hell, Mr. President, you got the answer to that when you were trying to implement your 'road map for Middle East peace.' All you got out of him was a little lip service. Knocked over a couple of trailer camps for the TV cameras; we know the trailers were set back up the next day."

"Maybe so, but apparently he did come around on the closing down the Gaza settlements," President Bush said. "And I think that's sincere—he certainly was willing to pay a big price politically for that plan.

"In any case," the President sighed, "this conversation is going to be a bitch alright. I guess we'd better get him on the line."

Condi did the preliminaries, then faxed the prepared text to Jerusalem.

"My God!" On reading it, Sharon exploded in the deep parade-ground voice for which he was noted. "This is the most outrageous, incredible effort at extortion, at blackmail, in history. As the leader of the world's only superpower you have only one choice open to you before history, before the world. Reveal this to the world immediately and denounce it for the horrible act of blackmail that it is."

"And put the lives of a million of my fellow Americans in New York at risk?"

"It is not you who is putting them at risk, Mr. President. It is these Islamic terrorists in Pakistan who are behind this. People surely tied to Osama bin Laden. You tell them publicly that if that bomb explodes, other and more powerful bombs will strike Pakistan's North-West Frontier Province and Baluchistan. The areas where these outrages are coming from will disappear from the face of the earth. And you won't have to worry about finding Osama bin Laden anymore. As you Americans say, he'll be toast."

"Ariel," the President replied—the two men had been on a first name basis for years now—"that's an appalling suggestion. Millions of Pakistanis would die! You have always chosen to downplay the hatred, the thirst for vengeance created by your retaliation against the Palestinians. Do this and Jews everywhere will face a murderous wave of anti-Semitism. You'll have the entire Muslim world, even those countries which have stayed on the sidelines, thirsting for vengeance against you."

"George, those people are the same ones who will cheer and dance in the streets if that bomb ever explodes in New York. Just like they did on 9/11."

"Look, Ariel, whether you like it or not, you and I have got to at least consider addressing the demands in that note. Every American president since Lyndon Johnson has opposed those settlements. We have to recognize that under international law they are unwarranted and illegal. My own father and his secretary of state, Jim Baker, were particularly opposed to them."

"That is absolutely out of the question, George. God gave those lands to the Jewish people. The Bible counts for more than international law. We, the Jewish people, have an historic right to the whole of the land of Israel. We are not going to surrender them in response to a heinous attempt at blackmail, at extortion, such as this. I have made my feelings on our rights to at least some of those lands clear to you often enough."

"Ariel, a majority of your own people are ready to dismantle most of those settlements, and you yourself are planning to close down the ones in Gaza. You know as well as I do that the settlements cost your nation five hundred sixty million dollars a year in subsidies of one form or another—subsidies which Americans have helped finance. We have always been your nation's best friend and closest ally. How much love do you think is going to be left for Israel in this country if that bomb explodes?"

"George, if I yield before this ghastly attempt at blackmail, it will be the end of Israel. I have never in the past made a concession with the security of Israel. I will make none now and none in the future. That is the historic responsibility that I bear for the future and fate of the Jewish people. You tell your friend Musharraf to announce to these criminals that if they go through with this, six million Pakistanis will die—and if you aren't willing to take them out with your weaponry, I will do it with our Jericho missiles. *Shalom.*"

Once again a stunned silence enveloped the American leaders in the Situation Room. "Dear God," murmured the CIA's Anderson. "Pray those New York cops and the Feds can find that damn thing in time!"

*   *   *

Two hundred miles from the crisis meeting in the White House Situation Room, the three terrorists who had smuggled their bomb into New York were finishing dinner. The remains of the Five Cheeses Pizza they had purchased from their nearby neighbor, Mimosa's Pizza, littered the living room of the terrorist's squalid Midtown Manhattan flat. The living room furniture consisted of the camp bed, table and three chairs they had bought that afternoon. The bedroom's furniture was mainly their atomic bomb, a two-foot-high cylindrical device looking a bit like an overweight barrel. Protruding from its top was the Nokia cell phone they had properly secured to it on their arrival, the phone that would receive the incoming detonation signal.

Omar Tahiri glanced at his watch. They could now safely make their call. A London colleague had equipped them with one of a pair of Nokia phones purchased at a computer warehouse for 450 pounds. Each phone had an identical SIM fitted into its base. The chips were encoded with a prepurchased fifty minutes of calling time. The beauty of the system was that the two phones could call each other but no one else. That meant they would rarely be used and calls made on them would be extremely difficult to trace. They, of course, had one. Imad Mugniyeh in Beirut had the other.

Omar used his first name when the phone was answered. Mugniyeh replied by simply saying "Your friend is listening."

"We are here. Everything has been set in place as instructed." He then proceeded to use a verbal code, given to them before they left, to give Mugniyeh the address and details of the building where they had the bomb.

"That is good," Mugniyeh said, "I will now take over."

Both men had been careful not to use any Arabic or any revealing Islamic-style phrases. Mugniyeh was particularly anxious to keep his part of the call brief because he knew the American NSA had multiple recordings of his voice. With them they could run a voiceprint analysis and could identify him as one of the speakers, if should they somehow decide to scrutinize the call after picking it up on their spy satellites.

The terrorist trio had rented rooms in a comfortable hotel not too far away, but there would always be one of them in this flat. On the table in the living room was an electric switch they had wired to the detonator. Should the police break down the door of their flat, the member of the trio babysitting the bomb would have only to press that button and the bomb would explode.

Omar had volunteered to take the first shift until mid-morning, allowing the others to get a reasonable night's sleep in their hotel room.

As they were preparing to leave, Khaled sat down beside Omar and squeezed his knee. Of the three, his experience in the struggle with their Israeli enemies was by far the freshest. "Listen," he said, "I know how the Israelis run most of their targeted assassinations. It's with these mobile phones. The Americans developed a technique they passed on to the Mossad. If they have your mobile phone number, they can call it. You won't know that the phone's been called but it will send back an answering message. Then they call the phone from somewhere else, and by triangulating they can pinpoint exactly where the phone—and presumably you—are. Boom! They hit you even if you're in a car with that mobile turned off. They can figure out what building you're in, even what room. We had to call Beirut and you can be sure that's one place their satellites are focused on. They get our number, and they may be able to trace us right to this room. I'm going to chuck this phone in a waste can on the way back to the hotel. We don't need it anymore, do we?"

*　　*　　*

The President pushed away his TV remote control with a weary gesture. "I'm exhausted," he announced to his wife, Laura, and to Condi Rice who had joined the couple in the White House living quarters for a final review of the day's work. "I don't have the strength or the desire to watch a ballgame tonight. What a day! The worst in my presidency since 9/11."

"Yes," Condi agreed. "It can't get much worse than today."

"Oh, yes it can," the President said with a sigh. "The only high point in the day was your talk with Dr. Khan."

"He did come around a bit, didn't he?" she noted.

"Because of you, your human touch with him." Suddenly the President sat up straight in his chair. "Of course," he said, "it was that human contact between the two of you that did it. What if we could set that up live, on a person-to-person basis? Condi, suppose we could get Musharraf to agree, would you be willing to fly out to Karachi and try to reason with Khan, you know, talk to him eyeball-to-eyeball? That just might be the way out of this damn mess."

"Mr. President, if Musharraf will agree and that's what you want me to do, of course I will. Obviously I'm ready to do anything to try solving this crisis."

"Let me handle Musharraf. I don't think he'll be a problem. He's being very helpful so far. I'll call Andy Card and have him get Air Force One at Bolling geared up to take you to Karachi. You get out there as fast as you can."

"Certainly." Condi closed her eyes for a second or two reflecting on the task she'd just been assigned. "One thing, Mr. President. Can we ask the Press Office to put together a package of the very best, the most moving videotape we have of 9/11? Not the shots of the planes hitting the towers and the buildings collapsing. Islamic extremists just love that footage. What needs to be on that tape are images of the anguish, the pain, the suffering, the faces of the women and children. That's what I want."

"Of course."

*   *   *

Detective Lieutenant T.F. O'Neill struggled to suppress the ill humor that had been building up in him for hours. Here he was, the commanding officer of the Midtown South Detective Squad, the elite unit assigned to protect what even Police Commissioner Kelly acknowledged was the most vulnerable part of New York City and what was he doing to stave off the menace threatening his city?

Not a damn thing he could see. He was parked in front of a computer screen in Port Elizabeth, New Jersey, methodically plodding his way through hundreds, soon to be thousands, of manifests and bills of lading of the ships that had called on the port in the thirty days before the threat note arrived at the White House. That tiresome, boring task was supposed, somehow, to allow O'Neill and his fifty fellow NYPD detectives, each of them paired off with an FBI agent, to spot a suspicious cargo in which the terrorists might somehow have smuggled their deadly device into New York.

The only consolation for T.F. in this grotesque misuse of his years of experience was sitting beside him. It was the FBI agent assigned to work with him—a relative rarity among the Feds, an African American female. What's more, she was stunning. In her tight black leather skirt and elegant blouse—with her full lips, beautifully combed hair and lithe, athletic figure—she could have done a centerfold for *Playboy.*

Not that he would pay her the compliment of suggesting that, of course. Not in these days when a compliment or a slip of the tongue could be taken as an unwanted sexual advance. And in the case of a government employee—could put his career at risk.

His FBI mate—her name was Olivia Phillips—was from Louisiana bayou country. The bureau had recruited her out of Tulane Law School, she had said, and sent her to their Quantico, Virginia, academy for training and a final polish.

He glanced at her as she peered intently at the manifest on her computer screen, then let his eyes fall to her slim legs protruding from her short, tight skirt. How times change, he thought. When he joined the force, Feds came in one sex: male. They all dressed alike, dark suits off the racks from Barneys—then a discount house—hair cut short, never any question of facial hair of any sort.

Now they came in sports shirts, wearing baseball caps turned fashionably backward, ill shaven. Hell, he had even seen one of them wearing an earring! And now, of course, some of them came in skirts and blouses like this lovely creature sitting next to him.

"Spot anything, Olivia?" he asked.

"Oh sure," she said, as bored by this task as he was, "another container full of bedsheets from Singapore for Wal-Mart." She shrugged and clicked the button on her computer to pull up yet another manifest for her appraising – and tiring – eyes.

When they had arrived at Port Elizabeth, a customs officer had assigned them to the first floor of the port's administration building. It housed a dozen gigantic offices, one for each of the port's terminals. They were given a large desk with two computers, its windows looking out across the towering cranes and warehouses of the port. Their charge was the 121 ships that had docked in berths 15 to 20 of Marine Terminal 4 in the last thirty days. That meant inspecting the paperwork on the cargoes discharged in those berths by all those ships—a total of close to five thousand containers.

As it happened, however, thirty-seven of those ships had been auto ferries bringing in 32,450 new German, British, Japanese and Korean cars. The cars came preloaded on trailers that were immediately driven off to the car dealerships on the eastern seaboard that had ordered them. Run those cars down to their dealers and check each one out to see if someone used it to smuggle a bomb into the country? An impossible task and probably a useless one besides, since it was hard to imagine a bomb that would fit in the trunk of a car.

That left T.F. and Olivia to scan the paperwork for the remaining containers. Olivia's eyes were now red with fatigue. She leaned back and rubbed them while T.F. gave her a sympathetic look. She glanced out the window at the forest of cranes lining the terminal piers. Never had she seen a port like this one before.

"Quite a place, isn't it?" she said.

T.F. laughed "*On the Waterfront* it ain't, that's for sure. You should have seen the old Brooklyn Docks I knew as a kid. The mob ran everything in those days, just like in that film. The morning shape-up was where they picked the longshoremen for the day. If you didn't have a cousin or uncle in a mob family, forget it. There'd be no work for you, pal. Now, like you see out there, it's all mechanized."

"What happened to that mob family?" Olivia asked.

"Dead. Or into new things like fake credit cards. Fortunately we've got a lot of them doing time upstate."

"Yes," she said, "they taught us a lot about that at the academy in Quantico. Gotti, the Gambinos. Did you get involved in all that?"

"Hell, yes. A lot of those wiseguys came from my precinct, downtown in Little Italy." T.F. took a deep breath. "Hey," he said, "that's a nice perfume you're wearing."

"Thanks," Olivia smiled. "It's Joy by Patou." Fascinating, she was thinking. How many people would expect a New York detective to pick up on something like that? Maybe he's been buying perfume for his wife or girlfriend for years. "Are you married, T.F.?" she asked.

"No," he said, "I'm a widower. I lost my wife in an automobile accident six years ago."

"Oh, how sad," she commiserated, "what a painful loss that must be."

T.F. sighed. "The holes in your life don't come any bigger than that. Well, I guess we better get back to this exciting job they've given us."

Olivia pulled another ship's manifest up on her screen. "Hey!" she exclaimed, "here's one that at least has got a nice name—'the *Jewel of India.*'"

"Yeah," said T.F. "Probably carrying curry as an easier way to poison New Yorkers than chlorine gas would be."

Twenty minutes later, Olivia laid her hand on T.F.'s wrist. "Take a look at this." She pointed to her computer screen. "Here we've got two containers off-loaded from this '*Jewel of India*' on the same day, one after another. According to their bills of lading they have identical cargoes—250 sacks of basmati rice, each weighing 50 kilos. The containers are identical, same model, same manufacturer. When the first one gets weighed on that scale on the dock, it weighs 31,000 kilos. Then the second one is weighed and it comes in at 31,150 kilos. Why the difference? How much do you suppose a barrel of chlorine gas weighs?"

T.F. studied her computer screen. "Now we finally have something interesting," he said. "Of course it could be anything but still . . ." He pulled up the *Jewel*'s consignment sheet for the containers:

NAME OF VESSEL	JEWEL OF INDIA
SHIPPER	MAHARASTRA ORIENTAL FOODS, BOMBAY
CONTENTS	BASMATI RICE
DESCRIPTION	250 SACKS 50 KILOS PER SACK
CONSIGNEE	EXOTIC GROCERY GOODS, CENTRAL WAREHOUSING GRAND AVE, ALBANY NY
IDENTIFICATION	LOS 8477/8484

Both consignment sheets were, as Olivia had indicated, identical. So why the difference in weight? Where had those containers gone? It was pretty certain they hadn't stayed up in Albany. They probably had been forwarded to a wholesaler or a large food store somewhere in the Northeast. And if that store were in New York?

"Well done, Olivia," he said. "This deserves a follow-up. Those 150 kilos are almost certain to be hash or hard drugs. Let's see if we can get somebody on the line up there in Albany."

A few minutes later, thanks to State Police headquarters in Albany, they had a sleep-befuddled night watchman at Exotic Grocery Goods on the line. He knew nothing about the containers in the warehouse yard.

"So what's the telephone number of the boss?" O'Neill asked.

"Hey, man," the watchman said. "Its one o'clock. He'll be sleeping now."

"I didn't ask you what he's doing. I want his phone number and I want it right now. Or I'll send a state trooper out there to get it from you. And to get you too, for failure to execute a lawful order."

Three minutes later the frightened watchman gave them the home phone number of the owner, Charles Osborne.

"Let me talk to him," Olivia suggested. "Sometimes guys will stand up a bit straighter when they hear the word *FBI.*"

Osborne had, indeed, been sound asleep when his wife got him, steaming angry, to the phone. He began to berate his caller when Olivia cut him short in her iciest voice, as she'd been trained to do at Quantico. "This is Special Agent Olivia Phillips of the Federal Bureau of Investigation. There is a national security concern involved here and I expect your immediate cooperation."

You could almost hear Mr. Osborne swallowing his distress at her words. "Of course, I am at your disposition," he assured Olivia in the meekest of tones while T.F. looked at her admiringly.

Olivia gave him the references of the containers of basmati rice and told him they had an urgent interest in determining where they had gone.

Osborne pondered the question. "We do a lot of basmati rice. There's a guy in Buffalo and one in Brooklyn who get it regularly but I don't have their addresses and numbers here."

"Can you get them for me? Urgently?" Olivia said.

"Well," said Osborne, "I live about an hour's drive from my warehouse. Say another hour or so to dig through the files and get you what you want. It's a helluva a chore at this time of night, but if my country needs me..."

"Yes," Olivia answered, "your country needs you and is grateful for your help, Mr. Osborne."

At T.F.'s suggestion they gave Osborne the phone number of his Manhattan South precinct to call. "If that container's in Brooklyn, we'll want to get out there as fast as we can. What we'll do now is drive back to the precinct. I have three female detectives in my squad so there's a women's section there where you can catch some sleep."

He quickly explained what they were doing to the customs officer running the manifest search and they were released. Before long they were heading for Manhattan through the Holland Tunnel.

"O'Neill. . . ," Olivia said. "I guess you must be Irish."

"Sure and *begorrah* . . . see, I can even talk with a Gaelic accent. On my father's side we go back to the potato famine and the Civil War. Later though I got a French Canadian grandmother and a Lithuanian great-grandmother."

"Did policing run in your family?"

"On my father's side. He and my grandfather were both on the force. How about policing in your family?"

Olivia laughed. She was starting to relax, now that they were out of that dreary office at the port. Besides, she realized that she enjoyed his company. "Oh sure. When they weren't picking cotton in massa's fields."

O'Neill smiled. He too was starting to feel an easy sense of camaraderie with this pleasant—and gorgeous—agent sitting next to him. "My grandmother loved to tell me the O'Neills were kings of Ireland. That and a buck will get you a beer in any pub in Dublin."

He was sorry that traffic had been light and they made it to the precinct so soon. But there would be other opportunities to get to know her better, he consoled himself.

After they pulled into the precinct parking area, O'Neill took her upstairs to the two rooms that had been set aside as living quarters for his female detectives when they had to work overnight. "It's not the Waldorf," he said as Olivia stretched out on one of the beds with a heavy sigh.

T.F. looked down at her fondly. "Well," he said, "get what sleep you can. As my mother used to say, 'Roses on your pillow.'" He switched off the lights and tiptoed out of the room.

CHAPTER

6

NEW YORK CITY
WASHINGTON D.C.
JERUSALEM
KARACHI

The Crisis—Day Three

Dawn had long since lifted night's chilly veil from the skyline of New York when T.F. O'Neill's unmarked police car took the exit ramp off the Brooklyn Bridge onto Flatbush Avenue. Beside him, the FBI's Olivia Phillips glanced back toward the skyline of Manhattan.

"How come these bastards always pick on New York?" she wondered aloud, her curiosity activated by the three steaming cups of black coffee T.F. had served her before leaving his precinct headquarters—the best coffee in the five boroughs, he had assured her. "Why don't they try Chicago or L.A. or even, God forbid, New Orleans?"

"Because we've got it all here, Olivia. The money, the people, the power. And for Islamic terrorists there's another big plus: a lot of Jews living here. People hate America? First thing that comes to mind is New York, that sight you just looked at back there."

At this early hour, the streets were nearly deserted and before long, they were gliding to a stop in the driveway of a red brick warehouse on which were painted the words *Birbaki Oriental Foods.*

"Looks deserted," Olivia said.

"Yeah," T.F. agreed. "We may be off on a wild-goose chase here. Still a place like this ought to have a guard. Crime may be down in New York, but it ain't down that much."

He walked to the garage door and began banging loudly on it with his fist.

"You don't shout *Police?*" Olivia asked.

"Hell no. If there's a watchman in there, let him think he's got a delivery."

After a few more imperative knocks, the sleep-befuddled guard opened the door. "Hey, man," he snarled, "we're closed. You want something you come back in an hour."

T.F. "gave him the gold"—flashed his detective's shield at the watchman. "Where's the boss?" he asked.

"He's asleep over in Greenpoint. You want I call him for you?"

That was the last thing T.F. wanted. He wanted to get the grocer cold, without allowing him a moment to reflect on a story if, indeed, he was a party to bringing a bomb—or much more likely, dope—into the city.

"Nope," he said, "what I want is to wait in here for him to show up. And you, pal, will just wait here for him with me and my friend."

Birbaki did indeed show up forty-five minutes later, stunned as he opened the door to his little office to find his two visitors and the guard waiting for him. Before he could say a word, Olivia stepped forward and flashed her ID. "Special Agent Olivia Phillips, the Federal Bureau of Investigation." As she articulated those words, T.F. studied Birbaki's facial expression, hoping to see there some telltale sign of fright that might hint at guilt.

He then flashed in turn his shield. "Police," he said. "We want to have a little talk with you."

"What the hell is this all about? I run an honest business here. Never had any trouble with you guys," Birbaki said, in a tone halfway between indignation and anxiety.

"It's about them two containers of basmati rice you got here forty-eight hours ago," T.F. said, still peering intently at Birbaki. Suddenly seeing what he was looking for, an intimation of fear mixed with the surprise on his face. Was the guy moving drugs, he wondered?

"There was something in one of those containers, my friend, that wasn't basmati rice. I want to know what it was and where it went."

Birbaki collapsed into his office armchair, grasping his head in his hands. Scared absolutely shitless, T.F. thought. You could almost smell the fear oozing out of his glands. Time to use a different tactic with the guy.

"Moving drugs," he said, "is gonna cost a guy like you, got a clean sheet and all, ten to fifteen years inside, depending on the judge."

"Officer, I don't know what it was," Birbaki pleaded. "I don't, so help me God."

"Look," T.F. said, "different guys got different ways of working. Me, I always say level with a guy, tell him where he's at. You help us, we help you; you know what I mean? I gotta know where the package that was in there with the rice went. What it looked like. Who got it. And by the way, I'm a downtown detective, not a narc, you know what I mean?"

"OK," said a somewhat relieved Birbaki. "I'll tell you everything I know." And he did, beginning with the Turk's first request, the subsequent deliveries and the final pickup.

"Now that Turk with the New York Yankees cap," O'Neill asked, "you got a name and number for him?"

Birbaki did and got it off his Rolodex. T.F. passed it to Olivia with a nod. She stepped out toward their car.

"Now that's a lot better," he said to Birbaki. "Let's go over all the details of that last pickup yesterday morning."

"Well," Birbaki replied, "the Turk always came for the stuff in a Hertz van. These two instead had an Easy Rent van. The woman was driving. She was wearing a kerchief on her head."

"A Muslim?" T.F. asked.

"Who's to know? It was chilly. The guy, he didn't have a left hand so my guys had to take the crate out of the container for him and load it into his van."

"Did you see it?"

"No, I was in here. My guys said it was a wooden crate maybe three feet long and heavy as hell. Couple of hundred pounds at least. T.F. frowned. Sounded like it was too heavy to be "horse," and for two hundred plus pounds of hash, you'd need three of those crates. Maybe it wasn't drugs after all.

Olivia, meanwhile, had returned from the car where she'd called FBI headquarters. "Our Turk has flown the coop," she said. "Flew back to Istanbul Thursday."

"Shit," T.F. groaned. A crate that looks too heavy for drugs. A Turk who conveniently disappears just when we need him. And a van from Easy Rent. That's where you didn't need a credit card to rent a truck. Just drop a thousand bucks deposit on the desk beside your fake driver's license and away you go. Maybe, he thought, this bright little FBI woman here had hit on something with those manifests last night.

"Look, Mr. Birbaki," he said, "I'd like you to come downtown with us and we'll just drop by Easy Rent and see if we can find out who rented that van and where it went."

*   *   *

A refreshing autumn breeze stirred the Aleppo pines lining the route of Ariel Sharon's three-car caravan as it sped past Saint John's Monastery of the Cross up the incline to the Israeli Knesset and the building housing the Jewish nation's principal government offices. As usual, a gaggle of journalists and TV cameramen were waiting as Sharon's car pulled to a stop in front of the Prime Minister's office.

Why, they shouted at him, had he convened this extraordinary meeting of his government? Sharon answered with an indifferent shrug of his shoulders and a dismissive wave of his hand meant to indicate it was a matter of no importance. He set off down the long corridor to his cabinet room with his usual heavy-footed, purposeful stride.

There was no such reticence, however, to soften his exposition of the crisis to his cabinet. At the start of the presentation, he passed out copies of the White House's Hebrew summary of the crisis, including the full text of the terrorist's threat note. Then he reviewed the transcript of his talk with the President from the tape recording he had made of their conversation.

The reaction of his cabinet colleagues was a mixture of horrified surprise and fury. Many of them, of course, were politically well to the right of the Prime Minister. The tourism minister, Yisrael Ephraim, was among them and he was the first to respond.

"You were absolutely right, Arik, to tell Bush we will incinerate Pakistan's North-West Frontier Province and Baluchistan if that bomb goes off. Those places are breeding grounds for the worst Islamic extremists on the planet: Bin Laden and the followers he trained in his camps, the leftover Talibans and the madrassas fueled by Saudi money, with their Wahhabite hate teachings. You can be sure that somehow they're behind this."

"Come on, Yisrael, you'd kill millions of innocent people?"

protested Henry Levy of the moderate Shinui Party, one of the few non-Likud members of the cabinet. "Do that and Islam—and not just Islam—will abominate this nation and the Jewish people for generations."

Yisrael Ephraim growled, "they already do. Besides, did you see the results of the last elections in Pakistan? They voted Islamic crazies into office."

Sharon turned to his defense minister, addressing him in the stiffly formal tone he always employed in these meetings. He prided himself in maintaining a profile distinctly different from the other Israeli leaders like Israel's founder, David Ben-Gurion, who didn't own a necktie. Since leaving the army he was inevitably well dressed in public, in a freshly pressed dark suit, a crisp white shirt and a necktie from the most elegant men's store in Tel Aviv.

"Mr. Mofaz, how about those Shaheen-II intermediate-range missiles the Paks tested a year ago? Could they hit us in a retaliatory strike? Three well-placed nuclear hits would sink us into the sea."

"Yes," Mofaz replied, "they certainly could. They have a range of twelve hundred miles, quite enough to reach Tel Aviv. We know from Mossad they have at least fifty Hiroshima-size nuclear warheads and they've had a year to manufacture the missiles to deliver them. Certainly long enough to turn out at least fifty of them."

"And what of our defense against a missile attack? Could we prevent those missiles from getting through?" Sharon asked.

"I would hope so," Mofaz replied. "The Patriot missiles we used in the Gulf War are now much improved. And more important, we have the Arrow anti-missile we developed with the Americans. It has been remarkably successful in all our testing. Still, nothing is certain in life. Even with all that, we have to assume that one or two would get through."

"What a prospect! Another Holocaust, after all the struggle to put Israel on the map and keep it there . . ." Sharon growled.

"Arik!" It was Sharon's great political rival Mishka Medev, sidelined since Israel's last election as the nation's finance minister, a task as challenging as it was certain to dim his political appeal to the Israeli voters. "There is no question—this is what we have all feared for years, the ultimate crisis in which the stakes are our nation's very existence. I don't think we have a choice. If we crumble before this threat," he continued, "our Zionist will to exist is going to be fatally compromised."

"Mishka, for God's sake," Levy interrupted. "This is no time for electoral speeches. Besides, you know as well as I do that the majority of our own citizens are opposed to those settlements in the first place."

"It's not the settlements that are the issue here. The issue is, will this nation back down before a terrorists' extortion threat?"

"Mishka, we are not being threatened. It's a million New Yorkers who are."

"But it is we who are being asked to pay the price of this blackmail," Medev continued. "Pay it and who knows what the next demands will be? Israel has survived in a sea of enemies because we've been tough minded and steadfast. And we have to deal with this in that same spirit."

"I'll tell you how we solve this crisis," barked Avigdor Beibelman. Together with his close friend, the Minister of Tourism, he was the most extremist member of the cabinet. "We go public and say 'If that bomb goes off, we will pack every Palestinian on the West Bank and Gaza into trucks and deport the lot of them to Jordan.'"

"Madness!" retorted Levy. "We will become a pariah

nation."

"We already are. And those terrorists will have solved the problem of Judea and Samaria for us once and for all."

"Look," Sharon intervened, "I must make one thing clear. I gave my word to President Bush that I would keep this threat a secret in view of the terms in that terrorist note. I hold you all honor bound to respect my pledge."

"Oh, Arik," interjected Beibelman, "the Americans will betray us. Just like Eisenhower did in 1957 after the Suez War when he forced us out of the Sinai that you helped take."

Sharon ignored him. "Since my conversation with the President, Mossad and Shin Bet have been working all out to help the Americans in their search for the bomb. We have to stay on the side of our most important ally."

"What do we tell the journalists outside was the reason for our meeting?" Mofaz asked.

Sharon thought a minute. "Tell them we were discussing a new program to bolster this faltering tourist industry of ours." Even in moments of crisis, the Prime Minister was not without a sense of humor. "I think, my friends," he continued, "we have reached a consensus. I will have to call the President and inform him that regretfully this government cannot and will not agree to dismantle the settlements despite the horror of the threat he faces."

Unnoticed by Sharon and unheard by anyone else in the room, Beibelman had turned to his colleague and fellow extremist, the Minister of Tourism. "I have an idea," he whispered. "An idea that will blow this crisis right out of the water."

* * *

T.F. O'Neill had planted his flashing blue "clear the streets'" light and siren on the roof of his car as he left the warehouse of Birbaki Oriental Foods. Now traffic was melting before his car as he raced up Hudson Street to its junction with lower Eighth Avenue and Bethune Street. There at the corner was his destination, the only Easy Rent garage in Manhattan, and fairly close to Birbaki's warehouse. Therefore, in O'Neill's judgment, it was the most likely source of the van that picked up the mysterious crate off-loaded from the *Jewel of India.*

The garage owner, alerted by a call from police headquarters, was waiting at the garage door for T.F., Olivia Phillips and Birbaki. As she and T.F. had agreed, Olivia flashed her government ID and laid the imposing phrase *Federal Bureau of Investigation* on the owner to make him "'stand up a bit straighter'" than he might have for a NYPD shield.

At the request of police headquarters, the owner had laid out for them in his office the rental agreements covering all the vans his agency had rented out in the last ten days. They were divided into two piles, one for male renters and a second, much smaller, for females.

T.F. sat Birbaki down at the owner's desk and pointed to the smaller pile. "OK, pal," he said, "see if you can find her in there."

Each rental agreement in the piles contained a photocopy of the driver's license presented by the renter with, as required by law, a photo of the renter, plus a copy of the credit card used as a deposit unless the renter had opted to give a thousand dollars cash deposit. Anxious to demonstrate the degree to which he was cooperating with O'Neill and Olivia's investigation, Birbaki earnestly studied the Easy Rent documents. At the third agreement, he paused.

"You know," he said, "I told you guys she was wearing a

head scarf. If I try to imagine a scarf on this woman, it could be her. He showed T.F. and Olivia the New Jersey license registered to a Sally Wonder, 1428 Carrolton Avenue, Hackensack, New Jersey. "This woman's about the right age, thirty-eight. And there's something about her eyes that rings a bell with me."

T.F. and Olivia stared at the agreement Birbaki was holding out to them. T.F. plucked his cell phone from his belt and called headquarters. "Listen, we may have a real break." Have the Hackensack police get a car out to 1428 Carrolton Avenue and see if they can get their hands on a Miss or Mrs. Sally Wonder."

Birbaki, in the meantime, continued to work his way through the stack of rental agreements on the desk while Olivia pondered the one he had selected from the pile. "Look, Mr. Chief Inspector," she said using the title she had playfully assigned T.F., "the timing on this agreement checks out pretty well. The van went out yesterday morning at nine thirty-seven and was brought back here to the garage at four thirty-two that afternoon."

"Remember what time they showed up at your warehouse, pal?" T.F. asked Birbaki.

"About ten thirty."

"Figures," said T.F. "That's about the time it would take them to get out there from here." The chorus from *Aida* rang out and T.F. grabbed his cell phone.

"Shit!" he announced, turning to Olivia. "Pardon my French, but that Jersey driver's license is a fake. Fourteen twenty-eight Carrolton Avenue is a vacant lot." He rubbed his forehead. "Until November 2002, we had a big problem with counterfeit Jersey driver's licenses. They were making them everywhere. This must be one of them."

"Well," said Olivia, "at least we now have an ID photo of the woman we can circulate."

"Yeah," said O'Neill, "and you can figure she isn't a Sunday school teacher. Where's the van now?" he asked the garage owner.

"Out back. It went out last night with a young couple who were moving house."

"OK," O'Neill said, "keep it there. We're going to have to ask some people to come by and take a look at it."

Olivia turned to the garage owner. "Did you get a good look at this woman?" she asked.

"I wasn't here when she checked it back in, but I did notice her in the morning when she checked it out. She was better looking than most of my customers."

"Did she say what she wanted it for?"

"Not really. She just said she had some errands to run."

"Was she alone?"

The owner frowned trying to recollect the moment. "No," he said, "there was a guy with her. An older guy."

"Can you remember anything about him?"

"He was just a guy, you know what I mean? But wait, there was one thing. He only had one hand. I had to light his cigarette for him because his lighter wasn't working."

"Bingo, Mr. Chief Inspector," Olivia laughed, grabbing T.F. by the forearm, "these are our people alright."

By now, a car from the NYPD's bomb squad, another bearing technicians from the FBI's criminal lab, plus a car carrying a pair of NEST inspectors, had arrived to examine the van. By common understanding, the NEST inspectors went first with their Geiger counters. They found nothing, although they had not expected to. Unless a piece of the device itself had somehow come loose and was lying in the van, there would be no telltale traces of gamma radiation to indicate what the van had transported twenty-four hours earlier. And neither the bomb squad nor the FBI's experts found paint scratches that might have signaled the vehicle had a scrape somewhere that could provide a lead.

When they left, Olivia gave T.F.'s forearm another playful tug. "Tell me, Mr. Chief Inspector, did they teach chemistry at Brooklyn College?"

"Yes but I was lousy at it. Why?"

"I was just wondering when they started to look for chlorine gas with a Geiger counter."

O'Neill looked at her with fresh admiration in his eyes.

"You've got a point," he said. "We were given an explanation at the meeting, remember? But I didn't really buy it. I think you just hit on something the honchos down in Washington want to keep a secret."

Olivia shrugged. Keeping secrets was part of your job when you were an FBI agent. She picked up the rental agreement. "But we've got something critical here," she said waving it. "They brought the van back in with eleven miles on the clock. And it took about one gallon to fill up its tank, so the reading must be right. How far do you figure it is from here to Charlie's warehouse?'

O'Neill went over to the big map of New York on the garage owner's wall. He traced out the distance using the scale at the bottom of the map. "Four and a bit miles."

Olivia turned to the owner. "Have you by any chance got a compass like those things you used as a kid in geometry class?"

"Yeah," he said, "I think so."

Fumbling around in his desk, he found one and passed it to Olivia.

"Okay," she said, "so about six of those sixteen miles were used getting out to Charlie's, allowing for a couple of wrong turns. That leaves us ten miles or so for the trip from Charlie's to their hideout and then back to Easy Rent to return the van. They kept it only a few hours, so they weren't doing any fancy sightseeing. Besides, would you with an atom bomb in your home?

Let's assume the place where they're holed up is somewhere in or near Mid-Manhattan. And this Easy Rent garage is down here in the West Village. So let's use six miles as the distance from the warehouse to the hideout, the same as from Easy Rent to the warehouse. That leaves four miles—about eighty city blocks.

She set the compass width to mark off a distance of four miles on the map. Then she put its pin on the corner of Bethune and Lower Eighth Avenue, where their garage was, and drew a circle with the four-mile radius. It included all of Manhattan up to Eighty-sixth Street, plus Brownsville and Williamsburg in Brooklyn, Long Island City and Woodside in Queens, and Hoboken in New Jersey.

"My dear Chief Inspector," she announced, in a voice that clearly was a caricature of movie detectives, "that barrel of radioactive chlorine gas we're looking for has got be somewhere inside that circle."

T.F. grabbed her in his arms. "You're terrific, Olivia! Next to you, J. Edgar Hoover was a Keystone Cop. Come on. We've got to get your map and the woman's photo to Police Plaza forthwith."

                    *   *   *

For Secretary of State Condoleezza Rice, it had been the voyage of a lifetime. Here she was, the only passenger on Air Force One, the personal airplane of the presidents of the United States, a huge jet fitted out with the most modern technical equipment and the most luxurious appointments in the sky. Sure, she had been in the plane before when she was National Security Advisor,

but always with the President, his other advisors and cabinet secretaries, plus usually the press. As secretary of state, she also had
a plane at her disposal, but there again there were always members of her staff and other officials. But on this flight from Bolling
Air Force Base outside Washington, D.C., to Karachi, she had
been alone, spoiled crazy by the plane's superbly trained Air Force
crew. At times, her experience made her think back to those quiz
programs she'd known as a kid—*Queen for a Day.* Here she was, in
the latest version of Air Force One.

With her sense of history, she kept thinking it was on an
earlier Air Force One that John F. Kennedy's body had been flown
back to Washington from Dallas and, on a far happier occasion,
that Ronald Reagan had flown to Iceland to meet Gorbachev and
to begin the process that would end the Cold War. And here she
was. Well, as her father had told her when she was a girl, in
America, with faith and perseverance, anything can happen.

As she sensed the pilot easing off on his engines as it came
time to start the descent pattern, she glanced out the window.
Sure enough, they were over land. Although she couldn't know it,
on the ground below, the Pakistan military was on full alert on
orders of President Musharraf himself. A tight cordon had been
laid down around the airfield. Musharraf was all too well aware
that hundreds of Stingers and Russian-made SAM-7s had disappeared in Iraq. What a nightmare it would be if one of them came
streaking out of the sky at the American president's plane as it was
landing on Pakistani soil!

When the plane finally taxied to a halt, a shiny, black,
pre–World War II Bentley, Musharraf's official presidential vehicle, drew up to the plane. The car had been a gift from the departing British to Pakistan's founder, Mohammed Ali Jinnah.
Musharraf's aide-de-camp, Colonel Lutfi Gibran, got out and

walked up the aircraft's stairs to officially greet Miss Rice, a small case in his hands.

After he'd showered President Musharraf's compliments and thanks on the young woman, the Colonel coughed nervously and opened the case. It contained a black *chador*, the all-enveloping garment that was practically obligatory for women when in public in strict Muslim countries, and a black head scarf. He explained that for her own security, the Pakistani president thought it was essential to keep her presence in Karachi a secret. Female visitors almost never came to visit his official Karachi residence dressed in anything other than strict Islamic garb. Would she, he asked, be willing to don the *chador* he held out to her?

To the Colonel's immense relief, Condi not only didn't object, she let out a charming laugh.

"Why sure," she said. It would be just like dressing up for the school play when she was a teenager. He stood by as she slipped the gown over her lithe and athletic form, then fitted the scarf to her head. Carefully, as prescribed by Islamic practice, he explained to her how to coax the few errant hairs dangling down her forehead back into the scarf's folds. Then he stood back to admire the result.

"Why, Miss Rice," he exclaimed, "you could be taken for a Mogul empress."

*   *   *

Thanks to energetic leadership from Police Commissioner Ray Kelly and some pushing and prodding by Paul Anscom, the New York City Office of Emergency Management under the base of the Brooklyn Bridge was fully operational just hours after the crisis started. It was handling an emergency exactly as intended by its founder, former mayor Rudi Giuliani.

Virtually every computer console at the half-dozen command stations ringing the room was manned. A soft undertone of muttered communications provided a sort of background music. Perhaps a hundred different images were blinking on the OEM's computers. No one was working harder than the agents of the FBI. Sensitive to the criticism leveled at the bureau for its shortcomings in the run-up to 9/11, both its Washington headquarters and its New York City bureau were determined that their behavior in this crisis would be above reproach.

Available to all was the bureau's new Terrorist Screening Center data bank of one hundred thousand plus names. It was created by merging a dozen existing lists maintained by nine different federal agencies, some of which previously had restricted access to their data even to their sister agencies. The merged lists included the Transportation Security Administration's "no fly" list of suspects barred from air travel, the State Department's massive TIPOFF list against which visa applications were screened, the FBI's National Crime Information Center list and the CIA's hitherto closed "Suspects File."

One team of agents was in constant computer communication with the immigration service in Washington and the Transport Security Administration, screening the landing cards and visas of everyone who had entered the country in the past month. Naturally enough, the agents paid particular attention to people coming in from the Middle East or other suspect areas of the globe.

That massive accumulation of personal data had been sharply criticized by civil libertarians. It was now, in an emergency like this, that its advocates maintained its worth would become apparent.

The OEM was Mayor Mike Bloomberg's first stop as soon as he arrived in the city from Washington. The Mayor was delighted to see that not a single press or TV vehicle was anywhere near the OEM's desolate and rather shabby location. After Kelly and Anscom had given him a tour of the building, he stopped fascinated at the command post supervising search operations at Port Elizabeth and Port Newark. It was adorned with huge photo-murals of the thirty-eight piers and seventy-seven miles of wharves making up the largest port facility in the United States and indeed the world. There was also a list posted for each of the ports' 142 docks showing every vessel that had unloaded cargo from the Middle East or any other suspect region at the dock in the past thirty days. It contained the date the ship had called on the port and an approximate list of the cargo it had off-loaded. As soon as one of the joint NYPD/FBI teams assigned to the docks spotted something suspicious in the multitude of manifests being scrutinized—just as T.F. O'Neill and Olivia Phillips had the night before—the cargo was signaled to the OEM office in Brooklyn. If the delivery had been scheduled for the metropolitan area, the OEM ordered the team that spotted the suspicious merchandise to track it down. If its destination was outside the metropolitan area, the FBI was instructed to get a team out to locate it.

The Mayor went from post to post in the command area offering his personal encouragement to the men and women running the search effort. A cackle of intercom communications signaled the progress of their work:

"Romeo Nineteen has just verified the twelve packs of sheepskin unloaded off the SS *Grace Three* from Latakia, Syria. No trace of any suspect merchandise was found."

"Scanner Four—*Scanner* was the code name for Customs—please verify the contents of two containers alleged to contain olive oil delivered yesterday to Exotic Supplies, 1148 Washington Avenue, Brooklyn. Port of origin, Beirut."

At another command post, a team of FBI agents and CIA officers were scrutinizing the personal dossiers of recent immigrants who might have some connection to al Qaeda or the Hezbollah. The names and addresses of those thought worth running down were radioed to FBI agents in unmarked cars to locate the individuals in question and verify their status and situation. To provide legal back-up, a brace of judges was on hand ready to furnish documents like a search warrant that the FBI teams might need.

"You're doing a great job!" Bloomberg said enthusiastically to Commissioner Kelly.

The PC felt obliged to temper the Mayor's excitement a bit. "All investigations begin like this, Your Honor," he said "but then we have to get down to the nitty-gritty, pounding the sidewalks, calling on the bars, coffee shops and grocery stores, looking for that one elusive clue that can lead us on. With a little bit of luck, all those efforts begin to converge on a precise point. Look what happened after the London bombings. The British scanned twenty-five hundred surveillance camera tapes and came up with the image that picked up the four terrorists. It took them just a week. An amazing success in that short a time. But that's more time than we've got. What you need, of course, is time—and time is the one thing those terrorist bastards didn't give us much of."

"Ray, your people are doing fine!" the Mayor assured Kelly. "Keep your chin up. You'll wind up finding that clue we need." Then Bloomberg's tone changed. "But listen, we still can't bank on that as an ironclad certainty. So we've got to at least prepare for an emergency evacuation of the city. How much time would we need to evacuate?"

"A minimum of twenty-four hours, and then it would

require a lot of preparation."

"These damn terrorists have given us until midday Friday. That means if worst comes to worst, we'll have to order the evacuation on Thursday, hoping we'll have time to save most if not all of the people."

The problem of evacuation had haunted the Mayor since the beginning of the crisis. Despite the terrorists' gruesome threat to detonate the bomb ahead of schedule if an evacuation started, how could he leave hundreds of thousands of his fellow citizens to their deaths without offering them even the slightest chance of an escape? It was an appalling moral dilemma, and a very personal one too, given the family, friends and colleagues living near the potential ground zero.

"There must be a plan for evacuating the city, no?"

"Sure," Kelly said, "it's two hundred-pages long and was drawn up in Cold War days when we were afraid of a thermonuclear strike. I haven't read it and most of my colleagues consider it worthless. I'll get the guy who drew it up in here to talk to us."

A few minutes later, a Washington bureaucrat flown in because of the crisis joined them. Charles Morningside was fifty-eight, his cheeks reddened by a long-standing taste for vodka and tonic. He was an example of a breed of person almost unique to Washington, a think-tank specialist whose work was subsidized by one of a score of well-meaning foundations. For years he had devoted his life to the study of evacuating urban populations in the event of a thermonuclear war. With the end of the Cold War, Morningside had had to reinvent his career in order to justify his substantial think-tank income. So he had convinced the leaders of the foundation that paid him that his studies could be—and should be—adapted to a more relevant problem: evacuating major American cities in case of a terrorist menace.

Kelly ushered him to the center of the command post from which they were working and said, "OK, Mr. Morningside, we're all ears."

"I don't think I need to tell you," he began, "that evacuating New York is a colossal enterprise. The first thing we would need to do is shut down all the access tunnels and bridges coming into the city. Or rather, make them all one-way. Only twenty-seven percent of the population of Manhattan Island has a car, which limits the potential for automotive evacuation, but we could require at least three people per car."

How the guy loves statistics, Kelly thought. "We'll requisition buses and trucks," Morningside said. "Fortunately, we have the subways. We'll run one-way traffic up to the outer Bronx and Queens, empty the cars, then turn them around to come back to the city for another load of people."

Driven by who? Kelly thought. The guys at the controls of the trains will have led the charge off the damn trains and headed for the suburbs themselves.

Morningside now placed a large poster on the easel beside him. TAKE, the title read. "We will display this card fairly constantly on television," he announced. It listed those things fleeing New Yorkers were supposed to take in their evacuation: a box of Tampax*, their cell phones, a bottle of water and a spare pair of socks and underwear."

Then he replaced his poster with a second one that read DO NOT TAKE. It listed three things—firearms, drugs, alcohol.

The guy's a genius, Kelly thought. He's listed the three things few New Yorkers would leave behind. And how about those thousands who won't go across the street without their pet dogs, cats or canaries?

*That was actually in the official text of the "TAKE" poster . . . what an example of product placement!

"Mr. Morningside," the Mayor intervened, "I recall that during the days of Governor Rockefeller the city had a vast, well-equipped series of air-raid shelters. Couldn't they be used in an emergency of this sort?"

An embarrassed silence greeted his words. Kelly found it difficult to repress a giggle. At the height of the Cold War, the city had possessed sixteen thousand shelters capable of housing in an emergency six and a half million people. Millions of dollars in federal aid had been spent equipping them with first aid kits, bottled water, nonperishable emergency food rations, even, in some instances, Geiger counters to allow survivors to scramble out after an air raid.

"I'm afraid, sir," Morningside answered, "their current state leaves something to be desired."

"Desired?" said Kelly. "When they had that earthquake down in the Dominican Republic a few years back, we pulled those rations out and sent them to the folks down there as a good-will gesture. What happened? Everybody who ate them got sick."

"What do you think of all this, Mr. Mayor," Kelly asked.

Bloomberg mopped his brow. "Think? I've given up thinking. I've decided to try praying instead."

The Commissioner's pocket cell phone jingled. He picked it up listened a second, then looked at Bloomberg. "You may be better at praying than you realize, Your Honor," he said. "That was my chief of detectives down at Police Plaza. We may have our first break in this case."

He opened up a computer circuit to Police Plaza and his chief of detectives appeared on his screen flanked by O'Neill and Olivia Phillips. "Commissioner," the Chief of Detectives said, "we mustn't jump to conclusions here. But what you are about to hear has all the earmarks of an important breakthrough in our search for this damn bomb. It could conceivably be a drug case, but I doubt it."

He turned to O'Neill. "I think you know T.F. O'Neill who runs our Midtown Manhattan South Detective Squad."

"T.F., we're listening."

Carefully and methodically, T.F. ran through the investigation he and the FBI's Phillips had been running since she had uncovered the discrepancy in the weight of the containers offloaded from the *Jewel of India*. He concluded by putting on the screen a map showing the New York area that fell inside the circle of probability based on the mileage used by the van that had made the pickup.

"Great work!" Kelly enthused. "What's the status of that woman's photo?"

"It's being printed up and distributed as we speak," replied the Chief of Detectives. "Sixteen thousand copies. We're getting it into the hands of every cop in the city with orders to show it all over town—to newspaper vendors, waiters, bar employees, every pizza parlor, fast-food shop, McDonald's and Burger King in their area, to the guys who sell *falafel* and hot dogs on street corners, to cleaning people in all public and private lavatories."

"Good. I want it run past the checkout counters from the crummiest food store in Harlem out to the best Safeway supermarket in Queens. Also to the men and women running the tollbooths of our bridges and tunnels. What cover story are we using to describe who she's supposed to be?"

"We've pegged her as the girlfriend of a couple of cop killers in Chicago."

"Good," Kelly said. "That ought to do it"

"How about the press?" Bloomberg asked "Should we pass the photo to them?"

"That," Paul Anscom declared, "is a question we will have to ask the White House."

The answer came back from Andrew Card almost immediately. Under no conditions was the photo to go to the press. The White House had no doubt that terrorist suicide bombers worked as a team; even if she were arrested, there'd be someone to carry out the explosion. The publication of the photo would only alert them to the fact the police were on their trail.

"He's right," Kelly said. He turned to the map on his computer screen. "That stretch of Brooklyn along Atlantic Avenue. That's a hotbed of Islamic extremist activity. It's 'Little Arabia' down there. 'Hubbly-bubbly' shops, backstreet mosques, women in veils, Arabic bookstores, the lot. They have a mosque, the Al Farooq Mosque, that we know raised over twenty million bucks for al Qaeda before 9/11. It's where that blind Egyptian *sheikh* was hanging out. If you wanted to hide that bomb someplace, that area is the ideal spot. Let's focus some intense search efforts down there—beginning right now."

*　　*　　*

In her elaborately furnished guest suite in Karachi, Condi Rice awaited the arrival of Dr. Abdul Qadeer Khan with a mixture of concern and curiosity. Curiosity as to what manner of man was this Islamic Oppenheimer, a scientist who could love roses and poetry and yet devote his life to endowing his people with the most terrible weapon man's mind had ever devised.

She was aware also that he was contradictory in other ways as well: genuinely devoted to the Islamic cause but suspected of making millions selling his country's secrets and peddling atomic materials.

Her major concern, of course, was about her ability to

strike a responsive chord in the man, to find some common area of sensitivity, which might allow them to find a way out of the terrible crisis menacing New York. The black *chador* in which she had arrived at the Pakistani President's Karachi guesthouse was neatly folded away. The clean-shaven Khan, she knew, was not a rigid follower of the traditions of Islam. Musharraf had explained that Khan was being kept under armed guard as a "guest" in the building, pending some resolution to the crisis caused by the theft of the Pakistani atomic bomb, an action in which he, of course, had been an accomplice.

At Condi's request, a videocassette player with a large screen had been installed in the room awaiting his arrival. To her immense relief, he was relaxed, almost friendly when an armed guard showed him into her suite. For a few moments, they chatted over green tea and cookies. Condi congratulated Khan on his work, which, she noted, had made him, in a sense, Pakistan's Oppenheimer. Had he, she wondered, studied the life of the father of the atomic bomb?

"Oh yes," Khan said. "I studied the Manhattan Project and its primary players, Oppenheimer, Groves, Teller, Szilard, at great length."

That was the opening she was looking for. "Oppenheimer, as you probably know," she said, "was in favor of employing the bomb on Japan."

Khan nodded his agreement.

"But when he went to Japan and saw the hell it had wrought, he was horrified. He bitterly regretted his decision to support using the bomb and that haunted and tortured him for the rest of his life."

"And fueled his opposition to the H-bomb," Khan observed.

"Indeed."

"I brought a videotape I'd like to show you, Dr. Kahn," she said, firing up her cassette player. For almost thirty minutes, a parade of terrifying images filtered by, children weeping and wailing—some, their little bodies mutilated—mothers embracing their dead in anguish, men weeping. The material damage of 9/11 was left aside—this was an agonizing portrayal of the human cost of the terrorists' action.

Abdul was understandably horrified.

"These are just the scars left upon three thousand people, Dr. Khan," Condi said. "If that atomic bomb explodes in New York, the cost it will exact in human suffering will be hundreds of times greater."

"Yes," the Pakistani scientist agreed, shaking his head in dismay, "it must not go off."

"We must each of us ask that of our God—I call him Lord Jesus, you call him Allah the Greatest—but at the end of the day it is the same divine entity. That horrible toll will be the consequence of the fruits of your genius. The images they will produce will haunt you, Dr. Khan, for the rest of your days."

"Of that," sighed Khan, "there is no doubt. The pictures on your cassette are horrifying indeed. But they are only one set of images. There is another set that you, Americans, do not want to see. You seldom screen them for your people on CNN and Fox News. They are the images of the suffering inflicted on my Palestinian brothers and sisters by your Israeli allies—of their homes destroyed, of Israeli tanks smashing through Palestinian farms and villages, of men cradling the bodies of their dead and mutilated women and children. Why don't you sit yourself down in front of these images, Dr. Rice, and try to understand the years upon years of suffering that lie behind the threat you now face?"

"Dr. Khan," Condi replied, "I have visited Palestine, I have met with the leaders there . . ."

"Please! Dr. Rice, do not take me for a fool. I have my sources, some of them inside your own government. I know how little sympathy you and people like your vice president and Secretary Rumsfeld have for the Palestinians. You are all tools of Sharon and the Jewish lobby. In July 2000, long before 9/11, you were saying that Arafat was a liar, someone the United States could not trust or work with."

"Arafat was in fact a lying incompetent, a liability to us, to the Israelis, but above all, to his own Palestinian people," replied Condi.

Khan snorted. "And your president's 'road map to Middle East peace'! What a farce that was! All Sharon had to do was sneeze and your Mr. Bush went off and cowered in a corner."

Their conversation was breaking down into sterile polemics, Condi saw, and if she wasn't careful, Dr. Khan could storm out of their meeting in a rage. Time to try another tactic, she thought, a dangerous one but one, which might shake the man in front of her into a grasp of reality.

"Look, Dr. Khan," she said. "Just what do you think are going to be the consequences if that bomb in New York goes off, as the terrorists are threatening, on Friday? Probably to coincide with the Friday prayers in Jerusalem."

"As you yourself have said, horrifying," said Khan. "That is why you must convince your Israeli friends to publicly declare their readiness to remove those settlements."

"I'm not talking about New York, Dr. Khan. I'm talking about right here in Pakistan."

Khan appeared taken aback by her words.

"Of course you are familiar with the concept of massive retaliation? What do you think Secretary Rumsfeld and Vice

President Cheney are going to advise President Bush to do if that bomb goes off in New York? Wipe Pakistan off the map of the world, that's what! And you know that the U.S. has the means and the will to do that if struck by a terrorist act that would make 9/11 seem like a school picnic."

She could see the shock of those words hitting home in the Pakistani scientist.

"And let me tell you something else, Dr. Khan. I know for a fact what Ariel Sharon's reaction to the terrorists' demand was. I heard it. If that bomb goes off in New York, maybe three hundred thousand of the dead will be Jews. If President Bush doesn't use our nuclear arms against you, Sharon will use Israel's. Maybe thirty, forty million of the Pakistanis to whom you devoted your life will die. Is that what you would like as the harvest of your life's work?"

Khan was shaken by her words. He turned away from Condi, his shoulders sagging. Clearly the Americans had found out it was a Pakistani bomb. But the whole idea was that it was to be an anonymous threat, that the Americans would never know against whom to retaliate.

"Help me, Dr. Khan!" Condi pleaded. "Help me to spare so many innocent people, Americans and Pakistanis. Just imagine if all those horrible images we just screened together—mutilated children, weeping mothers, the innocent dead frozen in their final agony—were Pakistani women and children."

Khan shook his head despairingly. "I don't know where the bomb is. I don't know who took it to your country or how they got it there. I only know one thing. I fitted a cellular phone to the detonator so that a call to that phone will set off the bomb. I have that phone number."

"Who else has it?"

"I assume at least two people, Osama bin Laden and a Lebanese named Imad Mugniyeh."

"Ah, yes," Miss Rice said, "I know who he is. Could you try to contact Bin Laden for us so we can try to reason with him?"

"That will not be easy—either finding him or reasoning with him. But I will try." Khan scribbled on a piece of paper. "Here's the number," he said. "But for God's sake don't tell anyone that I've given you that number. I know that I have just put my life in danger."

*   *   *

T.F. O'Neill led his FBI colleague into the "inner sanctum" of his police precinct at 357 West 35th Street. It was the detectives' canteen, a small, windowless room equipped with a coffeemaker, an ancient fridge, a table and a few chairs. The walls were decorated with the photos of some of Manhattan South's most sought-after criminals; the paint was peeling from both its walls and its ceilings; and a couple of dangling lightbulbs barely provided enough light to read by. Still, O'Neill assured Olivia Phillips, she was about to savor a cup of the best cappuccino to be found in New York City.

The FBI woman's eyes showed her surprise at the condition of the canteen. She looked very much out of place there. After returning from the Easy Rent garage she had changed into a new—and clinging—silk Calvin Klein blouse and a pair of elegantly cut black slacks. It wasn't wasted on O'Neill, who tried not to ogle her too obviously. This place, she thought, looked like one of those run-down police stations she'd visited in the outskirts of Mexico City during her FBI field training.

"Hey!" she laughed, "real third world, this place. What do

you use it for? Besides making coffee, I mean?"

"This is where we have our brainstorming sessions."

"Brainstorming? Here?" Olivia said, making no effort to conceal the touch of disbelief in her voice.

"Well, bullshitting sessions if you like," O'Neill said passing her a cappuccino. "You think this is something? Wait until you see the rest of the precinct headquarters. My guys still have to use those old Underwood stand up typewriters to type up their reports—when we have the money to repair them. We pay billions to make war on Iraq but we can't afford to fix the typewriters in New York's busiest police precinct.

"Come on," he said, "let's go see how our friend Mr. Birbaki is doing."

They had left the Brooklyn importer at the precinct's screening machine to run through all the photos the office had of criminals past, present and, perhaps, future. There were well over one thousand. To speed up the process, an officer entered the sex of the person sought, his or her approximate age and any identifying trait such as racial origin. The machine then filtered out the photos in the database and flashed them one by one on the screen.

Birbaki was scrutinizing that passing parade with no luck— it was a non-ending jumble of marijuana addicts or dealers, pickpockets, hustlers and petty thieves.

O'Neill gazed at him sympathetically. "Well," he said, "when you finish with these we'll call up the transvestite file. Then you'll see some really interesting pictures."

As he said that, the notes of *Aida* jingled on his cell phone.

It was the security officer of the New Yorker Hotel about a block away. Like most private security officers in New York, he was a retired NYPD officer riding the post-9/11 security gravy train. "T.F., I got something here you got to look at pronto," he said.

"Guy from Hamburg, Germany, checked in here forty-eight hours ago, hung his DO NOT DISTURB sign on the door and disappeared. Maid eventually knocked on the door, even tried calling. No answer, so she let herself in to check and see if he was okay. She found a laptop computer in there with wires hooked up to a device about the size of a VCR and what looks like an antenna wrapped up in tinfoil pointing out the window."

"Holy shit!" T.F. exclaimed. "Barricade the room and don't let anyone touch anything in there. I'm on my way."

"Come on," he said grabbing Olivia by the arm. "This may be what we're looking for!" As he headed for the door, he ordered his duty officer to get the NEST and the NYPD Bomb Squad to meet them at the hotel.

With its fifteen hundred rooms, the New Yorker Hotel is one of the largest in the city, known for its good and reasonably priced accommodations. Once it had belonged to the Moonies sect, but it had recently been taken over by the Marriott chain.

The security officer was waiting for them with a copy of the renter's registration card and his credit card. They confirmed that the man who had rented the room was, indeed, a German from Hamburg. To the hotel security officer's dismay, the NYPD's bomb squad and an anonymous NEST van were drawing up to the entrance. An excited crowd was the last thing he needed to promote his hotel business.

"Let's go, guys!" O'Neill ordered, and the team headed for the elevators and the twenty-fourth floor. They were equipped with suitcases containing detection devices and protective clothing, a sniffer dog and, for the NEST operatives, Geiger counters and gamma ray detectors.

Cautiously, the hotel security officer opened the door to 2408 with his passkey.

The sight that greeted them was enough to give someone an anxiety attack. As the security officer had said, a laptop computer was wired to a machine the size of a VCR and also connected to an antenna pointed at the half-open window. Several other devices, which looked like some kind of computers, were also wired to the central VCR-like machine.

The bomb squad officers let their dog sniff the device. He gave no bark indicating the potential presence of high explosives. The NEST men turned on their equipment and they, too, detected no telltale emanations. One of them pointed out, however, that whatever was in that device could have been wrapped in lead.

O'Neill sank to his knees and crawled along the carpet so he could look up at the principal device. At its base, he found a small metal plaque that read UNIVERSAL TIME CODE GENERATOR.

"That mean anything to any of you guys?" he asked.

It didn't.

He scribbled the words and the name of the manufacturer on a scrap of paper and handed it to Olivia. "Please get this to a phone and see if your FBI services can come up with anything on this firm."

"Could this be some kind of central timer?" he wondered.

"Yeah," said one of the bomb squad officers. "A centralized control that can synchronize the explosion of several bombs at once. Jesus . . ."

The NEST experts took the box's dimensions. It was conceivable that it could be a miniature nuclear device but it would have to be a very sophisticated one.

Suddenly Olivia appeared at the door. "Relax, guys," she said. "We got the number of that firm in Hamburg off the Internet. They make watches. Their top-of-the-line product is a watch that automatically reflects the change in time zones as its wearer travels. Their rep here installed this machine forty-eight hours ago because they haven't yet been able to adapt their watches for the automatic time changes needed on the eastern seaboard for Eastern Standard Time. The guy is on his way here now to explain the whole business to us."

A mixture of intense relief tainted with just a touch of disappointment greeted her words.

T.F. smiled and gave Olivia a hug. "Hey," he said, "people are much more suspicious since 9/11—which is what they should be. There's been a tremendous increase in things we have to respond to and there's a tendency in the police to become complacent because you're constantly reacting to false alarms. But complacent is one thing we can't afford to be." He looked at the other officers in the room. "Any of us."

*   *   *

"The President of the United States!"

The men and women gathered in the White House Situation Room jumped to their feet at those words barked out in his best parade-ground voice by the Marine Corps sergeant major in charge of security. Quite in contrast to the members of his Crisis Committee and their staff assistants gathered in the room, George W. Bush appeared alert and charged with energy. His close associates knew that he liked to take an ice-cold midday shower to give himself a hygienic shot of energy. Today, however, he had another reason to explain his energized manner and the smile that was lighting up his face.

"Ladies and Gentlemen," he announced, "Condi just called me over the secure phone on Air Force One as she left Karachi. Her visit to Pakistan was a complete success. After some initial reservations, Dr. Khan wound up being swayed by the arguments she presented to him." With a warm smile sweeping his face, the President took a slip of paper from his pocket and smoothed it out on the table before him.

Then he read the more formal text he had prepared for the meeting. "After an hour of sometimes difficult conversation, Secretary Rice was able to convince him not to tarnish his enormous prestige as a scholar and scientist by supporting a nuclear holocaust that could cause the deaths of hundreds of thousands of innocent victims. Above all, it seems that he was impressed by the thinly veiled menace of nuclear reprisals against his own Pakistani people."

"Be careful, Mr. President!" called a voice from the end of the table. Milt Anderson, the director of CIA, wanted to warn the chief executive against an overly optimistic interpretation of the position taken by the Pakistani scientist. "Dr. Khan is a very dangerous man. Believe me and my years of experience with people like him. If he put this bomb into the hands of the terrorists of Osama bin Laden, it's because he was absolutely convinced he was serving the higher interests of Islam. I don't think some shocking pictures of the suffering caused by 9/11 or even the specter of what reprisals could do to his own countrymen are going to lead a man like that to change his mind after a few hours of conversation. Mr. President, let me urge you to use extreme caution in assessing the actions of Dr. Khan."

No reproach was forthcoming from the President for being cautious and pessimistic—attitudes not often voiced in the gung ho atmosphere of Bush's inner circle—but instead he gave Anderson a warm smile. He picked up the piece of paper from his desk and continued reading.

"Ladies and Gentlemen, I think we can consider this terrible crisis resolved well short of the disaster that was threatening us. Dr. Khan has indeed accepted to help us save New York from disaster. He told Secretary Rice that he personally had attached a cell phone purchased in the markets of Islamabad to the bomb's detonator. A call to that cell phone will set off the bomb. And then, folks, he gave us the number of that phone. Only two other people have it—Osama bin Laden and probably a Hezbollah terrorist named Imad Mugniyeh. It is that number they intend to call Friday—just three days from now—if the ultimatum on the Israeli settlements on the West Bank has not been met."

The sense of relief sweeping the Situation Room was almost palpable. The President turned to the bespectacled computer whiz who represented the NSA at the table. "Moro," he commanded, "get this number to the director of the NSA immediately with my personal order to see that this number in New York City is isolated from all incoming communications from anywhere in the world. Make sure that nothing, no call whatsoever, can reach this number. I want the director's assurance in ten minutes that this is being done."

With a visible sense of relief, he turned to the gathering. "I want a full-scale review of this crisis to see what lessons we can learn from it for the future."

The group was deep in discussion of that topic when the nerdy young genius of the NSA reappeared.

"Mr. President," he said, "I'm afraid I have bad news. There is absolutely no way that the NSA or any other organization in this country can prevent a telephone call from abroad or anywhere else from reaching the number on that cell phone! Not unless we are right at the phone and can physically shield it."

*   *   *

At the Office of Emergency Management in Brooklyn, the near-frantic activity of the earlier part of the day had now been replaced by a slightly calmer air of determined, disciplined effort. The work of T.F. O'Neill and his FBI colleague, Olivia Phillips, allowed Police Commissioner Kelly to focus his search efforts on an area—however vast—that at least did not encompass all of New York's five boroughs. Assuming O'Neill and Olivia's calculations were correct, the bomb was in all probability somewhere on Manhattan Island between Eighty-sixth Street and the tip of the island, or in the adjacent parts of Brooklyn and Queens. Or maybe in the nearby areas of New Jersey.

As Commissioner Kelly was organizing the search, a team of FBI agents had swarmed into the Easy Rent garage to try getting the van the presumed terrorists had rented to "talk"—to come up with some indication of where its renters had taken it after making their pickup at Charles Birbaki's warehouse.

Hundreds of pieces of the van, stripped and broken down, covered the garage floor. The van had had thirty-seven known minor accidents, scrapes and dents, whose locations were circled in red. Every telltale trace of paint had been subjected to spectrographic analysis. All rental contracts on the van for the previous two weeks had been studied, the renters located and their itineraries reconstituted in as much detail as possible. The young couple who had rented the van the evening before had been located and brought to Police Plaza to see if they had found or noticed anything in the van—a discarded pack of matches, a soiled paper napkin from a restaurant, a newspaper—that might help trace back the vehicle's travels.

Experts had even vacuumed out the treads of the tires for anything that might help pinpoint where the vehicle had been.

Ditto for the floor mats. Since it was known that certain parts of the Brooklyn Bridge had received a coat of paint the day before, the Feds scrutinized every square inch of the vehicle's surface for a speck of paint that might indicate it had driven on the newly painted bridge.

The nuclear experts of NEST did their part by running Geiger counters and gamma ray detectors over every piece of the disassembled vehicle in the hope that a submicroscopic trace of radiation might somehow remain on one of them.

That enormous investigation failed to turn up a single bit of evidence that could help Commissioner Kelly tighten the area in which he had to search for the bomb. O'Neill's and Olivia's circle encompassed, however, some areas that his department already considered as prime targets for a terrorist's assault in the city—the Empire State and Chrysler Buildings, Madison Square Garden, Rockefeller Center, Penn and Grand Central stations, the Times Square area and non-Muslim houses of worship. For Kelly, for the leaders of the FBI, and for the hundreds of their agents and detectives already hard at work, it was an appalling challenge.

The PC wisely had decided to leave the setting of priorities in each of the areas encompassed in what was now being called "T.F.'s Circle" to the precinct commanders responsible for each area. After all, their officers patrolled those streets and neighborhoods daily and no one knew better than they did what might be hidden behind the facades of innocent looking buildings.

*   *   *

In the noise and tumult of the Emergency Operations Center, Mayor Mike Bloomberg was horrified to realize suddenly that the direct secure phone line to the President's Oval Office phone was blinking away unanswered. He grabbed it.

"Mr. President," he said, "please excuse us. We're so overwhelmed here we failed to catch your incoming signal." He gestured for silence at the center of the command module and transferred his call to the speakers around the command desk. "As you know, Mr. President, we feel we have at least been able to narrow down the area in which the terrorists' bomb could have been placed and are organizing a thorough and rapid search effort."

Still under the shock of learning that the most technologically advanced nation in the world was incapable of preventing a telephone call from somewhere overseas from reaching a cell phone somewhere on Manhattan Island, the President knew that now they had to find and disarm the terrorists' bomb. His contribution to the search was to exhort his New York forces to redouble their efforts to resolve this crisis in what seemed to be the only way left—other than getting Sharon to comply with the terrorists' demands. And that, President Bush suspected, might be even harder than finding the bomb.

He passed on the bad news he had just received. "Michael," he said, "I was hoping and praying that, knowing the number of the cell phone on the bomb, we could stop an incoming call from reaching it. That hope, alas, has evaporated. Our experts at the NSA say it is technically impossible."

"Well, Mr. President, that's not entirely correct," a voice at the command center desk observed. It belonged to David Graham, the head of the NEST search teams. "If we can surround that cell phone with a Faraday cage, that will prevent any incoming signal from reaching it."

"A what?" asked the President.

"Faraday cage. It's fundamentally a copper shield, which prevents any electromagnetic signal from passing through it. And that includes a call to that phone."

"Oh great!" exclaimed the President, "but we still have to find the damned bomb, don't we? In other words, we're still stuck here on square one."

"And," noted Commissioner Kelly, "the fact remains the search for this device is as delicate as it is dangerous. We just have to assume that these terrorists are babysitting their bomb. They will be holed up right there beside it ready to detonate it themselves if they pick up any indication that we are about to close in on them. The closer we come to success in finding them and their bomb, the more dangerous and critical our task becomes."

The President groaned out his agreement. He glanced at his watch. Condi would be landing soon. At least they might be able to relax for a few moments to watch an inning or two of the baseball play-offs.

*   *   *

In Manhattan, a young couple was walking hand in hand along Thirty-eighth Street toward Sixth Avenue, laughing at the absurdities of the film they had just watched, a crude effort to recapture the magic of the *Matrix* movies they had so much enjoyed. Jimmy Burke, a postgraduate student studying to become a computer engineer for Dell Computers, squeezed the hand of his live-in German girlfriend, Ingrid. "When you and I have kids, they'll still be trying to remake those flicks. With no more luck than they had tonight."

In his right hand, he clutched a crumpled up package of Oreo cookies they had just finished after leaving the theater. Halfway down the block, they passed under a streetlight below which had been set, conveniently enough, a green New York City trash basket.

"Hey!" Burke exulted. "Here comes the opening shot of the Knicks' new season. Watch! Hook shot!" he laughed, arching the crumpled cookie wrapper over his head toward the trash basket.

It flew through the lamplight, struck the rim of the basket—and tumbled to the sidewalk.

"Good shot!" laughed Ingrid. "Now we know why the Knicks can never make the play-offs." Well-brought-up young lady that she was, she bent down, picked the cookie wrapper from the sidewalk and leaned over to drop it into the trash basket.

"Look," she said, "What's this?"

She reached into the basket and pulled out a shiny new Nokia cell phone resting on a copy of the *Village Voice.* Jimmy studied it, then flipped open its rear.

"Hey," he said, "battery's gone but it's got a SIM card. I'll pick up a battery tomorrow and who's to know? Maybe we found ourselves a phone we can use to call your mother."

CHAPTER
7

WASHINGTON D.C.
NEW YORK CITY
JERUSALEM

The Crisis—Day Four

At precisely eight o'clock, his hair still wet from his ice-cold morning wake-up shower, the President stepped into the Oval Office. Andrew Card, his chief of staff, was waiting for him to begin the day with a regular little ritual. He set before the President the ten-page President's Daily Brief in its blue three-ring loose-leaf folder. Prepared overnight by the CIA, it was a digest of the latest information concerning world events and, in particular at this critical moment, the terrorist crisis facing his nation. He read through it swiftly. It contained nothing new or noteworthy. "OK," he ordered Card, "show the others in."

Vice President Cheney, Secretary of State Rice, Secretary of Defense Rumsfeld, CIA's Milt Anderson and Homeland Security's Michael Chertoff filed into the office. If there was going to be any information of note to mark day four of this crisis, the President knew, it was sitting opposite him in the person of Condi Rice.

Fourteen thousand miles, flown at over thirty thousand feet, a "clock-full" of time changes in less than three days, had not diminished in any way the cool demeanor of the Secretary of State. In her black sleeveless shirt, its neckline delineated by a string of pearls, the gabardine pants suit in which she so often appeared on television, she looked more like the dean of a graduate school at a good university than like the most powerful woman in the U.S. government.

"Condi didn't hesitate to fly out to meet the devil in the hope of finding a way out of this crisis," the President said to open his Crisis Committee meeting. "As you all know, she managed to convince Dr. Khan to give her the telephone number of the cell phone hooked up to the bomb hidden in New York.

"Alas, despite the billions of dollars we've invested in the NSA over the years, they are incapable of preventing a telephone call from getting through to that number. However, that in no way diminishes the enormity of Condi's achievement nor the hope that other positive results may grow out of her trip. Condi, let me turn this meeting over to you."

Her voice quiet and composed, Condi gave her colleagues a detailed account of her meeting with the scientist who had placed an atomic bomb in the hands of a group of terrorists. She acknowledged that President Musharraf's pressure had helped soften Khan's position. So, too, had the knowledge of the terrible retaliation that would strike Pakistan if that bomb exploded in New York.

"I'm sure that Dr. Khan," she said, "has some way of entering into contact with the terrorists who are behind this. At my request, he promised he would employ it to try to open up a line of communication for us to them."

"Bravo, Condi," said the President. "The idea of getting to reason with them may be nothing more than the faintest glimmer of hope, but at least it's that. And it is also the only glimmer of hope I can see in front of us this morning."

"We'll try to turn that glimmer into a light at the end of the tunnel," Secretary Rice said with a smile. "If Dr. Khan should indicate they are willing to at least speak with us, I'm ready to fly back to Pakistan on your orders immediately."

As she was speaking, Milt Anderson, the CIA director, had

plugged in the earphone of his cell phone. He held up his hand to get the group's attention.

"I have some devastating news," he said. "Our Islamabad station has just informed Langley that Dr. Khan was killed in an automobile crash near Waziristan in the North-West Frontier Province. And the circumstances surrounding the crash are highly suspicious."

"Murdered!" Condi gasped.

"So much for our morning's glimmer of hope!" groaned the President.

A heavy silence followed his words. Chief of Staff Andrew Card broke it. "We'd better get Paul Anscom up in New York onto our closed-circuit hookup and find out what's going on up there—if anything."

Seconds later, Anscom's face appeared on their TV screens. "We continue our all out efforts to find the terrorists' device," he said. "We have full mobilization of the FBI, the NYPD, the New York State police and all their supporting services. We've shown the photo of that woman to thousands of people. Our search of suspicious cargoes off-loaded at Port Elizabeth and Port Newark is almost complete. NEST has all its helicopters in service over the city, and its latest trucks from Livermore are in action. Unfortunately, I must tell you that all that effort has produced thus far has been a dozen false alarms."

Bush glanced at his watch. "Barely forty-eight hours left before the terrorists' deadline expires," he said. "And we are still at square one. No one to negotiate with, no lead to the bomb. We've got to do something. But what, God damn it, what?"

*   *   *

Nahed Jihari gave a discreet glance over her shoulder to be sure no one was watching her before she moved to the public phone at the corner of Fifth Avenue and Thirty-second Street. Although the Palestinian woman could not know it, of course, the photo taken from her fake New Jersey driver's license was at that moment being circulated all across the city. She dropped a quarter into the phone and dialed the number Imad Mugniyeh had given her before she left Beirut. She had no idea who she was calling or why. All she had in addition to the number was the password Mugniyeh had given her. It was the same word he had used to meet Osama bin Laden's aide at Karachi airport.

The phone rang for some time before a man's voice answered.

"*Seif*"—sword—Nahed said.

"*Al Islam*"—of Islam—the man replied.

"You may begin your operation," she said and hung up.

The man, his face pockmarked by smallpox, was a member of an al Qaeda sleeper cell planted in New York before 9/11. Chuckling with delight, he hurried toward a Lebanese grocery store on Brooklyn's Atlantic Avenue, in the heart of the area Police Commissioner Kelly had targeted for tight surveillance.

Two of his fellow cell members were waiting for him in the grocery's back room. "Our operation is on," he said smiling and went to an old stove in the corner of the room. From it he took a lead box. It was divided into two halves. One contained perhaps three-dozen rings about the size of a wedding band, to which were fixed small circular containers. The other had an equal number of tablets no larger than an aspirin. The tablets consisted of a mixture of various radioactive isotopes.

Carefully, they fixed a tablet into each of the containers, then went into the yard behind the grocery. Three cages awaited them filled with cackling pigeons. They were the most ordinary of gray New York pigeons, the kind that haunt almost every corner of the city. To a claw of each bird they attached a ring with its little tablet.

"Release a bird every fifteen minutes," the leader ordered. He looked at the squawking pigeons. "Fly away little birdies. Don't let the cats catch you. You've got work to do for the cause."

* * *

T.F. O'Neill's Manhattan South Detective Squad enjoyed the dubious distinction of covering the most important number of prime terrorist targets in New York City. They included Penn and Grand Central stations, Madison Square Garden, and the Empire State and Chrysler buildings. Its population was a puzzling anomaly. Officially, according to the 2000 Census, it contained only 16,179 permanent residents. Yet at midday on any day of the week, it housed well over a million people—shoppers, tourists and, above all, the office workers who trooped in daily by car, train, subway and bus.

Olivia Phillips watched as he poured her out another cup of New York's finest cappuccino. If we don't find that damn barrel pretty fast, she thought, he might start serving up New York's finest radioactive cappuccino.

How much longer, she wondered, is this bullshit story of a barrel of chlorine gas going to hold up? By now she had no doubts about what was really in the barrel they were looking for. She understood the panic just the use of the word *nuclear* could provoke. The mere thought that such a device might be in the barrel caused her own stomach to start fluttering.

She glanced affectionately at her NYPD partner. She smiled as she watched him chatting with one of his detectives. O'Neill was both good-looking and decent, she thought to herself. If they should survive, maybe there would be more to their partnership than just work.

O'Neill had begun to whack the map of his precinct on his canteen wall with a rubber-tipped pointer. "Look, guys," he said, "we're getting heavy flak from headquarters about this goddamned barrel of chlorine gas. Where is it? This may sound like a bullshit project to some of you but headquarters wants this damn thing found and found fast.

"I'm constantly thinking of past experience. Learning from past experience, we all know, is what police work is really all about. Think about some of these scumbags we've uncovered in the past three years who rent apartments to store their stolen goods or counterfeit CDs and DVDs. Where were they working out of? Times Square? Alphabet City down on the Lower East Side? Hell no. That's what the media still think. Times Square is gentrified now. You want to rent an apartment or a store up there? You sign a lease, pal. Same thing's true down in Alphabet City. In those parts of Manhattan, drugs and petty crime are way down now. The place is flooded with young people, foreign restaurants, discos.

"No. This is the area we've got to focus on here, Twenty-ninth Street to Forty-fifth Street between Fifth and Eighth avenues. About all you got there is commercial properties like they have in the Garment District. And you got dozens of supers or owners in that area who are ready to rent on a short-term basis, one, three, five months, cash in advance, no questions asked. Lease? ID? Forget it. As long as money's on the table no one cares who you are or what business you're in. The super is just going to stuff the dough into his pocket and as long as you don't make waves, he's not going to pay any attention to your comings or goings. Those places don't have any security people to get curious about who the hell you are. As long as you put the dough on the table, you're home free."

"Right," echoed O'Neill's senior detective, a pickpocket expert with twenty-six years on the force. "The other thing we got to do is scrub out the fleabag hotels in that area. Like the Culver on Forty-third Street. It's owned by a couple of Pakistanis and stuffed with short-term illegals. Go in there and half the towels say PROPERTY OF KINGS COUNTY HOSPITAL. I was parked over there a couple of weeks ago and some kid comes running out to play crying 'Hey, yesterday we were in Canada, today we're in America!' Got three illegal families thanks to that kid."

O'Neill knew that the Empire State and Chrysler buildings as well as a score of Midtown skyscrapers had already been scoured floor by floor and room by room by teams of the Joint Terrorism Task Force, backed up discreetly by NEST. They were clean. The professional basketball and ice hockey seasons had yet to start, so there were no events of importance at Madison Square Garden. By a fortunate fluke of scheduling, both the Yankees and the Mets were playing their baseball games on the road that week, so the PC and the Mayor were not faced with the drama of canceling games at Yankee or Shea Stadium and thus alerting the media to the crisis threatening the city.

Time, O'Neill well knew, was running out. In addition to the critical area he had signaled to his detectives, there were, of course, other areas of concern, like the gold stores at the Federal Reserve downtown and the financial center in general, and the old Jewish neighborhoods on the Lower East Side. Those were areas, however, where the kind of terrorists they were looking for would stand out—assuming they were not people of Western ori-

gin who had converted to a radical Islam like some of the terrorists involved in the London attacks. But in any case it was unlikely
that they would try to hide themselves or their weapon there.

No, O'Neill was convinced that if the terrorists and their
weapon were in Manhattan South, they would certainly be in the
area he had outlined, a jumble of commercial properties of every
ilk. That was where they would have to focus all their efforts.
O'Neill knew it would be a nightmare task at any time, and almost
impossible in the two days they had.

"Enough of that—it's time to get started, guys," O'Neill
said with a sigh. Divide up that Twenty-ninth to Forty-fifth Street
area among your teams and get to work, starting now. If ever there
was a time to honor that grand old NYPD slogan 'GOA GKD'—
'Get off your ass and go knock on doors'—it's now."

*   *   *

For Mayor Mike Bloomberg it was the most appalling
moral dilemma he had ever been called on to face. He left the
emergency headquarters in Brooklyn to pick up his helicopter at
City Hall and make an aerial survey of the city with Commissioner
Kelly and that paragon of bureaucratic orthodoxy, Charles
Morningside, the emergency evacuation expert.

But before boarding his chopper on the landing pad of
City Hall, he first met in his mayor's office with one of the two
human beings closest to his heart. Emma Bloomberg, twenty-
three, was the older of his two daughters. She had the same pale
blue eyes with tints of light brown as her father, and an elegant
neck and features as fine as in portraits by Modigliani. Like her
father she was a graduate of the Harvard Business School but had
turned down a number of challenging jobs in the financial world

to work at her father's side at city hall. If the NYPD failed to find that damned bomb before the terrorists' deadline expired, he knew she was condemned to die along with hundreds of thousands of their fellow New Yorkers. He had chosen of his own free will to stay in the city and face the same fate as his fellow citizens. Didn't that give him moral license to save his daughter? But how? Could he share with her the terrible secret that was given to him because of his position? Somehow, he had to find a way to get her out of the city without violating the trust that had been laid upon his shoulders.

"Emma, darling," he said as she entered his office and gave him an affectionate hug, "you look very tired. Worn. Are you burning the candle at both ends, staying out all night partying?"

The young woman looked at him with wondering eyes. She was, in fact, feeling particularly fresh and well rested this morning. She'd snapped her lights and TV off at eleven o'clock the night before. Never had her father made comments like these on her appearance.

"Why don't you get out of town for a few days?" her father suggested. "Go down to your mother's in Florida, get some sunshine, do some of the deep-sea diving you love."

"Mother's house?" Emma said surprised. She knew just how much her father disapproved of her mother's socialite lifestyle.

Emma got up. She circled around behind her father's desk so that she could rest her hands on his shoulders.

"Daddy," she asked, "what's going on? Why are you trying to get me to Florida? Or are you just anxious to get me out of New York?" She took out a Kleenex to wipe the beads of sweat glistening at his temples. Then slowly she asked, "Is it starting again? That 9/11 business?"

A long silence answered her query. "Emma darling," her

father said, "there are things I can't share without violating a trust. But it would be a load off my mind if I knew you were going away for a few days."

Sure, Emma thought, that's it. It's probably some terrorist thing. Her younger sister Georgina was well away from the city, out at the end of Long Island participating in a horse show.

"And you, Daddy? What are you going to do?"

"I have no choice. My place is here with my fellow New Yorkers."

"And in that case my place is here, too. As long as you stay, Daddy, I stay right here beside you."

*   *   *

By now more than a hundred NEST vans, representing a full deployment of the nuclear search organization's resources, were prowling the streets of Manhattan, Queens and Brooklyn. They bore the insignia of truck rental firms like Hertz or Avis to conceal their real nature. From the street there was nothing that would indicate they were anything other than normal rental vans. In fact, they were rolling laboratories, each equipped with the most modern detection devices known to nuclear science, all linked to the ordinary appearing antennas attached to their rooftops.

Their detectors were designed to pick up the slightest emanation of gamma rays or neutrons given off by plutonium or highly enriched uranium. Most important, their computers could screen out most of the false positives naturally found in any large metropolitan area.

In addition, a dozen NEST helicopters disguised with the names of imaginary firms were overflying the city hoping to pick up any telltale emanations coming from the rooftops below.

The whole operation was being run by NEST's director, David Graham, from the headquarters he had installed at the Office of Emergency Management in Brooklyn. He well knew as he puffed on cigarette after cigarette that he was looking for the proverbial nuclear needle in a haystack but he had confidence that the latest generation of his equipment would sooner or later pick up a trace of the terrorists' bomb. Unfortunately, it had to be "sooner" because "later" was likely to be too late. As for the hundreds of police and FBI officers doing their part in the search, they too were haunted by the relentless ticking of the clock.

Suddenly, the microphone beside his desk cackled. "Mr. Graham, one of your choppers is picking up radiation."

Graham grabbed the mike linking him to the helicopter in question. "What are you getting?" he asked the chopper's technicians.

"Ninety millirads."

Graham whistled. That was a helluva hit especially since in all probability the emanation had to pass through a number of floors.

"Where are you?"

"We're over a public housing project at Eleventh Avenue and Twenty-eighth Street, just a block away from the Hudson River." With two of the police officers who had been assigned to him, Graham quickly spotted the location on his map.

"OK," he ordered, "get out of there so you don't alert anybody that you're picking something up. I'll send in half a dozen vans to search the area."

He beckoned to the New York police officer assigned to him as a driver and ran out to the OEM parking lot and his unmarked police car.

"Listen," he said to the driver. "That's public housing down there so get on your radio and have city hall get me a full set of the plans and building specs and meet me with them when we arrive."

Twenty minutes later, as they pulled up to the first of the four apartment houses in the project, Graham recognized the woman getting out of the first of his vans to reach the scene. Gladys Simpson was a senior gamma ray specialist at the Livermore National Laboratory in California. She was married with two young children and had a doctorate in nuclear physics from Cal Tech. She was well tanned, and Graham was sure it was from her favorite pastime, climbing the slopes of the Sierra Morenas with her husband.

She had been filled in on the chopper's reading, of course. Glancing up at the fifteen-story building, she let out a low whistle. "Must have come from one of the top five or six stories," she observed.

"Yeah," Graham agreed. He knew from the plans he'd been given that the complex contained eight hundred apartments and probably five thousand inhabitants. Search that without drawing a crowd was going to be a damn difficult job. "You're right. We'll just do the top six floors in each building."

Gladys meanwhile had slung her portable detector on her back, looking, they all hoped, like a visitor to New York, backpack and all. Graham thought she was a little tense.

"You nervous? he asked.

"Yes," she said in a half whisper.

"Don't worry," he assured her. "We'll find the bomb. Our very first!"

"Bomb?" she said. "Who's worried about a bomb? I'm afraid some creep with a knife is going to try to jump me up there." NEST members traditionally were not armed.

Graham gestured to one of the FBI agents in civilian clothes. "He'll go with you," he said and the California woman set off to begin exploring the top floors of the building he had assigned her. He then organized similar teams to search the top six floors of the three other buildings.

Gladys was the first to finish. Her detector had picked up absolutely nothing, not even something as banal as the emanation given off by an old alarm clock with hands coated by a radioactive substance that glowed in the dark. Before long the other three teams were reporting back to him. They too had found absolutely nothing.

Graham was dumbfounded. Chopper picks up a shower of radiation and now they find not even a millirad!

"Get that chopper back down here," he ordered. A few minutes later, he heard the *whump, whump* of its rotors approaching. "Get over the precise spot where you picked up those emanations—and at the same altitude—and tell me what you're getting."

"Jesus, David!" the technician aboard the chopper called down. "I can't believe it! Now I'm getting nothing, absolutely nothing."

"You sure your detector is working properly?" Graham asked.

"Absolutely. I had it calibrated before we left Los Alamos."

Graham shook his head in disbelief. He turned to Gladys, "Go up there on the roof and have a look around."

"Yipes!" she said a minute later, "the elevator's not working."

"So what?" Graham said. "Climb up there. You're a mountain climber, aren't you?"

A few minutes later the young woman emerged onto the roof. Below her was the dark expanse of the Hudson and at her feet the asphalt covered roof speckled with pigeon droppings. Her detector was silent.

"David," she said, "there's absolutely nothing up here

except a lovely view and a lot of pigeon shit!"

*   *   *

Omar Tahiri waved his hand in disgust at the tawdry hotel room in which he and Amr bin Khaled waited, ready to detonate the bomb that would wipe out the heart of New York City. "We left our luxurious refugee camp in Lebanon to come and live here in this shit hole? Where they don't even know how to make the beds or change the sheets?"

"Well," Khaled acknowledged, "the Waldorf Astoria it's not. But don't worry. Just think about the green fields and flowing fountains that will be waiting for us when we enter the gates of paradise as martyrs."

"Oh, sure," Omar laughed, "and all those beautiful *houris* waiting to pleasure us for all eternity. You don't really believe in all that, do you? As far as I'm concerned, I'd just like some clean sheets and towels in this lousy hotel room."

"I believe in the cause," Khaled said. "I believe in our goal of restoring our land to our Palestinian people."

Omar gestured to their TV set, fixed as it had been for hours to New York One, the city's nonstop news channel. "It's not going to work, Khaled," he said. "There hasn't been a thing in the news. Not about a crisis in the Middle East, not about settlements, and certainly not about a terrorist alert here in New York. Nothing but how the President is supposed to be confined to bed in the White House with some kind of stomach trouble."

"That's probably just a cover story to hide what's really going on," Khaled said glancing at his watch. "We've still got almost forty-eight hours before the deadline we gave them expires. Plenty of time for Sharon to announce to the world that he's going to start withdrawing his settlements from the West Bank."

"He's not going to do it, Khaled," Omar replied. The third member of their trio, Nahed Jihari, was babysitting their bomb in the nearby apartment where they hid it. "We all know the Israelis. They'll never give in to a threat like this. Mugniyeh was dreaming when he cooked up this scheme."

Omar stood up and walked to the window looking down on Thirty-eighth Street. As he did, an image crowded into his mind—that of a woman cradling a baby in her arms, standing in the window of the building across the street from the apartment where the bomb was hidden. Down below, hundreds of shoppers and passersby jammed the street. Somewhere he'd read that at times five hundred people waited for some of the traffic lights in this neighborhood to change so they could cross the street. That bomb goes off and they all die, he thought, along with that mother and her baby. These last days spent in New York, sharing the daily lives of people so distant from the Palestinian problem, had begun to modify his vision of their mission. Was this really the way to win back their lost homeland, to advance Islam's cause? On a sea of corpses? It was a question disturbing him with growing urgency.

Khaled came over to join him by the window. He too, stared at the throngs in the street below. "You're probably right, Omar. Sharon and his gang won't do it. He smacked his right fist into the palm of his left hand. "And those poor, dumb bastards down there are going to pay the price for a monster's stubbornness. Because, I promise you, if the Israelis haven't caved in by the time the deadline expires, that bomb is going to go off. I'll see to that. If Mugniyeh for some damn reason doesn't manage to get a call through to the bomb, I'll be right there beside it. I'll set it off myself with the button we installed when we got here."

Omar studied his accomplice. Yes, he thought, Khaled will do it. There is nothing in that man's heart but hate. He glanced again down at the crowds thronging Thirty-eighth Street. If somehow this terrible gamble went wrong, as everything seemed to indicate it was going to, was he going to let Khaled exterminate that mass of innocent people? Somehow he had to find a way to disconnect the wire that linked the button on their living room table to the bomb's detonator.

*   *   *

For Avigdor Beibelman, the extremist member of the Knesset who had whispered to a cabinet colleague that he had an idea that would "blow this crisis right out of the water," the time had come to start putting that idea into action. To do it, he had come to the Israeli settlement of Kedumin, implanted not far from the Palestinian city of Nablus, the heartland of Palestinian nationalist aspirations.

Seven hundred settler families lived in Kedumin, most of them in small houses and bungalows built in three circling rows around the hilltop on which they had first planted their flag a decade ago. The site was surrounded by a rocky landscape sheltering centuries-old olive groves. They belonged to the residents of four small Palestinian communities clustered around the settlement. Some of those families had been cultivating their trees for generations, although Kedumin's extremist rabbi maintained that they were in fact stealing Jewish property "since God had given the land on which the trees were growing to the Jewish people two millenniums ago."

Almost a hundred of Kedumin's families were still living in

trailers and vans waiting for a chance to acquire the land on which to build a permanent home. That was exactly the chance Beibelman now proposed to offer them.

At the request of Kedumin's mayor, Yaacov Weiss, the heads of most of those families had gathered to meet Beibelman in the community hall of the settlement's synagogue. "My brethren," he began, "I cannot go into full detail for you from this platform without violating a trust, but what I can tell you is that our God-given right to settle our Jewish communities here in Yesha—he used the Hebrew word for the West Bank or Judea and Samaria—may soon be imperiled."

A gasp of dismay greeted his words.

"Yes," he continued, "but thanks to brave people like you, I know we will resist this effort to curtail our sacred rights from whatever source be it, our enemies or even Israel's leaders, or our closest and dearest friends. This is our homeland. Our rights to it are not subjected to or conditioned by any so-called peace plan or road map or international consensus. They were deeded to us by God and here we shall stay for generations to come in witness to the eternal covenant between God and his chosen people."

The entire assembly leapt to its feet, cheering as one. Beibelman beamed with pleasure. That was exactly the reaction he anticipated and wanted. "Devoted Zionists as you all are, you deserve a piece of our historic homeland for yourselves and your families. Well, I am here to tell you the time has come for you to have your land—not next week, not next month, not next year, but now—right now!"

He pointed to a huge aerial photograph of Kedumin and the Palestinian areas surrounding it, that he had placed on an easel. With his forefinger, he circled out a large swath of land adjoining the outer fringes of Kedumin. It encompassed dozens of olive groves.

"This is your land!" he shouted. "Tomorrow with your vans and your trailers, you will march forth and claim it, all of it, in the name of Zion and your sacred right to settle Yesha."

Those words could not have struck a more responsive chord among his audience. Most of the men and women before him had been clamoring for months for support to do exactly that—and now they had that support, not from some pro-settler extremist but from a member in good standing of the Sharon government. Again, they leapt to their feet, shouting, clapping and yelling their agreement.

"By sunset tomorrow, you will have firmly placed scores, even hundreds of vans and trailers on that land to let the world know that you, the sons and daughters of Zion, have exercised your historic rights to your homeland."

And, Beibelman thought happily, I will make sure the media are there to record their brave actions and let the world know as well that whatever blackmail may be attempted against us, our people will never abandon a square inch of our sacred homeland."

*   *   *

Moved and saddened in almost equal measure by his daughter Emma's determination to remain at his side, New York's mayor Mike Bloomberg clambered into his helicopter on the City Hall landing pad for an aerial inspection of his threatened city. Police Commissioner Ray Kelly was with him as was Charles Morningside, the Washington bureaucrat who specialized in the problems of evacuating urban centers.

As the chopper's rotors thrust the little craft into the bright blue autumn sky, Bloomberg felt his heartbeat quicken. In seconds New York was there at his feet, glistening in the fall sunshine, vibrant and so alive you could almost feel the dynamism of the city rising up to their helicopter. Was it possible that all that power and strength down there could be wiped off the face of the earth in seconds? Alas, he knew it was. He had in the last forty-eight hours studied a photo gallery of the remains of Hiroshima and Nagasaki. The pictures left no doubt in the Mayor's mind of the horrors of the threat they were facing.

The evacuation expert's voice intruded on his apocalyptic vision.

"Would it be possible somehow to order an evacuation of the city without giving the citizenry an explanation for it? Maybe by calling it a drill as part of our preparedness program?" he asked.

"Are you crazy?" Kelly replied. "You can't do anything in this city without telling the people why you're doing it. Besides, New Yorkers are not going to accept a phony reason like calling it a drill. Nine-eleven didn't change anything, my friend. New York is still New York, and New Yorkers are still New Yorkers, not sheep."

Moments later they were flying over the southern tip of Manhattan. They could see kids playing touch football in Battery Park. "Could we attempt an evacuation by motor vehicle, run the tunnels and bridges one way and do what you've done on occasion—insist on a minimum of three passengers per car? Of course, the police would have to be ready to employ force to keep order and prevent people from cutting into the evacuation lines."

Police Commissioner Kelly looked sideways at Morningside. *Employ force* was absurd, he knew. All you would accomplish by that would be to create hundreds of traffic jams when you wanted to keep cars moving swiftly.

The helicopter swung north paralleling the Hudson River

and the city's western flank. "Of course," Morningside droned on, "it will be easier here. The Lincoln Tunnel has six traffic lanes we can turn one way." But Mike Bloomberg had stopped listening to him.

"Ray," he said "it's just impossible to evacuate this city in any kind of a hurry, isn't it?"

"No way, Your Honor, no way—except maybe if the terrorists were kind enough to let us do it on a weekend when we won't have to deal with a million commuters on top of our own people. But the end of the forty-eight hours falls on a weekday, worse luck."

"And all those Rockefeller air-raid shelters? Nothing we can do with them?"

"Since the end of the Cold War, they've been abandoned, Mike. They're just relics from a bygone era. Hey," he said pointing to the left, "just down there you've got the New York State Office Building. They had the Rolls Royce of air-raid shelters. Why don't we drop down and have a look?"

The pilot set their chopper down beside the building and the three men walked inside. At the far end of the lobby, just beyond the elevator bank, was one of the old yellow and black air-raid shelter signs, faded and partially obscured by an AIDS-awareness poster. Kelly looked around and spotted a janitor. "We want to have a look at that air-raid shelter," he announced.

The janitor looked at him stunned. "Man," he said, "nobody's been down there for years!" Kelly insisted and the janitor took him to a wall board covered with keys. "Key gotta be on here somewhere." For a few minutes he studied the keys with no visible result. "Let me call another guy who's been here longer than me."

A few minutes later a scrawny, white-haired gentleman in a Mets baseball cap turned backward arrived. He was wearing a T-shirt covered with religious slogans like "The Redeemer is coming" and "Let Christ's way be your way." He, too, spent minutes studying the mass of keys before selecting two "probables." One of them worked. It opened a door giving onto a darkened stairwell. Guided by a flashlight, they made their way down a creaking wooden staircase ducking under heating pipes wrapped in cobwebs. When they reached the cellar, Bloomberg heard a series of scraping noises from the interior.

"What's that?" he asked.

"Rats," said their guide.

He turned his flashlight on an ancient Civil Defense poster. PROCEDURE TO FOLLOW IN THE EVENT OF A THERMONUCLEAR ATTACK it read. Below that admonition were six steps New Yorkers were advised to follow in such an event. They included such helpful suggestions as loosening neckties and unbuttoning restrictive clothing. The sixth and final admonition was *Immediately upon seeing the brilliant flash of a nuclear explosion, bend over and place your head firmly between your legs.*

Beneath, some jokester years ago had written *And kiss your ass goodbye.*

The floor of the shelter was littered with junk dumped there over the years. Barely visible were a dozen jerricans that had once been filled with water. On the pile of rubble were the remains of the first aid kits that had once been installed in the shelter.

"Junkies," Kelly said. "They learned there was morphine in those kits and came down here years ago to score a hit. Seen enough, Your Honor?" he asked.

"Enough to know how useless these places are. Let's get back to our chopper."

As they started to scramble their way back up the creaking

staircase, their guide took three pamphlets from a sack thrown over his shoulder and handed one to each of them. Bloomberg studied his. "Jesus saves," it said, "bring your problems to him." The Mayor couldn't help a wry smile. "Hey," he said, "maybe he's got something there. I'd even call on Allah or Buddha to come up with a solution."

They were buckling themselves back into the helicopter when Bloomberg's cell phone beeped. It was the White House.

Seconds later the President was on the line. "Michael," he said, "this is not a secure line so I must be brief. We need you here as fast as possible. Get over to McGuire Air Force Base urgently. There's an Air Force jet on standby there waiting to fly you down here."

*   *   *

The operation Sword of Islam launched by Nahed Jihari with her early morning phone call was beginning to pay dividends. The pigeons with their rings of radioactive material were now in full flight all over the city. David Graham, the chief of the Nuclear Emergency Search Team, was going crazy. Three times in the hour or so since going back to his desk in the Office of Emergency Management, his helicopters overflying New York had reported picking up important radioactive emanations. Yet those emanations had all mysteriously disappeared as soon as the Graham's vans arrived.

What the hell is going on, he asked himself, pacing the floor of his improvised headquarters. Suddenly, his angry meditation was interrupted by a call from another of his chopper pilots.

"This is Plume Three," the voice called. "I'm over Twenty-third Street near the corner of Madison Avenue and I'm picking up something."

Graham asked him to reconfirm his position, and as the pilot started to reply, he exploded. "God damn it! The radiation has disappeared!"

Graham swore in fury at this frustrating chase of emanations disappearing like ghosts.

"Hey, wait a minute, David," the pilot called. "I've picked them up again. They didn't disappear. Their location just shifted. Now they're moving up Sixth Avenue."

"Son of a bitch!" Graham growled. "Have those guys gone and stuffed their bomb in a truck? Are they moving it around the city?"

He contacted his FBI liaison and the two men ordered two-dozen disguised vehicles into the area in the hope that if the bomb was in a truck they could pick it up and follow it. The chopper in the meantime was following the movement of the emanations, up Sixth Avenue, then into Central Park where they veered west.

"The emanations have stopped, David!" the pilot shouted.

"Where are you?"

"Near the intersection of Broadway and Columbus Avenue."

Graham ordered his mobile teams to converge on the area. As the first one arrived on the scene, Graham recognized the voice of Gladys Simpson.

"Hey!" she said, "I'm getting radiation."

"Where are you?"

"Opposite Lincoln Center." Gladys got out of her Avis van, her portable gamma ray detector slung over her shoulders and contemplated the vast esplanade of Lincoln Center, with its opera house, concert hall and theater. Her detector gave her a steady reading of thirty-four millirads but there wasn't a car or truck in sight. In front of her there was only the monumental black marble fountain that was the centerpiece of the esplanade, surrounded by the usual noonday crowd of students, chewing on hot dogs bought from sidewalk vendors; shopgirls on their lunch hour; tourists and a few housewives walking their pets.

"Where in God's name are those emanations coming from," she asked herself. As she did, Graham arrived in a yellow Hertz van. He, too, got the same reading on his detector his colleague was getting on hers.

He grabbed a cigarette and studied the scene before him. Was it possible that somehow a truck had gotten to the esplanade before Gladys had arrived and ran a device into one of the buildings around the esplanade? That seemed impossible to Graham. Had they been shadowing some guy who had just had a massive dose of radiation for cancer? Still, Graham wasn't going to take chances. He ordered the follow-up teams reaching the esplanade to search all the buildings surrounding it.

"I think it's coming from that area around the fountain," one of his NEST inspectors observed. The two men started to walk slowly toward the lunchtime crowd when suddenly the emanations shifted to the left. An elderly woman in a shabby black coat had just broken off from the lunchers and was moving toward the left edge of the esplanade. Graham walked over to her. She was clutching a shopping bag from Macy's. As Graham got closer he saw that she was reaching into the bag and scattering chunks of stale bread. He barely had time to identify himself and show her his government ID when she said apologetically, "I'm sorry, Officer. I know it makes a mess but I didn't know it was forbidden. They're so hungry and they've come to expect me here each day." Around her was a flock of pigeons pecking at the bread. Some of them looked odd to Graham. They edged away from him as he got closer, but not before he noticed that some of the pigeons were wearing a sort of ring on the leg. Gladys, who had walked over to Graham with her equipment, yelped, "My God, it just jumped to sixty-two millirads."

Her voice startled most of the pigeons into flight, and she reported that the reading immediately began dropping toward zero. Then she also noticed the ring on some of the pigeons. She and Graham looked at each other and broke into a relieved laugh. It was crystal clear to both of them: all the false readings, the here-now, gone-now traces of radiation all had come from pigeons booby-trapped to drive him and his people crazy.

"Gladys, we've got to hand it to our terrorists—they're not only fanatics, they were damn clever too. If all this weren't so serious, I'd say they even have a sense of humor."

*   *   *

The sense of despair enshrouding the White House Oval Office was so palpable, so real, Mike Bloomberg felt he could almost reach out and touch it. The President gestured him to a chair beside Condi Rice and her successor as National Security advisor, Stephen Hadley, formerly her deputy. Also gathered around the President's desk were Vice President Cheney, Secretary of Defense Rumsfeld, Milt Anderson of the CIA, Michael Chertoff of Homeland Security and Andrew Card, the President's chief of staff.

"Mike," the President said in the tone of voice he might employ to announce the death of a dear friend, "we're up against a stone wall." He tapped his wristwatch. "The terrorists' deadline is going to expire in less than forty-eight hours and we're nowhere in our efforts to defuse this crisis. We thought we were going to be able to open up a line of communication to the people who are behind this. We failed. You know how hard the police, the FBI and our other agencies are working up in New York to find the bomb and the terrorists who brought it here. What have we found?" The President threw up his hands in despair. "Nothing. We haven't got a clue."

"Mr. President," Bloomberg noted, "I've got to tell you I spent the morning overflying the city in a helicopter. Evacuating New York in the little time we have left—even if we chose to ignore their 'don't evacuate' threat—is simply out of the question."

Bush gave a sad shrug of his shoulders to acknowledge the accuracy of Bloomberg's observation. "It's our feeling here, Mike, that you represent an important card we should now play. You know Ariel Sharon personally from your work with Jewish charities and the cultural activities you've sponsored in Israel. As mayor of New York, you represent the people whose lives are threatened by this menace, and that includes hundreds of thousands of Jewish people. You are in a unique position to try influencing Sharon's thinking, to convince him to work with me. We have to get him to adopt in public a position on those settlements that we can hope will at least allow us to open a dialogue with the people behind the terrorists. If that works, we can defuse this damn crisis. Will you please call him on my behalf and try to get him to modify his position?"

Bloomberg made a tight-lipped grimace. "Of course I will, Mr. President, but let's not have any illusions about the chances of my success. The terrorists behind this threat to New York are almost certainly fanatics, of the same ilk as those who did 9/11, who bombed that disco in Bali and synagogues and banks in Istanbul. They are likely to be deeply committed to their cause and beyond the reach of reason or compromises. I know Sharon and I'm sorry to say that he and most of his cabinet are equally committed and inflexible when they feel the security of Israel is at risk. But nonetheless, I will try, Mr. President, I will try."

Moments later, the Mayor had Sharon on the line at his Balfour Street residence in Jerusalem. It was a comfortable but far from opulent dwelling. No priceless paintings decorated its walls. Its principal artifact was a segment of the Dead Sea Scrolls presented to the residence by their discoverer, archaeologist Yigal Yadin. Sharon had, of course, placed the Israel Defense Forces on high alert but, given his nation's ongoing security concerns, that move had not stirred any particular attention. Furthermore, neither the Israeli nor the American media had picked up an indication of so serious a crisis.

In the circumstances, the Mayor's call hardly came as a surprise to Prime Minister Sharon. He settled into a comfortable armchair by his TV set for what he knew was going to be a painful conversation. After a ritual exchange of greetings, they mutually agreed to share their conversation by speakerphone with the American leaders assembled in the Oval Office.

Their conversation began exactly as Sharon had thought it would.

"Arik," Bloomberg said, employing Sharon's familiarized first name, "I speak to you as the Mayor of what in effect is the largest Jewish city in the world. But it is not just on behalf of the three million Jews living in the city that I am calling you. It is on behalf of every one of my fellow New Yorkers—Jews, Christians, Muslims, Hindus, Buddhists, nonbelievers, whites, African Americans, Chinese, Latinos. Everyone. Why are they menaced, Arik? Because this city symbolizes the power, the values of our nation, of the freedom and democratic values we represent to the world. And you know, Arik, that to many Islamic extremists this city represents the citadel of Jewish power in the world. That is why the lives of a million or more innocent men, women and children are threatened. Because there is no doubt, Arik, that if that bomb goes off a million people will die.

"I spent much of this morning flying over the city in a helicopter. Trying to evacuate the city in some kind of an emergency rush—even if we were to ignore what the terrorists said would happen if we tried evacuating—is a physical impossibility. There's a personal aspect too. Clearly it is my moral obligation to stay in the city with my fellow citizens and share whatever their fate is going to be. This morning, one of the two beings most precious to me, my older daughter Emma, was in my office. How could I violate my trust and give her a warning to get out of town when I can't give a similar warning to my fellow New Yorkers without causing a panic evacuation? If that explosion takes place, she will in all probability perish by my side. You're a father, Arik. Surely you can understand that this is the most terrible drama a father can face."

The Mayor paused feeling the tears smarting his eyes as he contemplated the horror his words had just captured.

"You, Arik, and only you, can now defuse this horrible crisis and save the lives of a million people. I'm asking you to make clear, publicly, your readiness to withdraw the settlers in the Occupied Territories. I know that would be terribly painful for you on many levels—moral, religious, political. But the settlers are on land that, whether we like it or not, has not belonged to the Jewish people for 2000 years, settlements a majority of your own countrymen have always opposed. And after all, you yourself proposed evacuating the Gaza settlements."

"My dear Michael," Sharon interrupted, "you know that

our pulling out of Gaza reflected many considerations—strategic, tactical, economic. But we chose unilaterally to do so. No one is more horrified than I am by the thought of so many innocent New Yorkers having their lives imperiled. But as I told your President, the issue here is not just some settlements. What you are asking me and my fellow Israelis to do is to surrender to the blackmail of a band of fanatics. Since 9/11, your president has not ceased proclaiming his determination never to yield to the menace of terrorism. Yet what are you asking us to do? Exactly what he has sworn never to do—yield to terrorism."

"Arik, please," Bloomberg rejoined, "Israel has no legitimate legal claim to those lands in the Occupied Territories."

"How can you say such a thing, Michael? You had a Jewish upbringing. You know as well as I do that God gave those lands to Moses and the Jewish people for all eternity."

"Arik, the world of the twenty-first century, of the thermonuclear age, cannot be run on the basis of forty-centuries-old religious beliefs. No more than the jihadists are justified in claiming the Koran as support for their terrorism. If you wish to invoke the principles of our faith, think of the Torah's command that if the life of a single being is in jeopardy, then the entire community must come to his aid. The lives of a million people are menaced, Arik, and you can help save them!"

In Jerusalem, Sharon stood up and began to pace his living room clutching his portable phone in his fist. "We are being asked to abandon the fundamentals of our national sovereignty in response to a criminal action which jeopardizes the foundations of peace and international order."

The Israeli prime minister took a deep breath. "I will tell you what the solution to this terrible crisis has to be, Michael, the only possible solution. Your president has to go on national television now, right now, and tell your country and the world the details of the terrorists' threat to New York. He must then make it clear that if those fanatics detonate the bomb, then the territories in Pakistan from which these Islamic murderers have been coming will cease to exist. Disappear."

"Killing an additional forty million people who will be as innocent as the million New Yorkers who will die? What kind of a solution is that?'

"The only one madmen like the people behind this can understand, Michael. Those of us who have lived alongside the Arab world know only too well that they respect force and determination, and exploit weakness and indecision. If we give in on this, it will be an encouragement to drive us out of all of Israel. There will be a murderous war with the Arab world and at the end, much of our population will die and our country will cease to exist.

"However painful the consequences may be, Michael, we are not going to remove those settlements in response to criminal blackmail. For a real and lasting peace with our Palestinian neighbors and the Muslim countries around us, yes, but not for this. I'm sorry. I will pray for both you and your daughter. Shalom." With that, Sharon hung up.

Bloomberg shook his head in despair. Condi Rice looking at him and thinking of what he had said about his daughter, took out a tissue to wipe a tear from her eye.

Milt Anderson of the CIA broke the stunned silence enveloping the room. "Mr. President," he said, "I think I speak for all of us here. The United States cannot allow a million Americans to be slaughtered because Sharon will not rectify the consequences of a policy opposed by the majority of his own citizens and by the world community. If Sharon's government won't remove those settlers, Mr. President, then you are going to have to do it."

"How the hell am I supposed to do that, Milt?"

"Mr. President, I suggest we get the Chiefs of Staff to come in here and lay out the options."

The President leaned back in his chair. "I'm afraid Milt has a point," he said to Rumsfeld. "Get the chiefs in here ready to brief us—right now!"

*　　*　　*

"Ah!" smiled Olivia Phillips, "another cup of New York's finest cappuccino from one of New York's finest!"

T.F. O'Neill placed a steaming cup of coffee on the desk of his FBI teammate at his Manhattan South headquarters. "Listen, Olivia," he said, "I've got to dash over to Brooklyn on a personal matter but I'll be back in an hour. You go on studying those Sixty-ones"—a Sixty-one was New York Police Department terminology for a criminal report—"to see if there are more locations we should check out when I get back."

Twenty minutes later O'Neill drove his unmarked police car up to the entrance of Our Lady of Sorrows Institution for Handicapped Children in Glendale, a pleasant suburb of Brooklyn. Sister Mary Francis Duchelle greeted him at the entrance.

"Nothing serious happening, I hope, Inspector," she said.

"No, Sister, not at all. I just have to take my daughter, Katy, out of school for two or three days to take her up to my parents in Connecticut."

"Oh, dear," the nun sighed, "I'm afraid that's quite against regulations. I'll have to take it up with Mother Superior."

"Well, you see, Sister," O'Neill insisted, "my wife's sister is arriving from her home in California for a brief visit. She's never seen Katy and we are very anxious that she meet her." He glanced at his watch. "I'm very busy, Sister. Could you be kind enough to get my daughter for me?"

"Couldn't you come back this evening after I've had a chance to talk to Mother Superior?"

"I'm afraid not, Sister. I have to deal with several pressing matters, and cannot get back here later today."

"Very well," the nun agreed, "just wait here for a few minutes while I go get Katy and pack her overnight bag." She guided O'Neill to the large bay window facing the school's playground. It was like that of any other school—a merry-go-round, a seesaw, a slide, swings. As always when looking at it, O'Neill felt tears stinging his eyes as he searched among the kids in the playground for his daughter Katy. He saw Sister Mary Francis cross the schoolyard, pick out Katy and, taking her by the hand, lead her to the dormitory.

O'Neill's heart tightened at the sight of all those other innocent children, some with the uncoordinated gestures of the seriously handicapped or with distorted faces. But they were playing happily, just like schoolchildren everywhere during recess. What about them, he thought, almost ready to burst into tears. I can save my own daughter—but what about them?

Five minutes later, Sister Mary Francis arrived at the entrance with Katy clutching her little valise.

Inspector O'Neill and his car had disappeared.

*   *   *

In view of the urgency of the situation, the Secretaries of Defense and State were able to get the Situation Room briefing organized in barely one hour. It was just before two thirty Washington time when the lead briefer, Lieutenant General Malcolm Touhy, commanding general of the U.S. Marine Corps, advanced to the speaker's stand.

"Ladies and Gentlemen," he began, "I want to stress that the preliminary proposals that I am about to put forward represent a joint State and Defense strategy for addressing this crisis, as the President requested."

Wow, half the occupants of the room thought without saying it aloud, that fast cooperation between those two bureaucracies is a new departure for this administration!

"Our proposal is to mount a two-stage assault in the hopes that, by carrying out the first, we will create a political situation in which the government of Israel will feel obliged to undertake the second of its own accord. However, I propose to brief you also on how we would execute both stages ourselves should that become necessary."

He turned to a large map of Israel beside his speaker's stand. "Our Sixth Fleet is fully deployed in the eastern Mediterranean right now, less than five hours sailing time from the Israeli seacoast. It contains two aircraft carrier battle groups, those surrounding the *George Washington* and the *Abraham Lincoln,* two of our largest and most modern carriers. It is our conviction that even given the acknowledged combat skills of the Israeli Air Force, those two carriers are capable of providing air cover for the first of our two assaults. However, if necessary, we can also call on additional air support from the Air Force combat squadrons at our Incirlik Air Force Base in Turkey. All those pilots have had recent combat experience in Iraq.

"Because of the tensions in the area, the fleet carries not one but two reinforced Marine Corps combat battalions, over eight thousand men in all. We propose to land both battalions here"—he thumped the map with his rubber-tipped pointer—"just north of Netzarim, right on the border between Israel and the area controlled by the Palestinian Authority. The seacoast there is shallow and will provide an excellent landing environment for our amphibious craft. The marine battalions will be equipped with armored personnel carriers, Humvees and Abrams tanks and they will head south to occupy Alai Sinai and Nisanet, taking control of the border crossing at Erez that commands access to the West Bank."

"And what about those fifteen thousand Israeli army troops stationed there? Are they going to sit there on their hands and watch all this happening?" Hadley, the National Security Advisor, asked.

General Touhy turned to the civilian seated at his left. "As I said, this is part of a joint Defense–State Department proposal. I'll let Defense's undersecretary for Middle Eastern Affairs, here, answer your question."

The Defense official stood up. "Shortly before our marine battalions board their landing craft," he said, "under the terms of our proposal, the President will address the nation and, by an international radio and TV hookup, the entire world. Prior to that he would have briefed the UN Secretary General and our major allies. He will reveal in full detail the threats the terrorists have made to New York City, and the fact that Sharon's intransigence has forced us to take this action ourselves in order to save the lives of hundreds of thousands of our citizens. The President's speech and the start of our subsequent action will take place three hours before the terrorists' deadline expires on Friday—just thirty-six hours from now. He will indicate that, if necessary, we will extend the operation to the West Bank as well. It is our hope that the speech and our action will lead the terrorists to give up their threat to New York and inform us of the bomb's whereabouts. However, as no one knows better than you, Secretary Rice, we have no line of communication open to the people behind this threat and no guarantee therefore that they will respond to the President's gesture."

"And what about the settlers?" Hadley pressed. "They are all armed, and they'll want to protect their families. Suppose they open fire?"

"The men we'll be landing are Marines. They will return any fire directed at them in quantity and quality."

"And if the Israeli army's field artillery fires at your landing crafts as they come ashore?"

"If they do, the fleet's warships will open up with their on-board cannon and missiles to suppress the Israelis' fire."

"In other words, for all effects and purposes we will be entering into war with Israel," Hadley pointed out, his voice turning solemn.

The officer grimaced. "We hope that it will not come to that and that ultimately reason will prevail."

"That," Condi snapped, "strikes me as an example of wishful thinking at its worst."

The President shook his head in despair and dismay. "So what's the second part of your proposal?" he asked.

General Touhy moved back to the speaker's stand, tall and straight, every inch a marine general. "If our forceful evacuation of Israeli settlers has not resolved the situation, then we will stage the 101st Airborne and the First Armored Division from their current assignments in Iraq into the West Bank. They will com-

plete the settlement evacuation, with the exception of huge settlements like Ariel north of Ramallah which everyone seems to
agree would become a part of Israel; the Palestinians in exchange
would receive an equal amount of territory from inside Israel's
1967 boundaries."

The President stood up indicating that the briefing, as far as
he was concerned, was over. "This whole thing is madness," he said.
"The world has gone crazy, completely crazy. Barely thirty-six hours
to go and we're nowhere near finding that bomb. What in God's
name are we going to do? Take a chance on ignoring the terms of
the terrorists' ultimatum and order a 'run as fast as you can' evacuation tomorrow? Let's adjourn for a spell. Condi, Rummy and Dick,
I want to talk with you upstairs in my living room."

*   *   *

Barely five minutes after the meeting had adjourned, the
telephone rang in the office of the Chief of Station of Mossad—
Israel's intelligence agency—in central Washington. Daniel
Olmert, the station chief, recognized the caller's voice before he
had even had to give him his code name. He was a high-ranking
official of the U.S. Defense Department.

"Turn your recorder on," he said. In a series of short con-
cise sentences he passed the Israeli spy chief a succinct account of
the White House meeting which has just ended. The United
States has few secrets from the Israeli government. Within minutes an encrypted copy of the report was on its way to Jerusalem.

*   *   *

The U.S. government has no facility more secret than the Menwith Hill Station of the U.S. Army's Intelligence and Security Command set in the Yorkshire hills, 170 miles north of Central London. Despite the term *Army* in its fifty-three-year-old designation, Menwith Hill is in fact an outpost of the National Security Agency. The station's mission is to suck every form of communication—satellite transmission of telephone calls and faxes, cell phone calls, encrypted wire transfers of billions of dollars, etc.—from the soup of cyberspace onto the NSA's massive computer data banks.

So restricted is Menwith Hill that not even members of the British Parliament have ever been allowed to visit it. The base is built on what legally is U.S. soil, sold to the United States under the terms of a still secret protocol signed by Harry Truman and Winston Churchill in 1951. No aspect of its ultrasecret work is more secret than the work performed in its SBI—Sensitive Background Information storage depot. Among other things, that depot houses all the information pulled from the skies by another secret NSA installation, the "big ears" in Bad Aibling, Germany. That installation is specifically responsible for intercepting all electronic communications going into and out of that most sensitive of areas, the Middle East.

The call made by the three terrorists in New York to Beirut to inform Imad Mugniyeh that their bomb had arrived and been installed in a hiding place was of course recorded on its computers. But because it contained no sensitive "red alert" words its content had not triggered an automatic alert. Nor was it made to a phone number on the NSA's watch list.

One thing, however, did set the call apart from the masses of calls stored on the computer. That was the fact that the call from New York was made by a cell phone that did not have a registered carrier service and owner. As a result, the NSA duty officer logging the call into the computer had flagged it with a special alert so that in the event another call should be made from the same Nokia cell phone, it would be immediately signaled to the NSA duty officer at Menwith Hill.

Shortly after seven o'clock London time on Wednesday night, the alert light flashed on the Menwith Hill duty officer's desk. A quick investigation revealed that the Nokia phone had just been used again, this time to call a number in Bremen, Germany. A swift check of the German phone directories revealed that the call had gone to a Frau Hildegard Helbling at 23 Wilhelmstrasse in Bremen.

The officer got onto the phone immediately to the CIA's Berlin station with orders to get someone to the Bremen address to find who in New York had made the call from the Nokia cell phone.

"Hey," the Berlin deskman said, "the chief ain't going to like that. We have to go accompanied by an officer from something called the Office for the Protection of the Constitution— BfV, the Bundesamt für Verfassungsschutz. Since Iraq, our relations with those guys are piss poor."

"I don't give a damn if they're in love with you," the NSA officer in England snapped. "This carries top White House priority. Get someone into that woman's house in Bremen pronto."

Frau Helbling was surprised when a pair of middle-aged gentlemen rang her doorbell. After they identified themselves, she was immediately cooperative. Of course she knew who had called her from New York. It was her daughter Ingrid who lived with her boyfriend, a young man named Jimmy Burke, on Thirty-seventh Street near Sixth Avenue.

*   *   *

His face puffed with stress and fatigue, his nervous fingertips beating a tattoo on the tabletop, Ariel Sharon opened the emergency session of his council of ministers. He had called it within minutes of receiving the secret Mossad cable from Washington revealing that the U.S. government intended to land the marines on Israeli soil.

"I am sorry I had to summon you all from your evening activities," he said, "but I have no doubt we are facing one of—if not the worst—crises in our nation's history." With that he turned to the Israel Defense Forces' chief of military intelligence, Nahum Milcham.

Milcham read out to the ministers the text of the secret Washington cable. "There can be no doubt of the American's intentions," declared the colonel who had crossed the Suez Canal with Sharon's armored column in the 1973 war. "Our aerial observers surveying the U.S. Sixth Fleet noted half an hour ago that they have already changed course and are now heading toward our shore."

His words provoked a reaction of stupor, anger and horror around the ministerial table.

"We must immediately inform the international press about what is happening!" thundered Jacob Levine, the minister of construction. "That will nail the Americans in place. Bush will have no choice but to turn his arms on Pakistan."

"Are you crazy?" shouted Deputy Prime Minister Shlomo Avriel. "If America learns that New York is about to be wiped out by an atomic bomb because of our settlements, you won't find a single American—not even an American Jew—who would oppose military action against us."

Henry Levy, the senior representative of the moderate Shinui Party in the cabinet, tried to impose his voice on the tumult in the council chamber. "Isn't it possible that just for once this nation of ours can recognize its mistakes? Why don't we clean out those settlements—all of them—ourselves? For years they've immobilized our army and cost us vast sums and eroded international goodwill." He turned to Benny Dan, chief of staff of the Israel Defense Forces. "Will the IDF get those settlers out of there like they did for the Gaza settlers?" he asked.

That was not a question General Benny Dan, a balding giant wearing his beret even in the meeting, was anxious to answer. "The West Bank is not Gaza. Our men are there to protect the settlers not uproot them by force. I'm afraid many of my soldiers won't obey an order to shoot their own people. So there goes the army's discipline and morale."

Mishka Medev, seated where he always liked to be, under the portrait of the founder of the Zionist movement, Theodor Herzl, intervened. "Look, as I have said from the outset of this crisis, this surrender to Islamic terrorists is something we cannot do and still survive as a nation."

"Mishka is right," Sharon agreed. "When I was forced to lead the evacuation of our Sinai colonies because of our peace treaty with Egypt, and later because of our decision to remove the Gaza colonies, I swore that never again would I have our army use force to drive Jews from land of Eretz Israel. I made that vow then and I intend to keep it today."

Suddenly the voice of Rabbi Avigdor Beibelman broke into the debate. No one around the table was aware that the extremist minister had already developed a scheme to flout the terrorists' demands. "Arik," he asked the Prime Minister, "landing the marines on our shoreline is nothing short of an act of war. Surely, in that event it must be your intention to order our troops to resist and if needs be, open fire at the Americans."

His question was so profoundly disturbing that for a few seconds there was no sound in the room except for the labored breathing of its occupants.

"Your question is one of the most difficult a prime minister can be called on to face," Sharon replied. "To order troops to fire on the troops of a nation's friends and allies is a horrible act. I know of only one such instance in history, when during the Second World War, Winston Churchill ordered the Royal Navy to sink the French fleet at Mers-el-Kebir after France's surrender, so that its ships would not fall into German hands. That order and the death of so many of the French crews haunted him for the rest of his life, and continues to this day as an obstacle to good French-British relations. I think that our answer to your question must come in a collective vote of the government. Will those who are in favor of our using force to repulse the Americans if they attempt to land on our national soil raise their hands?"

Sharon looked on solemnly counting the hands of his ministers. He too slowly raised his hand and then called for those opposed and abstentions. When the tally was completed, he turned to the government's secretary. "Please get President Bush on the phone urgently." In barely a minute he had the President on the line from his living quarters at the White House where he was still conferring with Condi Rice, Donald Rumsfeld and Dick Chaney.

"Mr. President," Sharon began his tone as sober as that of an undertaker, "I am obliged to inform you that the government of Israel after a long and painful discussion has just voted by twenty-nine votes to seven, with three abstentions, to order the armed forces of our nation to employ force if necessary to repulse your U.S. Marines should they attempt to land on our shores. It is a cruel and terrible decision, probably the most painful decision a government of Israel has ever been called on to make. I hope, Mr. President, that you and your advisors will measure, as we have, the extreme gravity of the situation, and that you will decide to cancel your projected invasion. However grave are the dangers this terrorist action poses to your fellow Americans, you must understand, dear friend, that history will never forgive you for ordering American and Jewish soldiers to shed their blood on the Holy Land of Moses and Jesus Christ. I pray, Mr. President, that God will grant you wisdom and enlightenment in this tragic hour."

"Arik," the President replied, "we too have been engaged in an excruciatingly painful debate here in my living quarters. However terrible the consequences, we cannot accept the deaths of hundreds of thousands of our fellow Americans because your government will not evacuate territories to which you have no right under international law or contemporary geopolitics. We are agreed, sir, that if this crisis has not been resolved by nine AM Washington time, Friday, I shall have no choice but to address the nation and the world, reveal the full dimensions and horror of the crisis before us, and order the Marines to land in Israel. I pray that it does not come to that."

There was a heavy silence at the other end of the line.

"As do I," said Sharon in a half whisper. "*Shalom*, George."

"Amen, Arik," the President answered.

CHAPTER

8

NEW YORK CITY WASHINGTON D.C. JERUSALEM

The Crisis—Day Five

THIS IS CNN, SEVEN AM EASTERN STANDARD TIME, THURSDAY. HERE ARE THE STORIES WE ARE FOL-LOWING THIS MORNING: PRESIDENT BUSH REMAINS CONFINED TO THE WHITE HOUSE LIVING QUARTERS WITH THE INTESTINAL UPSET THAT HAS BEDEVILED HIM SINCE SUNDAY. FRENCH PRES-IDENT JACQUES CHIRAC, AND BRITISH PRIME MIN-ISTER TONY BLAIR RESUME THEIR CONVERSATIONS ON ENGLAND JOINING THE EURO AT NOON IN LON-DON—AND THIS JUST IN FROM JERUSALEM—AS MANY AS THREE HUNDRED ISRAELI SETTLERS ARE PLANNING A MARCH FROM THEIR WEST BANK SET-TLEMENT IN KEDUMIN NEAR THE PALESTINIAN CITY OF NABLUS TO SET UP NEW, ILLEGAL HOMES ON THE OUTSKIRTS OF THE PALESTINIAN CITY. MORE ON THAT AND OUR OTHER STORIES ON OUR MORNING REPORT . . .

The occupants of room 312 of the Madison Hotel on Thirty-eighth Street near Sixth Avenue banged their feet on their bedroom floor in fury.

"I told you, Khaled," swore Omar Tahiri, "that bastard Sharon isn't going to evacuate those Israeli settlers. Never! In fact, he's letting them open new settlements. Not even the idea of turning a million New Yorkers into dust is going to make him change his mind. Mugniyeh's idea was a crazy dream. It was never going to work."

Khaled listened to his companion, his teeth clenched, his eyes burning with anger and hatred, a fervid desire to punish, to destroy. He was so obsessed with what he saw as the oppression of his people that he was eager to take vengeance even at the cost of his life.

"Listen, my brother," Omar continued, "as I told you, we can't build our homeland on the corpses of thousands of innocent people. You saw the people walking in the streets down there—Chinese, Hispanics, Italians, blacks—the lot. And there are Muslims down there too. Our enemies aren't those people. They're the Israelis back in Palestine, destroying our homes, stealing our land, chopping down our olive trees. Blowing off that bomb isn't going to change that. It's only going to make the whole world hate us. No one will support our claim to our homeland anymore. It would actually be counterproductive—as well as inhuman—to detonate that bomb."

"Well, whether you like it or not, it's going off if Bush and Sharon don't accept our conditions. I'll see to that, believe me."

"You would do such a thing, spit in the face of the world? In the end, hurt our own cause? I've been thinking a lot about that—and I'm afraid I can't let you do that, Khaled. I know we started on this path together, but now I see things differently. I was hoping you did too. But even if you don't, I have to stop you, so help me God."

"You what? Traitor! Why did you accept this mission if it was to desert and give up at the first occasion?"

Khaled swung out using the side of his hand like an axe,

striking Omar on the cheek.

Omar staggered under the blow, falling against a chair and toppling onto the floor between their beds. Khaled pounced on him and grabbed his neck with both hands, his thumbs digging into his throat.

Omar was choking, his mouth open, gasping for air. He managed to roll onto his side and with his good hand pulled out of his jacket pocket the small 6.35mm revolver given to him in Canada with their false papers. He clutched it in a trembling hand as Khaled banged his head against the floor. He pulled the trigger but his shot missed and lodged in the ceiling overhead.

Khaled put all his weight down on the hands that circled his companion's neck just below his Adam's apple. A spasm shook Omar. His mouth opened in a last desperate effort to gasp for air but he got none. A splash of spittle burst from Omar's mouth and he fell back unconscious. Khaled continued choking him for a long moment. When he released his grip, Omar was dead.

"That bomb is going off, Omar!" Khaled vowed. "I swear that to you. I will set it off myself if I have to. You lost, traitor!"

He pulled on his leather jacket, grabbed the revolver from his dead friend's hand and rushed out of the room.

*   *   *

It was Police Commissioner Ray Kelly's idea. Precisely at eight o'clock, every available detective, every FBI agent assigned to duty in the crisis shaking New York City, was ordered to report to the nearest precinct house anywhere in New York's five boroughs to watch a closed-circuit TV conference. That had never happened before in New York Police Department history, but there was no doubt in Kelly's mind that the situation demanded it, as the hours ran swiftly down to the terrorists' deadline.

T.F. O'Neill sat at the head of his officers of the Manhattan South Detective Squad. He was inordinately proud of those men and women. Budget cuts had reduced their number from forty to twenty-five but they were still running an arrest rate of over 25 percent, one of the best in the city.

He grasped a cup of New York's finest cappuccino in his hand and stared at the TV screen, waiting for the PC's image to appear. His mind, however, was not on the screen but on the playground of Our Lady of Sorrows school in Glendale and the adorable little girl he had felt obliged to leave at that school the day before. Would she survive the catastrophe threatening the city? Would he? Would his comrades in that room?

There was a commotion at the door of the squad room. A dozen FBI agents assigned to work with his officers had just arrived, his partner Olivia Phillips among them. He gestured to Olivia, pointing to the chair next to him that he had kept vacant for her.

The bureau had put her up in the nearby New Yorker Hotel for the crisis. He guessed she must have been up since seven despite the fact they had been working well past midnight. She was immaculate, every hair in her well-styled hair in place. Her athletic body filled out nicely her sleek Klein pantsuit. What a woman, O'Neill thought. She probably could have found some pretext to get back to her native New Orleans but here she was where duty called. She may end up dying for New York City, he thought, right along with me and our colleagues. He gave a long admiring look at her lovely figure.

Instinctively Olivia turned to him with a shy smile. It was almost as if she had read his thought. If that bomb is really here and goes off we will certainly go with it, me and my "Chief

Inspector, dear." What a shame, she thought. What might have been, what might have been! But supposing we do find it . . .

The lights flashing on the TV set interrupted their thoughts. Kelly's face appeared. "Ladies and Gentlemen," he began, "I'm going to be brief because time is of the essence. I must reveal to you something we have felt we had to keep secret until now. The terrorists who smuggled their barrel of chlorine gas into New York City have given us an ultimatum. If our national government does not respond to their demands by noon New York time tomorrow, the deadly chlorine gas in that barrel will be released on our city. That will cause immense pain and suffering—and countless deaths—not just in the neighborhood where it's been hidden, but wherever the wind carries that cloud of death. Therefore, for each and every one of us there must be no rest, no downtime, no diversions, no other tasks, however important, until we have found that barrel. I count on all of you to get out there right now; squeeze your sources, search stores and apartments, do whatever you need to do to get the job done. Waste no time on the niceties. Now get going!"

O'Neill stood up. "You all heard the PC," he said. "Get to work on the targets you were assigned in the critical area I showed you yesterday."

In the meantime Olivia's cell phone rang. She listened intently to her call, then beckoned to O'Neill. "It was FBI headquarters," she whispered. "The CIA has come up with the name and address of the guy that made that call to Beirut on the unregistered cell phone. Name's *Burke.* Supposedly works for Dell computers and lives in our area, Thirty-eighth Street near Sixth. They want us to get down there right away and check him out. See if he really is who he says he is."

*   *   *

Three sharp knocks, a pause, two more knocks, another pause and a final knock—that was the code they had established for entering the bomb's hideaway, where it waited for the signal that would end its existence, and that of much of New York City. Nahed edged open the door and Khaled slipped in. From the look of anxiety on his face, the young woman instantly realized something was wrong.

Khaled went to the wooden case in which the bomb had been shipped from Bombay, now an improvised half chair–half table. He slumped down on it and rested his head on his hands.

"I have killed Omar," he murmured. "He wanted to betray our mission. He wanted to prevent me from detonating the bomb."

Nahed gasped in shock.

"Turn on the radio," Khaled told her. "CNN said hundreds of Israeli settlers are getting ready to seize some more of our sacred homeland near Nablus. The Warriors of the Jihad have lost this phase of our struggle, but I am going to avenge them come what may."

He got back on his feet, grasped Nahed by her shoulders and fixed his gaze on hers. "Nahed," he whispered, "your presence here is no longer necessary. Omar is dead but I am going to stay right here in this room until the deadline expires at noon tomorrow. If the call doesn't come through to detonate our bomb then I will detonate it myself by pushing that button"—he gestured with his head to the device they had attached to their bomb as Mugniyeh had instructed them. "The enemies of our people will receive the punishment they deserve."

"Go up the street and buy me enough food and water so I can live in here without going outside until noon tomorrow." He took a wad of bills from his pocket and passed them to her. "You have your Canadian passport. Take this money and head for Canada. Palestine needs you still."

In five minutes she was back with a bundle of groceries, a pizza and Evian water. Tears in her eyes, she caressed Khaled's cheeks. She wanted to say something but the words would not escape her mouth. Finally in a half whisper she said, "May Allah welcome you to paradise as the hero and martyr you are."

She embraced him, eased open the door and hurried down the stairs. The Pakistani super was cleaning the entry hall but she brushed past him like a ghost, slid out the door and disappeared into the crowd of early morning shoppers in the street.

*   *   *

"It was right in here," Jimmy Burke said to T.F. O'Neill and Olivia Phillips, pointing out the green New York City trash basket near the corner of Thirty-eighth Street and Sixth Avenue.

"Yes," his German girlfriend Ingrid confirmed, "it was lying on top of a copy of the *Village Voice*."

"I picked it up, noticed it had a SIM card but no battery. I thought, 'Hey, maybe if I stick a battery in there it will have some time left on the card.'"

He had already handed the phone to Olivia. "That call I made to Ingrid's mother was the only time I used it so if there are any other calls on there. . . ," he shrugged, "they might be what you guys are looking for."

"Do you remember what time it was when you found it?" Olivia asked.

"Well, we went to the see the last *Matrix* film at the Rivoli over on Sixth and Thirty-fifth. The six o'clock show. We were walking home after the show so it must have been eight or just after."

"Bingo, dear Chief Inspector," Olivia said to O'Neill. "The NSA placed the Beirut call at seven-o-four, so those guys must have been somewhere no more than a one hour's walk from here."

"Right in the area we're concentrating on," he agreed. "I don't think we need to detain Mr. Burke and his lady friend anymore. They seem clean to me."

"OK, let me pass this on to the bureau supervisor at the OEM."

"Roger that," O'Neill agreed, "then let's get back to the precinct and focus our search efforts on the neighborhood around here. On the way there's one quick stop I'd like to make."

*   *   *

The President charged into the Situation Room of the White House with all the furious energy of a brave bull bursting into the bullring. He was so angry that he forgot the moment of prayerful silence with which he usually opened these meetings. He waved a blue binder, his daily CIA briefing, at them.

"Ladies and Gentlemen," he said, "with Milt Anderson's agreement, I've ordered a copy of this morning briefing paper prepared for each of you. Our latest report from Jerusalem informs me that over three hundred Israelis from the settlement of Kedumin are setting out to move their vans and mobile homes onto some thirty acres of Palestinian farmland near the city of Nablus. Their leader is Rabbi Avigdor Beibelman, the head of the radical National Religious Party. Its proclaimed goal is to drive the Palestinians now on the West Bank into Jordan. He has invited both the Israeli and the international press to cover the event. CNN is already announcing it. It is impossible to see this as anything other than an outrageous provocation, an irrevocable act designed to wipe out any hope of a peaceful resolution to the threat facing New York."

"Son of a bitch!" an angry voice muttered from the end of the room. "So now we lose New York for those three hundred settlers!"

"Can't Sharon stop them?" the Deputy Secretary of Defense asked.

"Perhaps," the CIA's Anderson answered, "but there is no indication he intends to."

As was so often the case, it was the quiet but firm voice of Condoleezza Rice that came forward with the next step to take.

"Mr. President," she said, "I think that you should get on the phone to Sharon immediately. You've got to make him see how outrageous this is."

The President nodded his agreement. "I think Condi's right. Try and get Sharon on the phone for us," he ordered the marine officer running the room's communications equipment.

After two agonizing minutes the voice of the Israeli prime minister came on the speakerphones ringing the table. "I'm listening, George," Sharon began, dispensing with the courtesy remarks that normally opened their calls. "I hope you are calling to inform me that your police have found that terrorists' bomb in New York."

"No, Arik," the President announced, making a determined effort to control his anger. "I am calling to tell you that this minister of yours, Avigdor Beibelman, is signing the death warrant of a million of my fellow Americans in New York with this mad plan of his to settle three hundred Israelis on Palestinian land in defiance of the terrorists' threat. I expect you to immediately order the Israeli Army to stop his action with force."

"Mr. President, that is out of the question. You are already threatening to land your Marines to forcibly evacuate our people from their homes. Do that and you will leave me no choice but to order my armed forces to oppose them. And now you ask me to use force against my fellow Israelis who are going out to occupy land that God gave them. The Israeli army's mission is to protect the lives and belongings of our people, not to fire on them as they are exercising their historic rights. If I give the army the order to stop them at the same time as I order them to oppose the landing of your marines, do you know what will happen? It will set off a civil war that could end with the destruction of my nation. Pray God your police can find that bomb in New York before it is too late, Mr. President, but do not ask me to sacrifice my nation if they fail to do so. Shalom."

There was a sharp click. Sharon had hung up.

"What in hell are we going to do?" Bush asked rhetorically. "What the hell can we do? General," he asked the Chairman of the Joint Chiefs of Staff, "how much advance notice does the Sixth Fleet need to get the marines ashore?"

"They will need to get the order eight hours before you want them to start hitting the beach."

The President acknowledged that with a nod and turned to his NSA advisor. "Your guys still haven't come up with a way to prevent an international call from getting through to the cell phone attached to that bomb in New York?"

"No, sir."

"Then," the President said, his voice constricting into something close to a sob, "what choice do we have? If we haven't found that bomb by midnight, twelve hours before their deadline expires, I will have to give notice to the UN and our allies that the tight deadline forces us to act unilaterally, but that as soon as possible we will come to the Security Council for authorization to proceed. Then I'll have to give the order to land the marines at eight tomorrow morning Eastern Standard Time. That will be early afternoon out there, four hours before the clock runs out on the ultimatum. At the same time, I will go on a national and international TV hookup to tell the nation and the world what we are about to do and why we are doing it. I'll ask Mike Bloomberg to stand by and as soon as I have finished I'll have him order an immediate evacuation of the city."

"Even at the risk of those terrorists detonating the bomb when they hear that word *evacuation?*" Condi Rice asked.

"I will make it very clear in my speech that our actions are just the first phase in an internationally supervised evacuation of the Israeli settlements in Palestinian post-1967 territory. We all have to pray that this will be enough to stay the hands of the terrorist madmen."

He looked with tear-filled eyes at the people around the table.

"Does anyone have a better idea? Can anyone think of another way of extracting us from this god-awful mess?"

A painful, heavy silence greeted his words.

"Then so be it," he said. "Pray God this will be enough to satisfy these fanatics, to save New York, to put an end to this damn crisis. Meeting   adjourned," he concluded in a voice that was barely a whisper.

*   *   *

Olivia Phillips looked up at the great Gothic spans of Saint Patrick's Cathedral and smiled. So this was the quick stop her "Chief Inspector, dear" had to make on the way back to Manhattan South. Well, she thought, following him into the shadowy interior of the great church, given how little luck we're having finding this damn barrel, we need help anywhere we can find it.

O'Neill dipped his fingertips into the Holy Water fount at the entrance, made the sign of the cross and started down the main aisle. He knew it well. He had walked its long expanse with his bride beside him after their wedding ceremony, and walked up it twice behind the coffins of both his mother and father. Not for nothing was Saint Patrick's the bastion of the Irish Catholic American community.

At the approach to the high altar, he turned toward the candle glowing in the red sacristy light, genuflected, again made the sign of the cross, then turned toward the bank of glowing candles in their small glass candleholders on the side altar. He slipped a bill into the repository, withdrew a candle, lit one of the lights and knelt at the *prie-dieu* facing them. Oh, Lord, he prayed, spare that small child I left entrusted to your care and help us in this our hour of need and pain.

Olivia watched fascinated at these rites so different from the spartan ways of her own Southern Baptist upbringing. "I'm ready to pray in anyone's church—or synagogue or even mosque. We can use all the help we can get," she said to O'Neill as they left.

They had almost reached his car when O'Neill's cell phone rang. It was the desk sergeant at Manhattan South.

"Hey, Chief," he said, "we got a homicide down at the Madison Hotel on Thirty-eighth Street."

"Well," O'Neill said, "homicides may normally be a top priority but with what we have on our plate today, they're in second place.."

"This one won't be, Chief," the desk sergeant said. "The dead guy has no left hand."

*   *   *

Within minutes O'Neill and Olivia were at the door of the Madison Hotel. The detective assigned to the case was waiting for him together with two uniformed patrolmen and the hotel proprietor.

"OK," O'Neill snapped, "so what have we got?"

"Guy's up in three-twelve. Looks he was strangled. There's a round lodged in the roof but no one in the building heard a gunshot. Maid found him when she came to clean the room."

"I immediately called nine-one-one," the proprietor assured them, anxious to display his law-abiding nature.

"Let's have a look," O'Neill said, heading for the elevator.

"You know," Olivia murmured as they got in, "I've never seen a cadaver."

"Not to worry," O'Neill assured her, "some of these bad guys look better dead than alive."

The police officer standing guard at the door let them into 312. It consisted of a small sitting room and a bedroom with twin beds. Omar's body, mouth agape, was sprawled on the floor between the beds.

"Get me a Polaroid of this guy's face right away," O'Neill ordered.

There was a woman's brassiere and panties on one of the beds. "You had a couple living in here?" he asked the proprietor.

"Three of them rented the suite, Inspector," the proprietor said.

"And two of them slept together on one of these rickety little beds?"

The proprietor ignored his observation. "I don't think the three of them were ever here together. Sometimes the woman spent the night here with one or the other of the guys. Once maybe, the two guys were here for the night. Where they went or what they did the rest of the time, I don't know. We don't try to keep track of their comings and goings. You know, what's their business is their business not ours."

"Sure," O'Neill said taking out the ID photo from the woman's Easy Rent driver's license. "Was this by any chance the woman?"

The hotel owner put on his glasses and studied the photo. "Yeah, I think so," he said. "Although she didn't always wear a scarf."

"What did they give you for ID when they checked in?"

"Canadian passports. We have the details downstairs in the office.

O'Neill looked at Olivia. "Probably every bit as good as that driver's license from Jersey. How did they pay? Credit card?"

"No, they gave us cash a week in advance."

"Figures. Lets look around."

The two began to study the little sitting room, the ashtrays and the wastebaskets, the drawers of the closet and bureau. "Hey!" Olivia said. "Look at this!"

Delicately, so as not to leave her fingerprints, she pulled a soiled carton from the sitting room wastebasket. MIMOSA'S PIZZA PARLOR, it read, 314 FIFTH AVENUE. "Must have been our friend over there's last supper," she said.

O'Neill looked at it. "I know the place. It's over by Thirty-second Street. Just six blocks from here. Lets go check it out."

He turned to the detective from his precinct. "Give this place a thorough going over. Dust for fingerprints, the lot. I'll be in touch."

As they got down to the front door, they could hear the wail of sirens in the distance. "What's that?" he asked the patrolman on the door.

"I think someone called the bomb squad to have a look,"

he replied.

"Damn it—tell them to turn their honker off and park their bus around the corner. We don't want to draw a crowd. And certainly not the press. Come on, Olivia. Let's get to our pizza parlor."

Within minutes they were walking into the front door of Mimosa's Pizza, its air redolent with the smell of baking pizzas. The owner became particularly welcoming when O'Neill flashed his shield. They took out the woman's license photo and the Polaroid print of Omar.

"Santa Maria," the owner exclaimed, looking at Omar's photo, "what happened to him?"

"Had a little trouble getting his breath," O'Neill said. "Recognize either of these two?"

"Yeah. The lady she came in a few times. Always asked for the pizza with five cheeses for three people."

"Never had it delivered?"

"No. I think she lives right near here."

"Thanks, pal," O'Neill smiled. "Appreciate your help."

The pair walked out and up to the corner of Fifth and Thirty-second Street. O'Neill paused and stared down Thirty-second through the tangle of delivery trucks—FedEx, UPS, Worldwide Delivery Service, Seoul Pom Inc.—jamming the street near the corner of Fifth. "You know, this place rings a bell in my memory. We had a little problem here two years ago at Three-sixteen Fifth. The entrance is just down there." He indicated the building next door on Thirty-second Street.

"What happened?" Olivia asked

"Super's a Pakistani. Real venal bastard. He'll rent anything to anybody for cash, no ID, no papers, nothing. So these two African guys come in, rent two rooms from him and fill them up with counterfeit CDs and DVDs. They're doing a booming business selling their stuff up and down the street when some of the African American brothers see what's going on and figure they ought to have a share of the traffic. Dumb Africans don't agree and the brothers come in with their thirty-eights to make them see the folly of their ways. One of the Africans goes out the window and his pal dies of a gunshot wound. Twenty thousand counterfeit DVDs we find in there."

"So you figure this might be our guys' hideout?"

"Why not? Look what's just up the street. The Empire State Building. With the Towers gone could they have a more tempting target than that?"

O'Neill gestured toward the building entrance. OFFICE FOR RENT read a big sign. Next to it in Korean and English was a sign reading KOREAN HAIRSTYLIST.

"Look," O'Neill suggested, "let's go in there like boyfriend and girlfriend so no one picks up on us. You can get your hair combed out at the salon. While you're doing that I'll slip out and have a word with my friend the Super."

"Let's do it," Olivia agreed, taking T.F.'s hand in a properly girlfriend-like gesture.

Once they'd settled inside the beauty parlor, T.F. pretended to leaf through a magazine, then announced, "I'm going to go out in the street for a smoke."

Nothing could have seemed more natural given the city's smoking laws. Once outside, he spun back in and into the Super's little cubbyhole. The Super looked up, recognition dawning on his face as O'Neill flashed his badge.

"Hey, I know you," he said, trying hard to look like a solid citizen. "I'm clean. No fake CDs here today."

"Screw CDs," O'Neill said pulling out his photos of Nahed and Omar. "It's these two people who interest me. You seen them?

Rent to them?"

The Super began to mumble a vague answer.

"Look, my friend," O'Neill said, "I'm not the housing police, you know what I mean? I just want to know one thing. Did you rent to these guys?'

"Yeah. And they had a friend, a younger guy. I think he's up there now. They took the little office next to the Afghan carpet dealer on the fourth floor. You remember him. The woman, she walked out a couple of hours ago."

"What do they do?"

The Super shrugged. "Man, I don't know. They come, they go, they don't make trouble. What do I care?"

"They get mail?'

"Never. But when they came in about a week ago, they had a package, big one, heavy son of a bitch. I have to help them get it to the elevator because that guy with his mouth open in your picture, he had only one hand."

"Listen, friend. I'll be back in a few moments with some pals. In the meantime, you don't tell no one I was here. No one. And especially not that guy up on the fourth floor. I'm going upstairs to talk to my friend who has that Afghan carpet shop opposite their place."

O'Neill and the Afghan, who had been particularly helpful during the investigation into the counterfeit DVDs, recognized each other immediately. "Hey, Inspector," he said, "come in, have a cup of Afghan coffee."

"I'm afraid I haven't got time for that, my friend, but just between us, what have you observed about the comings and goings of your new neighbors across the hall?"

"Nothing really. Since they arrived with their big package, they stay locked up in there almost all the time, night and day."

"Any idea where they're from?"

The Afghan shrugged his shoulders. "No. They not friendly. They say nothing to me when they come out. And always use the stairs, not the elevator. But I think probably they're Arabs."

"Why do you say that?"

"Me, I'm Muslim. OK? I only go to the mosque now once in a while, for Ramadan and Aid el Kebir. But our Koran is in Arabic. So even if I don't speak Arabic, I recognize it when I hear it. It's Arabic they were speaking."

"Thanks for your help, friend. Don't say anything to anybody about my interest in those people, OK?"

O'Neill went back downstairs to the Korean hairdresser's salon. Olivia was almost finished. He indicated with a gesture that they should get going.

Once they stepped out onto the street, he said, "Olivia, I think this is the package we've all been looking for; you and I are going to be the ones to solve this thing! We've got to get to a secure telephone as fast as possible."

"Your car?"

"Not secure. Press can sometimes pick up those calls. We'll have to go back to the precinct."

Ten minutes later, they had Commissioner Kelly, Paul Anscom, NEST's David Graham and the Chief of Detectives on a secure video-phone tie to the Office of Emergency Management in Brooklyn. "Commissioner," O'Neill said, "we've found the package that was smuggled into New York in a container of basmati rice, the one Agent Phillips and I were assigned to track down. It's in a fourth floor apartment at Three-sixteen Fifth, which is really on Thirty-second Street."

He then described how the place had been rented for cash with no ID. "Most important, Chief, that guy without a left hand that we described in our earlier report was found this morning in his hotel room. DOA, strangled."

"OK," Kelly said, "but how can we be sure it's a bomb in there and not drugs?"

O'Neill gave the suggestion of a laugh. "Or the kind of chlorine gas you go looking for with Geiger counters, right? I have a witness who says they were speaking Arabic."

"Arabs smuggle drugs," Kelly observed.

"Listen," said the Chief of Detectives, "that's an ideal place for the kind of stuff we're looking for. The Empire State's around the corner and that building's sitting on top of two subway lines and the Long Island Railroad tracks. To say nothing of the city's main gas and electric cables."

"Commissioner," Anscom added, "I think your Inspector O'Neill and Agent Phillips have done great work. I think we're close enough now to a solution that we had better bring the President up to speed. I'm going to ask Andrew Card to pass the news to Mr. Bush. I have a hunch he'll want to put a hold on the confrontation with the Israelis. And I'd like to have his authorization to go ahead with breaking into that room, including the use of deadly force."

Kelly followed with "Let's get a team of our emergency service people in there ASAP, bust down that door, grab or take out the guy who's in there and find out for sure what the hell is in the package . . . if we're out of the woods now or if the search still has to go on."

"NO!" The words were screamed over the OEM's hookup to the White House Situation Room by Lisa Holmgren, the National Security Agency's nuclear terrorism expert. "For God's sake, don't do that! If there is a nuclear device in there, that guy will detonate it as soon as he hears the word *police*. You've got to go in there on tiptoes, disarm him and then render that bomb safe once he's out of the way."

Kelly reflected a moment. "Yes," he said, "she's right. We need speed and we need silence. We've got to go on tiptoes so that guy doesn't figure we're onto him. No squad cars with sirens howling, and for God's sake no media! O'Neill, you're there on the spot. I'm putting you in charge. Any officers you call on to come and help have to be in civilian clothes. I'll send you the Special Operations Division team from Fort Totten. Find an underground garage near that building that they can use so no one can spot their vehicle."

"And I'll send you a NEST van right away," Graham said. "If the device in the place does turn out to be nuclear, NEST would be in charge of operations."

"Maybe there's a window across the street from which we can get a picture with one of our high-resolution, low-light infrared cameras," the Chief of Detectives suggested.

"Right," O'Neill agreed, "and there's an Afghan carpet dealer that shares that fourth floor with them. I think he'll let us use his place as our HQ."

"OK," Kelly said, "get going right now. But remember silence is golden."

*   *   *

Kelly's first act was to call Captain Jack Walton, commander of the police department's Special Operations Division, or TARU (for Technical Assistance Response Unit), at Fort Totten, Queens. His orders to Walton were simple: get his men with all their sophisticated eavesdropping devices over to Thirty-second Street as fast as possible. Their job: to find out who and what was inside that fourth floor apartment at 316 Fifth Avenue, and to do it without letting anyone suspect what they were up to.

The secrecy shrouding the operation was no surprise to Walton. His officers usually worked in civilian clothes, moving around the city in unmarked cars.

"How much time have we got?" Walton asked.

"None," said Kelly, "but under no circumstances are you to go busting in there without my express orders to do so."

Mmm . . . Afghan carpet dealer, Walton thought, reflecting on the mission briefing Kelly had given him. Among his many contacts was a Broadway costume rental company that provided the city's theaters with costumes for their productions. In view of the urgency of Kelly's request, Walton decided to give the job to his Emergency Services A-team, the elite of the NYPD. He would send them to 316 Fifth dressed as Middle Easterners coming to do business with the carpet dealer. Yeah, he thought, and I'll get my hands on half a dozen carpets. The team can roll their equipment up in the carpets and tote them into that Afghan's shop without arousing any suspicions. He smiled as he remembered the scene in *Cleopatra,* where Elizabeth Taylor gets carried secretly into Caesar's tent rolled up in a carpet. Funny how life sometimes copies art.

He got O'Neill on his cell phone and instructed him to find an underground garage in a nearby building. His team could park their truck with its NYPD markings there without drawing the attention of curious pedestrians.

T.F. was in a fourth floor office of the building across the street from 316 Fifth with an NYPD cameraman using a high-intensity infrared camera to photograph the rooms in the facing building where Khaled was babysitting the bomb.

They could see his figure in the front room, his back to the door, sitting on what seemed to be the remains of a big crate, hunched over what was probably a radio. The door to the next room was open. There was a bulky object of some sort inside that room, but there wasn't enough light to get a good image of it.

O'Neill said to the photographer, "Focus tight on the crate. See if you can make out any markings or lettering on it."

The cameraman scrutinized the crate as best he could. "It's been busted apart," he told O'Neill. "Take a look. I think you can just make out below the guys knee, the end of what was a word. I can see three letters: *ODS*."

O'Neill studied the image in the camera. Sure, he thought, *Oriental Foods*. Has to be Birbaki's case.

"Listen," he ordered, "you stay here and keep that zoom focused on the guy over there. If he gets up to leave the flat, buzz this beeper number." It belonged to an armed patrolman T.F. had secretly placed in the Afghan's shop across the hall from Khaled. "If he opens the door of that office, our guy will nail him."

With that, he went back down to Thirty-second Street to wait for the NEST van to arrive. The driver of the van with its AVIS markings pulled up two doors down from the entrance to 316 Fifth. Gladys Simpson sat beside him.

"We've got some heavy, sophisticated stuff in here," she told O'Neill. "I hope we can park close to the scene."

"Not to worry," O'Neill assured her. "Park right here for the time being." He glanced down the street. "What the hell, everybody else does. Besides if some guy gives you a ticket, we'll ask George W. to take care of it. Come on. Let me take you upstairs to show you the place we're going to be working from."

Gladys glided like a cat into the Afghan's carpet shop, her Geiger counter slung over her back looking as if she were a backpacker out shopping. She immediately unslung it and took a reading.

"Nothing," she said, "but if there is a bomb in there they could very well have shielded it with lead to seal in the emissions."

With Gladys installed, T.F. went down the block to the underground garage he had located. He led the van to the garage entrance, then waved it down to a parking space.

He smiled when he saw that the four officers of the Emergency Services A-team who climbed out of the van were dressed in a variety of Middle Eastern apparel. One had a turban, another a robe. "You guys look like the old Taliban, or Iranian carpet peddlers."

"That's the idea," the team leader said. He pointed to the interior of the van. Six rolled carpets were stacked on its floor. "Our stuff's in there. We'll take them up to the shop you're using as your headquarters one by one so we don't draw a crowd. Tell me, they got any ATM cameras in that suspect building?"

"Just one. Super says it hasn't worked for six years."

"Figures. We'll have to get the Super's master key and take him into custody while the operation's going on."

"He's been pretty cooperative," O'Neill remarked.

"Makes no difference. It's SOP."

O'Neill shrugged. These were guys you didn't argue with. A few minutes later they were unrolling the first of their carpets in the back room of the Afghan's shop while its proprietor looked on fascinated. The array of Special Operations Division eavesdropping equipment was mind-boggling. It included microphones no bigger than a pinhead that could be inserted into a keyhole to pick up every sound coming out of a room under surveillance. There were cameras so small they were encapsulated in a wire that could be threaded through the building's electrical conduits. There were also high-speed drills to pierce a tiny hole in the wall into which the miniature camera or microphone could be inserted.

The team's pride was a flat camera so thin it could be slid under a closed door. "Bad guys got no secrets from us," the team leader told O'Neill. Nor on occasion did people's pets. One of the team's exploits involved a gentleman's pet tiger. The man had died in his sleep and the tiger, roaring out his grief and hunger, was roaming the apartment. The team drew him to the inside of the door with the odor of cooking meat then knocked him out with a hypodermic needle inserted through the keyhole.

"How many people they got in there?" the team leader asked.

"Far as we know, only one. A male."

"Well, let's confirm that." They did it by placing against the wall a new type of thermal imaging device sensitive enough to pick up the slightest differences in body heat.

"You're right. One person, a male."

Next, a pinhead microphone was slipped into the keyhole of the front door. It revealed that Khaled was listening to a radio broadcasting in Arabic. Since the photo images being shot by the police cameraman across the street showed he was sitting with his back to the door, the team leader decided to use their newest and sexiest toy. It was the incredibly thin camera that could be slipped under the closed apartment door.

It was connected by fiber-optic cable to a computer in the Afghan's backroom that relayed its images over a cell phone line to the Emergency Response Vehicle parked in the basement garage at 37 Thirty-second Street, where it was again relayed to the Office of Emergency Management in Brooklyn. There, Kelly, Anscom and Graham huddled around their computer screen, mesmerized by the technology and becoming, in a sense, part of the crime scene themselves.

While the photographer across the street kept his camera trained on Khaled to make sure he didn't get up or move, a Special Operations officer in his stocking feet crossed the hallway and slowly slipped the camera under the door of Khaled's apartment.

Gladys watched intently as the images began to form on her computer screen with astonishing clarity. The officer manipulating the camera slowly moved it to scan the front room in which Khaled was sitting, then focused it on the double doors leading into the adjoining room. Just inside the door was the bulky device which the cameraman across the street had spotted but was unable to photograph clearly.

"Hold on that!" Gladys ordered. She studied the object with all the concentration she had employed as a nuclear physicist, studying its form, its dimensions and then the giveaway outline of the detonation device topping it.

"That's it!" she said with an intensity that carried her voice through the communication circuitry to the OEM in Brooklyn. "That's what we're looking for! That's their atomic bomb!"

*   *   *

A joyous near pandemonium broke out in the Office of Emergency Management as her words came over its speakers. "Let's get the President right away," Paul Anscom shouted over his hookup to the White House Situation Room. "Give him the good news."

"Wait a minute!" broke in David Graham, the director of NEST. "Remember that until we've gotten in there, isolated the bomb and rendered it safe, this crisis isn't over. Mugniyeh or Osama bin Laden could pick up a phone wherever the hell they are right now and call the cell phone fixed to that bomb. They do that, and New York will go! Besides, the guy in there must be primed to set it off if he thinks his mission's in danger. Or who's to know, some accomplice down on Thirty-second Street may have a beeper that can send in a detonation signal, the way these suicide bombers do with cars they've booby-trapped."

"Commissioner," Anscom asked, "what do we do now that we know where the bomb is? How do we get in there to neutralize it? Look, you've got a photographer across the street with a clear view of the guy. Why don't we get some sharpshooters up there too and nail him now?"

"Because if they miss him or just wound him, he's going to detonate it in a second," answered Kelly. "Fortunately, the best guys in the world to take him out are already over there on the site, the A-team of our Special Operations Division. They have a device down in their van called a Porta Power. It releases a huge blast of compressed air that will blow the door off its hinges— *whoosh!*—before you can say *bingo*. Or before our friend in there can react and blow the bomb. The A-team guys go in right behind the door as it sails across the room. With shotguns. They have orders to "shoot to stop" rather than "shoot to kill," to calm the civil liberty folks. What that really means is that if that guy so much as raises an eyebrow, they blow him away."

"Can they do all that without alerting the guy to the fact they're on to him?" Anscom asked.

"We'll sure try. The whole thing is designed for a silent operation. They've done it a dozen times. The Porta Power's on felt runners that don't make a sound. Nothing actually touches the door they're going to blow in."

"How fast can they do it?"

"Ten minutes max."

"I say do it," Anscom said. "Right now."

"Shouldn't we get the President's OK first?" someone in the Situation Room asked.

"He'll agree. Let's not waste time. We need to give Kelly the go-ahead right now."

No one dissented and Anscom gave Kelly the nod.

Less than two minutes later the Special Operations men were carrying their Porta Power out of their van and up the staircase of 316 Fifth. On the fourth floor, their waiting colleagues had stripped off their Middle Eastern clothes and pulled on black sweatshirts with *Police* stenciled in large white letters.

The Porta Power was already fully charged and all the team had to do was glide it silently up to the door of Khaled's flat. The huge charge of compressed air it contained was unleashed by a radio signal. There was a quick, sharp explosion. Then the door literally flew off its hinges and sailed into the room.

Shouting "Police! Don't move!" the A-team, with shotguns aimed, sprang into the room. Khaled lunged for the detonation button next to the bomb but four simultaneous shotgun shots flung his body, blasted to shreds, across the room.

Gladys Simpson, the NEST technician burst into the room right behind them, She immediately fixed her eyes on the button Khaled had died trying to push.

"You!" she ordered one of the police officers. "Stand guard on that button. For God's sake don't let anybody touch it or even breathe on it!' Everyone understood that as the representative of NEST she was now in charge of the operation.

She pulled back and cast her expert eyes on the device before her. Holy shit! she thought sizing up its dimensions. No doubt about what that is. The faces of her two young children back in California crowded into her mind. Don't panic! she warned herself. Think systematically the way you've been taught, even when fear is threatening to overwhelm you. Panic is the enemy. You mustn't let panic get in the way. Her legs were weak and shaking, perspiration forming on her forehead. This was it, the nightmare come true, the horror she'd been trained to deal with since, against her husband's wishes, she'd joined NEST. She was standing in front of a fully operational atomic bomb, one whose power surely equaled the one that reduced Hiroshima to a smoking pile of rubble. I have got to eliminate any possibility of igniting it. I don't dare move it. It might be booby-trapped. And how much time do I have to do it?

Always assume the worse. That was how NEST approached any situation. She quickly called her boss, David Graham, the head of NEST, at the Office of Emergency Management. He in turn got on a phone link to a pair of senior nuclear weapons designers at the Livermore National Laboratory in California.

"Should we warn the police and suggest they order an evacuation?" was her first question to Graham.

"No," he replied, "that will only get the media involved and generate chaos on top of chaos. What I want you to do is walk and talk us through that bomb from top to bottom, estimating each of its key measurements as you go along but without touching anything."

She immediately spotted the cell phone, installed where Dr. Khan had said to Condi Rice.

"Quick!" she called to Graham. "Get me a Faraday cage."

"One's already on its way. It should be downstairs by now. What exactly is that cell phone connected to?"

"There's a wire about a foot long that runs down to a black plastic ball, a little bit bigger than a softball."

"That would be the energy source or what we call the 'fire

set,'" said the voice of one of the weapons designers at Livermore. "Inside that black ball is a capacitor that stores up an enormous charge of electrical power. When a call comes into that cell phone, it answers it and in doing so it sends a signal to the capacitor that instantly releases all that power stored there in a single blast into the detonator. It should be a big cylinder wired to your black plastic ball. When that electric charge hits it, the detonator sets off its high explosives which in turn start the chain reaction and an atomic explosion."

"Hey!" Gladys shouted to Graham, "two of your guys just arrived with a Faraday cage."

"Great," he replied. "They'll fit it into place for you. They've done it dozens of times."

As she always did, Gladys thought the cage looked like the helmets hairdressers use when doing a woman's permanent. On its top was a hook that would be connected to an eight-foot-high stand from which the cage could be lowered over the cell phone. It was crucial that it not be touched, in case it was booby trapped. At the cage's base was a copper skirt that could be tucked into place almost touching the base of the phone to keep out signals coming from underneath.

Her two NEST colleagues flown in from Livermore forty-eight hours earlier worked with fast but sure hands, lowering the cage in place. In less than five minutes, their job was done and the phone was surrounded on all sides by a copper sheath. OK, they told Gladys, it's now completely cut off from any signal that could activate the bomb.

"They've done it," she told Graham with a jubilant shout. "The bomb can't be detonated by a phone call anymore. Now what we've got to do is render it safe."

The air of euphoria in the Emergency Operations Center

in Brooklyn and in the Afghan's rooms was tempered by the knowledge that the most dangerous and unpredictable part of the operation still awaited them: rendering the bomb safe. Gladys had rehearsed these operations dozens of time at Livermore and Los Alamos, but it was never the same and never certain. Cold sweat now glistening on her brow, she listened to Graham's voice.

"There's no reason to make life complicated here, and time is critical," he said. "We'll get a PAN up there."

"A what?"

"Its full name is 'percussion-activated non-electric disrupter.' It's basically a super-high-pressure hose that will blast out a huge stream of water at that energy source and literally blow it apart. Even if it releases its stored up electrical charge, with all that water flooding it all you will get is *poof*, maybe a blue flash and a massive short circuit. The charge just won't get down to the detonator with the power it needs to set off the bomb."

Five minutes later the firemen in helmets and slickers arrived. "Focus them on that black ball and tell them to blast it away," Graham ordered.

The burst of high-pressure water literally flooded the small room. The black plastic ball was torn from the base of the cell phone and flung across the room. A blue flash accompanied its flight. Gladys, her voice trembling, described the scene over the phone.

"OK," said the weapons designer at Livermore, "now take a close look at the detonator to which the black ball was attached. You should see three wires, probably one red, one green, one blue, running from it into the bomb sphere. See them?"

"Yes."

"OK, are they color-coded like I said?"

"Looks like it."

"Cut the red one."

Her hands shaking, the images of her children before her, she did.

"Done," she said.

"OK, now cut the green one."

"Done."

"And now the blue one."

"Done."

"Congratulations. You have now disarmed the bomb. It can no longer explode."

His words echoed through the Office of Emergency Management, most of whose members had been tuned into the Brooklyn-Livermore conversation. Strangely, the reaction of the men and women in the main room of the headquarters was not a jubilant outburst of shouting and cheering—like after a successful launch at Cape Canaveral—but an almost reverential silence, a mute expression of gratitude for what had just been accomplished and for the enormity of the tragedy New York had so narrowly escaped.

"Bravo, Gladys!" Graham said adding his congratulations to those of the experts at Livermore. "I knew you could do it. Yours is a NEST first.

"Paul," he called to his colleague Paul Anscom sitting opposite him at the command console. "Now you can call the President. This time you can tell him it's all over."

*   *   *

Andrew Card intercepted the President with the news as he was heading down from his living quarters to the Situation Room. He stopped, almost staggered under its impact, then leaned briefly against the wall. "Thank God, oh, thank God!" he murmured.

The members of his Crisis Committee who had also just heard the news stood as he entered the Situation Room. They, too, did not cheer or shout in triumph but instead just clapped their hands to welcome him.

The President acknowledged their gesture with a grateful nod. He took his seat and laid his hands on the table. For a moment he glanced at his colleagues, a suggestion of tears in his eyes.

"I think it would be appropriate," he said, "if each of us in his or her way paused for a moment of silence in thanks for the extraordinary deliverance that has just been given us." Then he nodded in prayer.

When he'd finished, he glanced down the table to the Chairman of the Joint Chiefs. "General," he said, "clearly our first order of business now is to stand down the Marine landing and to order the Sixth Fleet to begin steaming west instead of east."

The officer sprang to his feet. "Done, sir," he said.

The President next turned to Andrew Card. "Please convey my personal congratulations and heartfelt thanks to everyone in New York who helped defuse this terrible situation."

He paused a moment then continued. "I want you to appoint a blue ribbon committee to study every aspect of this crisis, what went wrong, where, how and why. We must learn everything there is to know from it, because there could be a next time. I will want to talk to Mike Bloomberg, but my next priority has to be to talk to Ariel Sharon. Would you please get him for me?" he asked the marine communications officer.

"Arik!" the President boomed into the phone as soon as he had Sharon on the line, "it's over, the crisis is finished. Our police and FBI agents have found the terrorists' bomb and rendered it safe. Two of the three terrorists are dead. The third, a woman with false Canadian papers, is trying to escape via Canada, but our Canadian neighbors should be able to intercept her. And of course I have issued the order to cancel the marine landing."

"Wonderful, George! Congratulations. Thank God this ghastly moment is behind us."

"I share your sentiments, Arik, but you and I have now got to think through the lessons this terrible crisis teaches us, and begin to apply them."

"I agree. George, what do you think those lessons are?"

President Bush paused a moment to reflect. "Arik, we must acknowledge that there are people out there with the technical knowledge and the resources to make and deliver weapons of mass destruction. They are filled with hate and madness, and ready to use those weapons against us. All the security procedures in the world cannot guarantee safety. It's up to you and me, working with the new Palestinian leadership, to do whatever it takes to bring peace to the Middle East. Think of how that would change the lives of your citizens."

"George, it's not just the Palestinian problem. There are a dozen places in the world—Chechnya, Indonesia, Afghanistan, Iraq and so on—where Islamic terrorism is thriving," replied Sharon.

"Arik, I am not so naïve as to think that finding a just solution to the Israeli-Palestinian issue will end the threat of extremist Islamic terrorism. But it would be a huge step toward that goal . . . a step that the world is waiting for you and Abbas to take. Believe me, Arik, for all the sympathy I bear you personally and for the State of Israel, I am not prepared to see another American city menaced as New York was because of our failure to come to grips with this problem."

"George, now that the Palestinians have a more reasonable and trustworthy leadership, we'll try, however difficult I
think it still is. *Shalom.*

"Yes, Arik, *shalom,* peace."

*   *   *

For some time, the hidden grotto sheltering the most wanted man on the planet had been gripped with frantic energy.
Clambering up the rocky trail hewn into the cliffs of Waziristan,
the Pashtun tribal chiefs who had pledged to shelter Osama bin
Laden had been bringing alarming news. The commanding officers of the Pakistan Army, under pressure from General
Musharraf, who in turn was being pressured by the Americans,
were beginning to crumble.

Some Pakistan Special Forces units were now prowling the
tribal zones of the North-West Frontier Province trying to capture
ex-Taliban fighters and members of Osama's al Qaeda forces.
There were reports that up to a hundred people already had been
seized. Bin Laden's own safety was imperiled, and he knew that he
might at any moment be captured. After all, it would only take
minutes for the American's helicopters to fly to his refuge from
their bases in Afghanistan if they could squeeze his location out of
one of their prisoners.

Come deeper into the mountains of the Hindu Kush, the
tribal chiefs urged, and be protected by greater distance and
other no less friendly tribal leaders. When the Americans gave up
their search, he could return to this hideaway.

Bin Laden reflected on their advice. He knew how much
his bitter enemy George W. Bush wanted to capture him, as Bush
had promised his countrymen. If that traitor Musharraf was giving

in to Bush, then there was the risk he might succeed. Nothing, no prospect on earth, would be so utterly demeaning.

He ordered his followers to prepare for a sudden flight once night had shrouded the area. But before leaving this grotto for another hiding place, he was determined to carry out one last nightly ritual.

He reached down, twisted a dial which sent power from a simple twelve-volt car battery into his TV set. Its antenna was fixed to a tree on a crest of the mountain's flank outside. The precautions were designed to render Osama's TV viewings immune to any electronic detection devices of his American foes.

The set was tuned not to Al Jazeera or Al Arabiya but to CNN's *Your World Tonight.* For the past three days, he had watched the evening broadcast with growing anxiety, as the hours to the expiration of his nuclear ultimatum ticked away. Nothing in the reports of the network's correspondents in Washington or Jerusalem had yet indicated that the evacuation of Jewish settlements on the West Bank had begun.

Mugniyeh's idea—that our plan had to be tied to the demand that the United States force the settlements to be cleaned out—was a terrible mistake, he thought. No, the only thing those infidels understand is an action like the World Trade Center. Well, now that the clock has run out on Mugniyeh's plan, it's time to take that action. If it's terror they understand, then it's terror they will get.

Leaning on his cane, he got up and went over to the small safe placed beside the carpet he used as a bed. He took out a cell phone, stuffed it into the pocket of his *djellaba* and hobbled out of the grotto to where a mule was tied up. He untethered the animal, mounted his saddle and rode down to the valley where his jeep and driver were waiting with a cluster of armed tribesmen.

He ordered the driver to head for the little community of Oudja some ten miles away. The action he was about to take could endanger his life if the American's listening satellites were able to pin down the location from which his call came, but then, like others before him, he would become a *shahid*, a martyr.

When the minaret of the town's mosque came into sight, he ordered his driver to pull over and stop. He turned on his cell phone and slowly, almost tenderly, he keyed in the fatal phone number of the cell phone he knew had been wired to the detonator. He pressed the phone to his ear and listened in what was close to a state of ecstasy as the number began ringing.

Then to his utter astonishment, he heard not the answering *click* he was expecting but the voice of a woman speaking English. "We are sorry," she said, "but the number you are calling is temporarily out of service. If you wish to leave a message, you may do so after the tone."

POSTSCRIPT

A month after the terrorists' bomb was discovered and defused, Detective Lieutenant T.F. O'Neill, FBI Agent Olivia Phillips and NEST's Gladys Simpson were invited to a small ceremony at the White House. Andrew Card welcomed them at the West Gate and took them to a small room adjacent to the Oval Office. Only one other person was present, Gina Newhouse of the Associated Press, a pool photographer for the White House Correspondent's organization.

Shortly after they arrived, the President appeared. In a few brief and well-chosen words, he thanked them all for the services to the nation they had recently provided in New York. Then, with Andrew Card's help, he hung around each person's neck a Medal of Freedom, the nation's highest civilian honor. He shook each one's hand, embraced the two women, and left.

"Hey, Little Pal," O'Neill said, "could you celebrate these trinkets by spending a little off-duty time up in New York with an old widower?"

Olivia smiled. "You know," she said, "that might be nice."

Card took them back to the West Gate where a car waited to drive them to Reagan National airport. On the way out the door, the AP photographer turned to Gladys.

"Where are you from?" she asked.

"Livermore, California."

"Wow!" the reporter said, "A long way from New York. What do you do?"

"I'm a nuclear physicist."

The photographer stood gaping as the trio got into their

car. Hey, she thought, there must have been a hell of a story up there in New York that we people from the media somehow we didn't get.

ACKNOWLEDGEMENTS

We wish, first and foremost, to express our immense gratitude to our wives, Nadia and Dominique, who shared all the moments of our long and difficult research months, and were our irreplaceable collaborators during the writing of our book.

We also wish to express our thanks to Colette Modiano, Antoine Caro and Victor M. Kramer, who spent long hours correcting and editing the manuscript and encouraged us with their words and thoughts.

We could also not have written this book without the confidence and enthusiasm of our publishers Leonello Brandolini in Paris, Gianni Ferrari in Milano, Carlos Reves and Berta Noy in Barcelona, Shekhar and Poonam Malhotra in New Delhi, Michael Viner in Beverly Hills, and our dear agent Alan Nevins, also in Beverly Hills.

The reader will understand that, given the highly sensitive nature of much of the information to be found on the pages of this book, we cannot cite, for security reasons, the names of all of those who contributed to the more secret aspects of our research. We wish, however, to acknowledge the help we received from among others, Dr. Frank N. Barnaby, a distinguished British nuclear weapons designer who now, in his retirement, devotes much of his energy to the problems of nuclear proliferation; Dr. Ralph James, deputy director of the National Laboratory in Brookhaven, New York; Senator Christopher Shays (Connecticut) who presided over a sub committee of the Senate devoted to the problems of national security and, in particular, some of those related to certain aspects of nuclear terrorism, as well as his Chief of Staff, Larry Halloran.

We would also like to acknowledge the help of Brian Wilkes, Rick Arkin and Deborah Wilkes of the Homeland Security Department's Emergency Response Team whose challenging task it would be to confront a national emergency of the sort described in this book. We also owe a thank you to Dr. Lisa Holmgren, former director of NEST and, for years, an expert on nuclear issues for the National Security Council, as well as a number of very thoughtful people at the Nuclear Threat Initiative of the Carnegie Foundation.

And special thanks to two old friends, Milt Beardon, who ran the war against the Soviets in Afghanistan for some years and is now a distinguished author in his own right, and Frank Bolz Jr. who was the mainstay of our research at the New York Police Department.

Larry Collins and Dominique Lapierre

BOOKS BY THE SAME AUTHORS

Is Paris Burning?
…Or I'll Dress You In Mourning
O Jerusalem
Freedom at Midnight
The Fifth Horseman

LARRY COLLINS
Fall From Grace
Maze
Black Eagles
D. Day—The Day of Miracles
The Road to Armageddon

DOMINIQUE LAPIERRE
The City of Joy
Beyond Love
A Thousand Suns
Five Past Midnight in Bhopal *(with Javier Moro)*